Missing Persons

MISSING PERSONS

A Crime Writers' Association Anthology

edited by Martin Edwards

with a foreword by Ian Rankin

Constable · London

First published in Great Britain 1999
by Constable & Company Limited
3 The Lanchesters, 162 Fulham Palace Road
London W6 9ER

Copyright © 1999
The right of the contributors to be
identified as the authors of this work
has been asserted by them in accordance
with the Copyright, Designs and Patents Act 1988

ISBN 0 094 79930 X

Set in Palatino 10 pt by
SetSystems Ltd, Saffron Walden, Essex
Printed and bound in Great Britain
by MPG Books Ltd, Bodmin, Cornwall

A CIP catalogue record for this book
is available from the British Library

Contents

Foreword	7
Introduction	11
Nowhere to be Found by Mat Coward	15
Flying Pigs by Judith Cutler	33
Miss You Nights by Carol Anne Davis	41
Three's Company by Eileen Dewhurst	53
The Search for Otto Wagner by Marjorie Eccles	65
A Stolen Life by Martin Edwards	77
Raffles and Miss Morris by John Hall	95
The Laddie Vanishes by Edward D. Hoch	113
Missing by Bill Kirton	125
A Small Problem at the Gallery by Janet Laurence	141
After the Sega by Peter Lewis	149
Trust Me by Phil Lovesey	167
By the Time You Read This by Keith Miles	181
People Don't Do Such Things by Ruth Rendell	197
Coming Home by June Thomson	211
A Busy Afternoon by Alison White	223

Foreword

I first became interested in MisPers (as police refer to missing persons) almost accidentally. I was living in France and trying to write a novel about the Bible John case. This was a real-life Scottish serial killer case of the late 1960s. Fellow writer and Crime Writers Association member Jerry Sykes sent me a book he thought I might find useful. (CWA members are like that.) The book was called *The Missing* and was by Andrew O'Hagan. It dealt with missing persons, beginning with a true case from O'Hagan's family history, but taking in the Bible John and Fred West cases along the way. O'Hagan asked a lot of searching questions about MisPers: why do they leave? Where do they go? How can society allow them to just disappear?

Of course, not every missing person case will involve foul play. People run away from home for all sorts of reasons. In fact, if someone is of adult age, and there's no reason to be suspicious, then police are loath even to open the most cursory investigation into any disappearance. Walking away from the world seems to be one option open to all of us. But acceptance of this means we must also accept that there is another world out there, a parallel world where people have started new lives; a whole community of them. Tens of thousands of people leave home every year. The vast majority turn up after time, but hundreds, perhaps even a few thousand will not. How many of these are in fact murders we may never know. If no one's investigating, and no body is ever recovered, then you've pulled off the perfect crime.

There's one notorious case in Scotland as I speak. A woman disappeared from her home in Elgin, leaving the place 'like the *Marie Céleste*', according to one CID officer. She hadn't taken her glasses or her prescription medicine with her. She had left no note. Police waited a couple of weeks before deciding to open an investigation. They now fear the worst, and meantime the community has become a less comfortable place. We all like to think that we have a place in this world, that our lives mean something. A disappearance negates these comforters. I'm reminded of Milan Kundera's description of an Eastern Bloc politician who had fallen out of favour to such an extent that his image was removed from all the official photographs, leaving in one case just his hat as evidence that he had once existed. The Elgin 'victim' left us her glasses and a jar of pills.

As I became fascinated by the questions posed in O'Hagan's book, so I used them to good effect by writing a novella, and then a novel, both dealing to some extent with MisPers. I spoke to police, social workers and the homeless, and even finally plucked up the courage to talk to one or two families whose lives had been affected by one member's disappearance. I found that what troubles these families most is the lack of any sort of closure. They had an abiding need to know why their loved one had left, and where that person was now. As long as these questions remained in the realm of mystery, the families could never know peace.

It is the same in cases of unsolved murders. Two teenage girls were found dead on the outskirts of Edinburgh in October 1977. One of the largest ever murder investigations in Scotland was launched. The girls had last been seen drinking in a crowded city centre bar. Despite a slew of leads and thousands of hours of hard graft, no one was ever brought to trial. In these cases, the investigators become victims, too: obsessed by a need to know the truth, yet stymied and frustrated at every turn. Unsolveds can stay with them till the grave.

However, the case of the two teenagers was reopened last year. Innovations in DNA testing had led to forensic scientists being able to produce a genetic fingerprint of the killer. The same thing has happened with the Bible John killings. Though he last struck in 1968, scientists now have a genetic fingerprint of Bible John. A DNA database is being compiled: anyone convicted of certain crimes in Scotland now has a swab taken from the inside of their mouth. It is hoped that eventually this just might reveal the identities of these unknown killers, people who thought for twenty and thirty years that they had 'got away with murder'.

The missing person case is perfect for crime fiction because it allows the author so many possibilities. You can concentrate on the mystery itself and the effect it has on the person doing the detecting; or you can focus on the lives affected by the person's disappearance. Twists at the end are catered for – whether the MisPers turns up to reveal all, or turns out never to have existed in the first place (think of Graham Greene's *The Third Man*). In a recent Hollywood thriller, *Wild Things*, it was almost impossible to keep up with who was really dead, who was playing a game, and who was the ultimate victim.

These stories will, I hope, stimulate and entertain you. They're by some of the greatest names on the current crime scene, courtesy of the Crime Writers Association.

Ian Rankin
Chairman, CWA

Introduction

The missing person story is a staple of crime fiction. It has over the years continued to capture the imagination of notable writers, perhaps because it offers almost unlimited possibilities. When someone goes missing unexpectedly, there can be so many explanations. Has there been a kidnapping, a murder, a Reggie Perrin-style scam to flee family and friends? Even where the plot seems familiar, it may be given new life by an author of distinction. For example, Julian Symons, one of my predecessors as editor of the CWA annual anthology, pointed out that in *The Thin Man*, Dashiell Hammett used a device similar to that employed seventy years earlier by Joseph Sheridan Le Fanu in *Wylder's Hand*. Yet in most respects, the books are a world apart and each in its own way ranks as a minor classic.

I received a clear indication that missing person stories are as popular as ever when I invited members of the CWA to contribute to the present anthology. Never have I received so many positive responses. The manuscripts that I received more than lived up to expectations and, not for the first time since I took over the editorship of the anthology four years ago, I found that the most difficult part of my task was to choose between stories that were very varied in content but similar in quality. It was fascinating, and a source of much pleasure, to see the ingenuity – in some cases, downright deviousness – with which my crime-writing colleagues had approached my chosen theme. In contrast to previous years, none of the members who submitted a manuscript gave their series detective an outing, although I did select for inclusion a brand new Raffles story. The emphasis for the most part was on suspense and the working of the criminal mind rather than on ingenious detection. It is a sign of changing fashions in the genre that there were no takes on the 'impossible crime', although many of the finest missing person stories of the past (including Ed Hoch's deservedly famous 'The Vanishing of Velma') were puzzlers which fell into that category.

My hope was that, as in previous years, I would be able to combine contributions from major contemporary crime writers with work by those who are just beginning to make their way in the mystery world. Happily, enjoyable stories from young writers were in plentiful supply; I conclude that there is no shortage of fresh blood in the CWA. As a result, I have been able to include, on the ground of sheer merit, as many as half a dozen contributions penned by members who have never before had a story in their Association's flagship publication.

One important development over the past twelve months is that the anthology has found a new home. Constable have for many years boasted a splendid crime list, adorned in recent times by such celebrated writers as June Thomson, R. D. Wingfield, Jessica Mann and Nicholas Rhea. I hope that their decision to take on the anthology will mark the start of a long and happy relationship; certainly, it seems to me to have got off to a very good start.

As ever, I owe a great deal to a good many people. First, I would like to thank Ian Rankin for his foreword and everyone who wrote a story for the book, whether or not it was ultimately accepted for publication. The anthology enjoys a wonderful reputation amongst connoisseurs of short crime fiction, and that is because CWA members fill it year after year with truly excellent tales of mystery and imagination. I am also grateful to Helena Edwards and Eileen Dewhurst for their support work and to Tara Lawrence, the editor at Constable who adopted the project at an early stage and whose enthusiasm for it has been so encouraging. We all hope that everyone who reads and enjoys *Missing Persons* will succumb to the temptation further to sample the work of the writers whose stories appear in it.

Martin Edwards

Mat Coward

Mat Coward is that rarity, a crime writer who specialises in short fiction. His work is notable for its variety of tone and subject matter, although humour is never too far below the surface even of his bleakest stories. 'Nowhere to be Found' is a story of friendship, its mood quietly melancholic. The narrator, Jerry, is not a detective by profession, but he is seized all the same by the urge to find a solution to the missing person mystery that puzzles him: 'I've got to know.'

NOWHERE TO BE FOUND

by Mat Coward

The last word he said to me was 'topography'.

When the phone rings late at night I always look at the clock first and *then* answer the phone. A sign of chronic pessimism, according to my last girlfriend – always anticipating bad news. Well, there's an obvious retort to that.

'Jerry? You've got to come and get me. How soon can you get here?'

Seven minutes past two in the morning. It was November, and big winds were herding hailstones against my bedroom window. 'Alan? What do you mean, come and get you? Where are you?'

'I'm at home, of course. Wake *up*, Jerry. I really need your help here, man. I'm leaving Jackie, right now, and I . . . are you *awake*, Jerry?'

'I'm awake, calm down. You and Jackie are splitting up? What's happened?'

'I'm leaving her, you've got to come and get me. You should be here in under two hours if you put your foot down. OK?'

He rang off. I sat there thinking for a while, feeling slightly sick from a combination of the sudden awakening and the beer I'd drunk the night before. Then I had a shower, got dressed, and set off for Wiltshire.

The drive down from London took me just over three hours door to door, in terrible weather and over unfamiliar terrain. Alan was hopping by the time I arrived.

'Where have you *been*, Jerry? I've been leaving messages on your bloody machine for the last hour and a half.' He didn't shake hands, or smile, or even say hello. He'd been waiting for me outside the cottage, at the far end of what was little more than a mud lane. I was impressed with myself for having found the place; I'd only been there once before, when I'd helped Alan and Jackie move in.

'Got here as quick as I could, mate,' I said, opening the car door but not getting out – I wasn't sure if I was *supposed* to get out or not. 'So, what's the plan? Got any luggage?'

'Yeah. Wait here.' He turned and walked back up the path towards the cottage. His back was as soaked through as his front. He looked freezing cold, but he also looked as if he was unaware that he was freezing cold.

Just as he reached the cottage door, I called after him. 'Alan?'

He paused without turning, his irritation visible even through that weather. 'Yeah?'

'Good to see you, mate.'

'Just wait there, OK?'

I waited there, the car radio playing, the motor thrumming, for five minutes before I eventually thought, Sod it, the least I'm due is a slash and a cigarette. I got out of the car, walked up the path and knocked on the door. Cup of tea and a piece of toast wouldn't hurt, either.

Jackie opened the door. She yanked it towards her as if it was sticking from flood damage, then let her hand slide off the door knob as she turned and walked away. She didn't look at me.

I followed her into the kitchen, at the back of the house. She was wearing a dressing-gown over a pink nylon nightie. Blue nylon slippers. The general air of someone who has realised that giving up smoking all those years earlier did not, after all, placate the gods sufficiently that they would evermore keep sadness from her hearth. Her face was grey, except where it was red. If a half-decent paramedic had turned up at that moment, he'd have prescribed a dozen full-strength fags and a pint of vodka. *Then* breakfast.

'Sorry to intrude, Jackie,' I said, from the kitchen doorway. She sat at the table, her back to me. 'I just wanted to ... obviously, I don't know what's going on here, that's your business. I just wanted to use the loo, if that's all right?'

She didn't answer, but then it was a pretty daft question. No matter how much someone's life is falling apart, they're hardly likely to respond to such a request with: 'No, you bastard! Go and do it on the compost heap!'

I had a pee, a bit of a wash and brush up, drank some cold water from the tap in cupped hands; I didn't reckon a pot of tea and a plate of scones were going to be appearing in that kitchen any time in the near future.

I could hear Alan still moving about upstairs, so I sat down at the kitchen table. Eventually Jackie did look at me, but she needn't have bothered; there was nothing in the look that said anything.

'Well,' I said. 'This is a bad day.'

She began crying, silently, her eyes fixed on mine. Now that she'd started looking at me, it seemed, she couldn't stop.

'Do you know where I'm taking him to, at all?' I asked. 'Because I don't.'

She shook her head, very short, suprisingly careful shakes, and wrinkled up her face and cried some more. I'd thought she *wouldn't* speak, but I realised now that she couldn't speak. Another gulping of sobs caught her by surprise, like sudden vomit. She clamped two fingers over her lips, as if fearful that if she allowed her mouth to fall open a crack, all her vitals would slip-slide out and pool around her feet.

I reached over and patted her arm, which didn't seem to help enormously. I didn't know what else to do – I hardly knew the girl, for God's sake, I'd only met her once before. Twice, maybe.

Footsteps clattered on the carpetless stairs, and Alan appeared. He was carrying nothing but a duffel bag. 'What are you doing here? I said wait in the car.'

'I needed to use the loo,' I said, and immediately wished I hadn't offered him an explanation at all. The rude, ungrateful bastard! It wasn't even as if we were close friends. We were *old* friends, certainly, known each other for ever, and I loved him like a brother. But your brother isn't usually your closest friend, is he?

We went out and got into the car. Neither of us said goodbye to Jackie, and she didn't speak to, or look at, either of us. It was still raining. People often say, 'I must be mad to do this,' but at that moment I really did wonder if I was actually mad. Or if one of us was, anyway.

'Is that all you've got? One duffel bag?'

Alan looked down at the duffel bag between his knees. 'That's it,' he said. He didn't seem inclined to say more, so after a brief pause to search for loose cigarettes in the glove compartment (there weren't any), I fired up the motor and headed off in what I hoped was the direction of the motorway.

'You got any smokes, Alan? I ran out on the way down.'

He shook his head. 'I packed it in.'

'All right,' I said. 'I'll stop somewhere. Anyway, be breakfast time soon, right?'

He wasn't talkative – he wasn't in fact saying anything, which is untalkative by anybody's standards – but that didn't surprise me. He'd been with Jackie a good few years, on and off, and any break-up that occurs in the early hours of the morning is, by definition, a sudden break-up.

I couldn't keep silent, though. Not on a journey of that length. Not with no sleep, no breakfast and no cigarettes. Time dragged. So did distance – I didn't know my way around there, the weather was no better, I was driving slowly.

Every minute or so I'd say something like 'Well, this is a bad night,' or 'Maybe things'll look better in a day or two.' But I had to be careful what I said; careful not to sound too disapproving. Because the truth was, I *did* disapprove. I didn't know the ins and outs of this particular situation, obviously, but I couldn't help feeling that a man like Alan, who'd had three wives before he was thirty, was more often than not likely to be the author of his own misfortunes.

And he knew I disapproved. Which is why I tried to keep things light.

'So where is it I'm taking you?' I said, after a few more silent miles, and with the bloody motorway still playing hide and seek in the country darkness. 'Back to my place, is it? Because that's fine if it is, goes without saying, my floor is your floor. Might even find you a spare pillow if you're good.'

'Stop here,' said Alan, and I was so shocked that I obeyed him immediately. He started struggling with the seat belt. Its release catch had always been dodgy.

'What's the matter? You feel sick?'

'You can drop me here,' he said.

I peered out of the windscreen. I couldn't see much because of the weather, but I got the impression that there wouldn't be much to see even on a clear day. Just hedges and fields. No houses for miles around. 'Alan, we're in the middle of nowhere. We're on a road with no pavements, for God's sake. We're on a road with no pavements, it's raining and we're Londoners.'

He freed himself from the death-trap seat belt, and started struggling with the door handle. A deeply non-mechanical man, Alan; never learned how to ride a bike, let alone drive a car.

'Look, Alan, I don't feel happy about leaving you here. I mean, at this time of night, in this weather – what are you going to do, hitch-hike? I can take you where you want to go.'

He got out of the car, slung his duffel bag over his shoulder, and ducked his head down to speak to me. He started with a half-smile, the nearest thing to a friendly face I'd seen all night. 'No, don't worry, Jerry, I'm not hitching. I've got a friend lives just near, I'll crash there for a day or two while I sort myself out.'

I'd never seen anyone lie so obviously in all my life, but what could I do? 'What's this place called, then?' I asked, trying for a tone somewhere between sceptical and jokey.

Alan shook his head. 'I don't know it by name, exactly, I just recognise the topography.' He began walking in the opposite direction to the one in which the car was pointing. Within a very short time he was invisible.

I called after him, 'I can drive you to your friend's house, that's no problem,' but I don't know if he heard me.

What could I do? You can't force a grown man to stay in a car, no matter how hard it's raining. As I leant over to close the door that he'd left ajar, I spotted a cigarette, bent but unbroken, under the passenger seat. So I sat and smoked that, and after a while the sky became lighter and I was able to find my way back to the motorway and home.

*

It wasn't until three years later that I went looking for Alan. Perhaps I should explain that.

Alan never became a Missing Person, except in the crudely literal sense that he was a person, who was missing. No official body ever listed him as missing, because nobody ever reported him gone. He hadn't had a regular job in years. He had no mortgage, no driving licence, no credit cards, no bank account. Alan Hallsworth was one of those people whose only proof of existence is their heartbeat, who never trouble the computers of the world, either with their presence or their absence.

His parents had divorced when he was twenty, long after he'd left home, and Alan had achieved the impressive feat of becoming permanently estranged from both of them. I remember him boasting to me about that, one sober night. 'I have literally,' he told me, *'literally* got an address book with no addresses in it.' Another night, equilibrium restored by Guinness, he'd changed his mind about that. 'I didn't mean that I'd *literally* got an empty address book,' he explained. 'I just meant that I don't know where my parents live, either of them, and don't wish to know. I haven't actually got a *literal* address book, empty or otherwise. Don't need one – don't know anyone.'

His wife, of course, might have reported him missing, but when I once suggested it to Jackie, on the phone, she sounded puzzled. 'But I kicked him out, Jerry. I mean, you know, him not being here sort of goes without saying, doesn't it?'

Missing Person, of course, is a definition rather than an occupation, and it's one that not every person fits, even when they do happen to be missing.

And me? I never reported Alan missing because I never believed for a moment that he was a missing *person*. Almost from the start, I thought of him as a missing corpse.

Two weeks after my pointless journey to and from Wiltshire, I still hadn't heard from Alan and I was beginning to get worried. He didn't know many people, and I'd been certain that he and his duffel bag would end up on my sofa before long. After all, where else do you go when you're running away from home but to London? No offence to Wiltshire, but it's definitely a *from* place, not a *to* place.

That was when I phoned Jackie. She was no longer unable to speak without crying, and made it unambiguously clear to me that her marriage, her husband, her husband's duffel bag, and her husband's friends were all part of her past, not her present. Goodbye.

So, I thought: he must be dead. If he was alive and well, he'd have been in touch with me. If he was alive and in trouble, the authorities would have been in touch with his wife. Therefore, he must be dead – and undiscovered. A missing ex-person.

As weeks and months passed, Alan's supposed death and disappearance faded from the forefront of my mind, the way even the biggest things in life will under the daily onslaught of little matters. I thought of him most at Christmastimes, when he didn't send me a card. He never *had* sent me a card, you see, not once in all his life, and I'd always sent him one, and it had always rankled. But now, I couldn't really blame him for not sending me a card, because there wasn't really much he could do about it.

And then, as the fourth Christmas approached, I suddenly thought, I've got to know. Just like that, really: I've got to know. After all, it was my car he got out of.

The drive down still took me three hours. The weather was OK this time, but I still didn't know the way.

The cottage in which Alan and Jackie had served the greater part of their marital sentence was uninhabited now, empty and boarded up. I sat outside it for a while, smoking, listening to the shipping forecast, wondering where to start.

Three years earlier, I'd asked Jackie on the phone, 'Was there another woman?'

'Another woman?' she'd replied. 'There were *several* other women. But not one that'd have taken him in.'

If Alan was alive he'd have been in touch. I'd known him since we were both kids, and I don't think there'd ever been a period of three consecutive months during which we didn't speak to each other at least once.

He had been killed deliberately, because if it had been an accident his body would have been found, and word would have trickled through to me eventually, through one twisting conduit or another.

I finished my cigarette, turned the car in the craterous road, and set off slowly to try and retrace the route we'd driven on the night he left. After about an hour of dawdling, reversing, peering and swearing, I gave up. One bit of rural road looks much like another, unless it's where you live.

Once winter's early darkness had turned my mission from futile to farcical, I stopped at the next pub, which happened to be one I'd seen a few hours before, on my drive down. I reckoned it was about ten minutes' walk from Alan and Jackie's old place. Their local, by any chance?

I needed a drink. Until that day, I hadn't said the word 'murder' to myself – not out loud, so to speak. The logic was solid enough, and had been there all along, but I suppose acknowledging it was just one of those jobs I'd preferred to put off indefinitely, like fixing a leaky tap.

Murder, I thought, as I sipped a pint slowly. In which case, given the truncated nature of Alan's social circle, there could only be two categories of suspect: his wife, or one of his girlfriends. (Not a wronged husband? No – Alan put it about a bit, before, during and after his various marriages, but he never to my knowledge slept with anyone else's wife. 'I have my standards,' he used to say. 'They're twisted ones, I know, but they're the only ones I've got, so I keep 'em.')

In my mind, as I drank, I auditioned Jackie for the part of vengeful assassin. Supposing, when Alan got out of my car, he had walked or hitched back to the cottage. He'd changed his mind, he wasn't leaving home after all. It had just been one of those rows that ignite in marriages, and then burn themselves out. Now I thought about it, his lack of luggage perhaps suggested a certain lack of resolution. You don't walk out of a marriage with just a duffel bag, do you?

All right, I thought, towards the bottom of the beer. He arrives back on his own doorstep, tells his briefly abandoned wife the good news: 'I've decided to give you another chance, you lucky cow.' So why does she kill him?

Well, for all I knew he performed the same show once a month. Leaving, coming back, expecting (demanding?) gratitude. And this time was once too often. Being left by your husband would be bad enough, I imagined, but being left on a regular basis would be even more humiliating. Worse – it'd be *irritating*.

So much for the wife. What about the mistress?

When he insisted on getting out of my car, Alan had claimed that he was going to seek shelter with a friend. At the time, I hadn't believed him. It had crossed my mind then that perhaps he was going home, and was embarrassed to have me drive him there, but now it struck me that there really could have been a friend. She'd have had long, dark hair and big buttocks, no doubt, as did Jackie, and Susan before Jackie, and the Spanish one, whose name I could never recall, before Susan.

But then, what was the story there? Alan gets out of the car, walks to his girlfriend's house, says, 'I've finally left my wife, let me in, it's raining' – and she kills him? No, that doesn't work. All she'd have to say, if she wasn't keen on the idea, was 'Grow up, Alan. Go home and sleep it off, kiddo.'

By the time my pint was dead beyond doubt, I'd talked myself out of the murdering mistress scenario. Which, unavoidably, meant that I'd talked myself into the murdering missus ...

I needed another drink, and maybe a sandwich to soak it up. While I was waiting for the sole barmaid to serve a man at the other end of the counter with a bag of peanuts (a transaction which seemed to involve a longer conversation than most people have with their mothers on Christmas Day), I eavesdropped a large, red-faced man with a local accent giving directions to an elderly couple who had wandered into the pub holding a road map upside down.

'Excuse me,' I said, when the old folk had departed smiling, with their map the right way up. 'You seem to know your way around these parts.'

'I should do, yeah. Been running deliveries round here for years. Plus I live just up the road. Why – you lost?'

'Well, not exactly. Look, could I buy you a drink, if you've got a moment? I'd really like to pick your brains a bit.'

He shrugged. 'I wouldn't say no to a lager top.'

We took our drinks over to a table, and I pondered my approach. *I need some village gossip* probably wasn't tactful. I decided to rely on ritual and feel my way.

'Cheers.'

'Cheers.'

'Jerry, by the way.' I stuck out my hand.

'Oh, right. Norman. Cheers.'

'Cheers.' We drank, smacked our respective lips, put down our respective glasses. I leant my elbows on the table. 'Look, Norman, hope you don't mind me waylaying you like this. Thing is, I've driven all the way down here from London to look up some old friends.'

'Round here?'

'Right, yep, just up the road here. Haven't seen them for ages, and obviously I should have phoned first, because when I got to their cottage I found it was abandoned. I mean, you know, actually boarded up!'

Norman shook his head sadly. 'Lot of that round this way. No jobs, see?'

'Ah? Right, right. Terrible, really, what's happening to the countryside. But the thing was, I was wondering if you might have known them – might know what happened to them. Alan and Jackie Hallsworth.'

He looked at me suspiciously, then, I thought, and I wondered if I'd underdone the subtlety, or whether I was merely receiving the standard amount of suspicion awarded by a villager to an outsider who asks questions. I couldn't tell, having never lived in a village.

Norman took his time swallowing a few mouthfuls of beer before he replied. 'Well ... Alan and Jackie. Yes, I did know them. Not to talk to, like, but to nod to. They used to come in here now and then, weekends and that.'

'How long have they been gone?'

'You're an old friend, you say?'

'Yeah, you know, we sort of lost touch. The way you do, you know.'

He drank some more, and watched me over the rim of his glass as he did so. 'Well,' he said eventually. 'If you've not been in touch for some while, then you probably won't know. They split up.'

'Alan and Jackie?'

'Yeah. Afraid so. Few years ago now, must be.'

'Oh God, that's awful! What happened, do you know?'

Norman shook his head. 'Didn't know them that well. From what I heard at the time, Alan just walked out one night, and a month or so later Jackie was gone, too. Back to her mother's, apparently. She waited around for a while, I daresay, just to see if he was coming back.'

'Which he never did?' I asked.

Norman studied me again, but this time without using the beer as camouflage. His suspicion now was overt, though not, I thought, hostile. 'Never saw him again. Took off with one of his women, I suppose. No offence, what with you being a mate of his, but – well, he was a bit of a lad, if you know what I mean.'

I couldn't believe my luck. This was exactly the conversation I wanted: a discussion of Alan's infidelities, preferably with names and places. But as I started to assure Norman that I knew exactly what he meant about my old friend's ways, he abruptly stood up.

'Got to be going now. She'll be expecting me back soon.' He stuck out his hand. 'Nice to meet you. My advice, look for Jackie at her mum's. Cardiff, somewhere, I seem to recall. Can't help beyond that, I'm afraid.'

Damn, I thought. I must have asked one question too many. Enough to turn a natural gossip into a loyal neighbour. Even so, I felt that what Norman had said – and what he had presumably left the pub in order to avoid saying – told me quite a lot. Alan was a known philanderer, active locally. He had disappeared, and shortly afterwards, so had his wife.

I left my second pint half-finished on the table, and walked out to my car. I couldn't put this off any longer: it was time to visit the scene of the crime.

Whoever had boarded up Jackie and Alan's cottage – the landlord, presumably – had done a thorough job. I quickly saw that I wouldn't be able to get into the house without some difficulty, not to mention some tools. For now, I'd have to make do with a quick look round the garden. The body was more likely to be in the garden than the house, anyway, I figured. I couldn't really imagine Jackie burying her husband beneath the floorboards.

There was a fair bit of garden, very overgrown now. Most of the land was at the side of the house, with only a small stretch at the front. The front yard was mainly laid to patio – and that, I remembered, had already been there when Alan and Jackie moved in.

I kept a torch in the car, but not a spade, so a proper search was out of the immediate question. As I prodded around more or less aimlessly amid the brambles and frost-blackened weeds, I felt fear, as well as frustration – fear that I wouldn't have the guts or the constancy to come back again, better prepared. And fear that I would.

To do either would be to confront a question about myself that I would sooner have left unanswered: was I a man who believed that one is obliged to make sense of death? I'd never made, or especially tried to make, any sense out of life. But death, especially someone else's death, was somehow a different kettle of ball games.

'I've got a spade here.'

The words, quietly spoken somewhere behind my left shoulder, made me leap, gasp and drop the torch, which landed a few yards away in a patch of mud. Norman picked it up and shone it in my face.

'I saw you here earlier today, sitting outside in your car. I come by once or twice a week, to check everything's still as it was. I followed you around the lanes, and into the pub. I'd have spoken to you if you hadn't spoken to me. And now here you are, back again. Didn't need to follow you this time. Guessed where you were headed.'

I cleared my voice before speaking, but still it croaked. 'From what I said in the pub?'

Norman dropped the torch's beam from my face, to the ground between us. 'Didn't know how much you knew. Still don't know how you found out. But you know something, that's clear.' He passed me a heavy, agricultural spade, blade end first, and said, 'Over here.'

The spot he led me to was deep in a small thicket of horticultural neglect, hidden from any view, not too near the house or the road. I could see his logic. As I took a moment to gather my thoughts before beginning the sweaty task of digging my own grave, I went through the motions of considering my options. What it came down to was this: Norman was a big bloke, a physical-looking man, and I wasn't. I hoped he had a gun, or a blunt object, or at worst a knife. He hadn't struck me as the naturally violent type. If I did what he wanted me to do, I hoped he'd end it quickly. End *me* quickly. If I tried to escape, he'd catch me, and probably finish me with the spade.

That was what it came down to, my last attempt to make sense of death: that I'd rather die by a gun than by a spade.

'It was your wife, then, was it? Alan was seeing your wife?' I was playing for time, of course, but only for more time to rest before beginning the digging. I was too far gone in fear and listless despair to try for a higher prize.

'My wife?' said Norman. 'I'm not married. I can't be, see, I have to look after my mum, she's been poorly.'

As I turned the first sod, I was thinking, I don't know that many more people than Alan did. How long will it take them to realise I'm dead? And I was thinking, If this bloke's a psycho killer, he's a bloody bone idle one. Two victims in three years? You wouldn't think they'd allow it in these deregulated days. You'd think they'd have got some guy in Korea to do it for half the wages, twice the productivity.

But then I realised that I was making too many assumptions. Norman had only two victims that I knew of – he could have had four hundred that I didn't know of. I might be doing him an injustice, he might be the archetypal New Model Worker. I was pleased to think that. There's comfort in numbers, even when there isn't safety. Stupid, but true. Stupid, but human.

Anyway, I dug down a few more feet, and after a while I unearthed Alan.

'I'm to be sharing then, am I?' I said, putting down my spade. I was quite pleased with that. It showed a certain character, I thought, to go out with a quip on your lips.

Norman reached into his coat pocket. Gun or knife, I wondered. Gun, I hoped. Blades are too personal.

It was a mobile phone.

'You call them,' said Norman, handing me the phone. 'I'm no good at all that.'

'Call them . . .?' My croak became a whisper.

'The police,' said Norman. 'Would you mind? I get all, you know, tongue-tied. With officials.'

I looked at the phone. I didn't know what it meant. I looked at Norman. I didn't know what he meant, either. 'You *didn't* kill Alan?'

'I didn't mean to!' he said, his face flushing in the torchlight as if I'd offended or embarrassed him. 'You know what these roads are like, round here, in winter. I never even saw him. First I saw of him, was when I stopped and went back to see what the noise was.' He choked, snorted his nose clear. 'I thought it was a badger.'

'When was this?' I said. To my relief, I found that my hands had stopped shaking sufficiently for me to light a cigarette. I drew the smoke in deep, and felt it save my life. I offered the packet to Norman.

'Ta. I'm supposed to have given up last Christmas, but you know . . . When was it? Three years ago. Found out later Jackie'd kicked him out that same night. He must have been hitching, I suppose, though he was going in the wrong direction, silly bugger. Probably pissed or stoned, he usually was.'

He took the cigarette down like a marathon runner gulping water. I lit him another. 'Ta, you sure you got enough? Ta, then.'

'Why didn't you call the police? After the accident, I mean.'

Norman shook his head, as if to dislodge the shame from his face. 'I'd been made redundant three times in five years. Company I was with then, they've got this policy – you have an accident and you're out. Doesn't matter if it's your fault or not. I couldn't allow it, do you see that?' He nodded towards the open grave. 'If I'd lost that job just then, the debt would have buried us. I'm not kidding, me and my mother, we'd have been buried alive.' He laughed. 'Got the push a year later, anyway. Rationalisation. It's just me and my old van now.'

'So you put him here.'

'Not straight off. I kept him in my shed for a while, but then when Jackie handed in the keys to this place – well, it belongs to my mum, you see. And I knew we'd not be able to let it again in a hurry, not with the way things are.'

I was still holding the phone, and I still couldn't make sense of it. 'I thought you were going to kill me, Norman. I thought that was what the spade was all about.'

'Jesus!' Norman threw his cigarette away. 'Bloody hell, man, where could you get an idea like that? I'm not a nutter!'

'Of course not,' I said, quickly. 'It's only that – '

'It was you asking questions, see? I mean this – ' again he nodded towards the grave – 'this was never intended to be permanent. Just until, you know . . . my mum. But then you came down, looking for Alan.'

'I don't get it.' What I meant was: I don't get why you're not going to kill me. Always assuming you're not.

'I knew Alan and Jackie a bit. More than what I said earlier in the pub. We weren't real mates or anything, but when I came round to get the rent sometimes we used to have a drink, like, a bit of a smoke, bit of a chat. So I knew Jackie wouldn't miss him, see what I mean? Even if she hadn't kicked him out, she'd just have thought he'd walked out. He would have sooner or later, too.'

True, I thought. Alan wasn't one for sticking at things.

'And I knew there was no one else gave a shit about him, dead or alive. No family, nothing like that. So I thought – well, bit hard on him, bit hard on me, but no point in making matters worse. It wasn't as if I was causing anyone else pain, do you see? By keeping quiet.'

'But then I showed up.'

Norman nodded, and tears appeared on his cheeks. 'At first I thought maybe you were a debt collector. Child Support, whatever. But debt collectors don't go looking for bodies in gardens. See, if he had someone who cared about him enough to come looking . . . well, that changes everything, doesn't it?'

He gave a huge, rasping sigh, and sat down on the wet earth. 'You call the police, then, will you?'

The mobile phone still didn't make sense. It did to Norman, perhaps, but not to me. I gave it back to him. I gave him the spade, too.

'You can fill in,' I said. 'I've done enough digging for one lifetime.'

When I got home, there was a Christmas card waiting for me. Just one. It had a return name and address on the back: Jackie Peters, ex-Hallsworth, Cardiff. I read it without taking my coat off.

'Sorry not to have been in touch for so long,' she wrote, 'but it's taken me a while to sort myself out. Hope you're still at the same address! I hope also that things are OK with you, and that you might drop me a line sometime.' Then she came to the point. 'Are you in touch with Alan at all? I don't have an address for him. If you hear from him, could you give him my address? Tell him not to panic, nothing heavy, it's just that I feel we have some unfinished business.'

I got myself a drink, opened a new packet of cigarettes. Finally I took my coat off, and switched the central heating on.

It had occurred to me during the drive home that the only reason Alan got out of my car on the night he died was that he was being driven mad by my silent nagging. So he'd got out, walked along a country road in the dark, and got himself killed.

'Dear Jackie,' I wrote. 'It's good to hear from you. I have often wondered what became of you. I'm afraid I can't help you regarding Alan. I haven't spoken to him since the night you and he parted. I have come to believe, Jackie, that it's not always possible to make sense of death – '

I swore, screwed up the letter, and started again.

'... not always possible to make sense of loss, and that sometimes it's best not to try. It sounds like you've got yourself a life there in Wales, and I truly believe that you should concentrate on the present, not the past. I hope you don't find my advice impertinent. And I do hope you'll keep in touch.

There's not many of the old crowd left, we should stick together! With love from Jerry.'

I hadn't bought any Christmas cards, so I put the letter in an ordinary envelope, addressed it and stamped it and went out to post it before I had a chance to do a lot of useless thinking.

Judith Cutler

Judith Cutler has emerged over the last few years as one of our most reliably entertaining crime novelists, but until she submitted this story to me, I had not realised that she is an enthusiastic and accomplished writer of short fiction. This typically witty piece of work introduces us to a new and distinctive protagonist, Wedgwood, truly a 'pig of the world'.

FLYING PIGS

by Judith Cutler

We pigs have always had a bad press. What do humans say? *Her room's a pigsty. He eats like a pig. You're as thick as pig muck.* Not very nice, is it, being a pig with comparisons like these flying round you? You don't even think we're worth stealing: *Might as well,* you say, *be hanged for a sheep as for a lamb.* The only time a pig's brought into the conversation in favourable terms is when someone *brings home the bacon*. And what is bacon, but dead pig?

All right, it's our destiny. You keep us and feed us and kill us and eat us. You're pretty rotten to some of my relatives, keeping them penned up like battery hens. Others have whole fields to root through. I'm somewhere in between – I occupy a sty about fifty yards from their cottage. Of course I'm organic! None of your food pellets for me. I'm mash and scrap fed: regular food but a nice varied diet. Well, varied. She prides herself on trying everything from one of these flash cooking magazines. One month it's a hundred ways with pasta; next it's all fancy salads. All the same, you'll say, for a pig: it all goes down regardless. But I have my likes and dislikes, in food as in everything else. Take Malaysian chicken curry: loathsome stuff, in my humble opinion; on the other hand, a bit of rare steak goes down a treat. I suppose I should worry in case I get BSE, but the way I look at it, I probably won't be here to find out. Not if she has her way, anyway. Can't wait for me to go to that great pen in the sky. You can see the way she looks at me, rather like the way she looks at him, working out the ham to the last pound – that's the only reason she condescends to feed me. I'm a dirty smelly creature, see. All she does is slap the food in my trough and she's slamming into the car, her and her silly high heels. No manners. Him, now. He's different. He's John. Sometimes John, sometimes John Dear, and sometimes John You Bastard. Mostly, I suppose. She's Alison Love most of the time. He looks at her the way I'd eye up a truffle, but she never looks at him that way. No, she saves that for this man in the green car. Gavin My Angel. When he arrives, even if she's just about to fill my trough, she bangs the bucket down and runs off indoors with him. Once or twice she's left it almost within reach. I tried to climb over my wall, but I wasn't quite tall enough. And then I had a worry at the gate. In fact, I've had a number of goes at that since; you never know when a gate that you can open yourself might be useful.

John hasn't noticed it yet. He's a townie too. An artist. Makes pots in his workshop at the other side of the yard. He thought living on a small-holding would be green, you see, which is where I come in, of course. A wonderful recycler, in deed as well as in thought. And he's grateful. He likes to feed me bits and pieces by hand, and scratch my ears. I've managed to persuade him not to stuff me with over-ripe pears – terrible wind, they gave me – and convince him that an orange makes a nice aperitif. He talks to me while he scratches and feeds me. About his debts, and the big cheque he got the other day. And how he wishes Gavin didn't come here, rubbing his nose in it, whatever it might be. No wonder he's bitter: I wouldn't want to share a sow of mine with another boar.

Look at the poor man. Trails across to me as if he's carrying the burdens of the world instead of a bucket of – now what on earth is that?

'Yes, Wedgwood, you may well snuffle,' he says, tipping it into my trough. 'It was a spinach lasagne, but it ended up on the floor. Via the wall. I made sure there wasn't any broken crockery in it when I scraped it up: I didn't want to give you indigestion, now, did I?'

I agree. But he needn't have worried. We pigs can digest almost everything, though we draw the line at metal, of course.

'You know,' he continues, 'I reckon you can understand every word I say. And why they should talk about little piggy eyes, I don't know: you look very kind to me.'

I agree again, and put my head under his hand. As scratches go, it's pretty half-hearted, but it seems to make him feel better.

'I wish I could just divorce her,' he continues. 'But that'd mean selling up so she could have half. There's no way I could afford to buy her out, you see, Wedgwood. None at all.' He sighs.

I wiggle my ears, and sigh in sympathy. And self-interest. There's no way out of becoming a recipe ingredient eventually, but no one wants to rush such things. After all, a good healthy boar like me might have other destinies to fulfil. I'm blood-stock: I'm a Wessex Saddleback. Worth more alive than dead, I like to think. It would be terrible to be minced for sausages before I passed on my genes.

Now, being a pig on your own gives you plenty of time to think. Apart from eating – and notice, I don't add, *like a pig* – you roll in the mud. You have to roll, to keep clean. I prefer a nice deep scrape, so I can have a slow, sensuous wallow. And while I wallow I think.

What we've got to do is get rid of Alison. For good. I'm a pig of the world, and I know that if she disappeared, the first person the police would suspect is John. Motive, opportunity – they'd want to talk. They might even dig up the whole of the small-holding to see if he'd buried her. Now, there are areas of suspiciously lush growth in various places – the leek patch, for instance – but no one would persuade them that they weren't a result of human burial but of my recycling. They'd want to see for themselves, wouldn't they? They might even detain John while they looked, and then what would become of me?

A little more work on the catch on my gate gives me another opportunity to think. What I have to do is wait for John to be well clear of the premises. We need a witness to be able to testify that Alison was alive and well when he left for the market town with his pots. No problem there. He's usually collected by a mate with a big old van.

So we have a witness.

It's all plain sailing from there on. Except for one thing. The bits of metal. You know, her ring, her bra fastenings. I'm not sure how pigs deal with shoes, but I'll find a way. What I must do is watch and wait, and when my chance comes – snatch it!

Meanwhile, more work on that gate, plenty of stretching on the wall, and solid chomping to exercise the jaw. Oh, and make sure my scrape's really deep.

Today could be the day! It's a sunshine and heavy showers day, so my mud is lovely and liquid. I have a little roll to test it: excellent. Now, there's obviously a row going on in the house – his voice is rumbling away, while hers rises in great screams. At this rate he'll be late when his friend comes. And what about my breakfast? I squeal a couple of times.

He comes out with last night's peelings: 'Sorry, Wedgwood,' he says. 'I'll get you some nice mash tonight. But there's been a bit of a row.'

I lift an ear.

'Well, a lot of a row. Do you know, she actually threw her wedding ring at me. She'll have to wait till tonight before I can get it back – it's right behind the dresser.'

Is it now?

'See you tonight, Wedgwood – my goodness, Tom's here already!'

He's forgotten to stack the crates for his mate to load into the van; they must be late. So late they're hardly out of the yard before Gavin My Darling's green car appears. Better and better – they must have met in the lane. Gavin My Darling, we now have a witness that Alison was alive when you arrived. Excellent.

Alison must have heard the car. Still in her dressing-gown she shoots out the house into his arms, and then virtually drags him inside. What about my breakfast?

She's still – or again! – in her dressing-gown when Gavin Darling emerges into the yard. After an enormous embrace, he gets into his car and, waving, sets off. She waves him out of sight. How romantic. How touching. How vulnerable.

By this time I really am hungry and decide to let her know it. My squeals would rend the heart of a harder woman than Alison. OK, she'd rather slit my throat than feed me, but she's too squeamish to try. So I squeal more loudly. In between squeals I open the catch on my gate.

'Shut up, you bloody pig!'

I do have a name, madam.

'I don't know why he keeps you! If you don't stop that noise I'll take you down to the slaughterhouse!'

I'd like to see her try! We Wessex Saddlebacks are big, powerful animals, and it'd take more than a bit of hysterical ranting to get me into the pick-up truck.

This time I make my squeals more pathetic.

'Don't say you're ill!'

For a minute I'm silent. The last thing I want is a visit from the vet who might well be carrying humane killer.

I produce something between a whine and a snuffle and bang my trough.

'I suppose that stupid bastard forgot to feed you. It'd serve him right if I left you to starve.'

More whines.

'OK. OK. You'll just have to put up with this.' She comes pattering across the yard.

Excellent. Still in her dressing-gown and – how stupid can you get in a muddy, cobbled yard? – slippers. She tips a white sliced loaf into my trough and picks her way back. Or tries to. One rush from me and she's flat on her face. The whole thing's very quick. I wouldn't want you to think I'm any less efficient than the average abattoir. The fall stuns her. Then I lie on her – and a boar of my build lying on top of a small human body can extinguish life within a minute. In fact, I'd say her heart's stopped beating by the time I drag her back into my sty. Just to make sure, I arrange her face down in my scrape.

Before I lock my gate, I have a look round the yard. Hmph. Tracks. What can I do about that? I sit and think. Intelligent as I am, I can't manage a broom, and in any case, that would leave traces too. To my delight the sun goes in, and another shower swirls across the yard. Not enough water, though. How about the water butt? The tap's always dripped – one of the things John's been meaning to fix. I reckon I could push it a little further. There. Not a footprint, not a drag mark in sight. Resisting the temptation to help things along – being an artist, they say, is knowing where to stop – I withdraw to my scrape and lie down again.

At last John comes home. The first thing he does is check my trough, and he tuts when he sees only the nasty white bread, still, of course, untouched. 'I'm sure I can do better than that,' he says.

I grunt and let him scratch my ear.

When he comes with a bucket of mash – 'No, leave it a bit, Wedgwood, it's still hot' – it's clear he hasn't missed her. Soon he'll notice though. Later on he'll find her bag, and that'll worry him. Why should she go without her keys and purse? He'll start to worry. Eventually he'll call the police – another of the little insults they regale us with, calling these men pigs. I wonder how long it'll take to make them decide she's a missing person? A couple of days? Pretty uncomfortable ones for Gavin Green Car. And for John. But John's got witnesses, remember. I shall have to eat pretty solidly for a bit. I reckon I've got a week before they decide they really do have to check my sty, though they won't want to disturb me – I can look a bit mean if called on – and they certainly won't enjoy shifting all my waste products. Let's hope they have the sense to put them on the rose bed.

Conscience? Of course not! I've made the world a better place by getting rid of her. And now I shall have a better chance of fathering particularly healthy, intelligent litters. No, when my time for the bacon slicer comes, I confidently expect to go to heaven. After all, pigs do have wings.

Carol Anne Davis

One bonus of editing the CWA anthology is the chance I am afforded, from time to time, to sample the writing of talented writers whose work I have not previously encountered. 'Miss You Nights' is a good example. At the time I received the manuscript, I had not read Carol Anne Davis's acclaimed début *Shrouded*, but I enjoyed the story so much – and not just because I have a weakness for crime stories with pop song titles – that I determined to seek out her novel. I hope others may react in the same way after reading this tale with a splendid twist.

MISS YOU NIGHTS

by Carol Anne Davis

Twenty-four hours ago I made Melanie disappear, so now she's officially a missing person. It's that many hours before they start making enquiries – I've seen it on *Heartbeat* and *The Bill*. Some missing people stick a pin on the map, usually when they're sitting crying on a train just before the adverts. Not Melanie, though – she's chained by her ankle in the basement as I write. I'd have chained her by her waist because I bought the biggest piece of chain that the Garden Centre had in their Everything Must Go sale, but it might have interfered with the last stages of her pregnancy.

Not that it's one of those shadowy basements where the coffin creaks open as the clock strikes twelve. No, it's got proper lights, and I'll eventually put her in a plastic tub rather than an oakwood coffin. I've also covered the floor with my best pink rug and a good-as-new futon. I'd have got her a double bed but can you imagine a woman like myself carrying a double bed down fifty stairs? Still, the charity shop futon is very nice and they were also selling Mills and Boons so I got her ten of those to keep her company. She wasn't best pleased when I ushered her into the basement, but I'm sure that she'll come round.

Most people come round to your way of thinking if you're nice enough, at least eventually. Take my Henry. He's said he doesn't believe in marriage unless there are little ones involved so I imagine we'll have a summer wedding now. That'll give me time to lose a little weight and choose a lacy white dress and find somebody to take the baby for a half-day. Henry won't want a honeymoon. He's never been big on going out.

Melanie's very big. Eight months. I asked. She said that it's going to be a boy, that she saw it on a scan. She was shifting her weight from foot to foot and moving her key towards her door as she said it. Getting ready to put that door between me and my child. 'Oh, I've taken in a parcel for you,' I fibbed. She turned back to me then, moved her eyebrows high up her face, said, 'Oh thank you, Miss Lammar. Do you want to give it to me now?'

'My arm's not quite right. Could you come in and get it?' I asked. I saw that bit on the Saturday première, the *Inspired by Actual Events* season. The guy pretended that he'd hurt his arm and got a girl to help him lift a square brown box into his car. Then he pushed her inside and she screamed and the screen went dark and next thing you know he was whistling as he cleaned all the seats and then finding another girl.

'All right. But I'll have to make it quick. You know – the baby's pressing on my bladder.' Really, I didn't think it was right her talking about such matters. But I'd already put Mum's old commode in the cellar for her, so that she could stay down there until the natural birth.

Later that day I dropped the knife into the duck pond by the cemetery. No one can blame me if a duck is stupid enough to cut itself – I mean, you see on *Pet Rescue* that they get injured all the time. Providing they don't call the divers in, the water will hide the blade and wash away Melanie's DNA. Just the one smear, mind, because the silly girl pulled back and grazed her throat against the knife when I opened the door leading to the basement. She whimpered so much that you'd have thought I was some stranger rather than the woman next door.

Not that we often spoke. No, she'd just say, 'Nice again today,' or 'Not so nice today,' and I'd nod because Mum always said that a person should keep themselves to themselves and not be beholden to others. So I didn't want her asking to borrow my umbrella or my good summer dress, depending on what the weather was like.

She'll be warm and dry down there, no matter what the weather's like. If it wasn't for the fact that lodgers always murder their landladies, I could charge someone rent for it. But Melanie can have it rent-free until the birth. She can have pies and that tea where the flavour floods out and walks on her chain and books and those free newspapers that they put through the door every Thursday until she has her child.

Well, it's my baby now. My baby and Henry's. He'll be so pleased to hear he's a daddy when he next calls round. He can't call so often now, of course. You know what it's like, being in the army. They're often on secret manoeuvres and get flown to pastures new all the time.

'All that gadding about's not for me,' I once said.

'Wendy,' Henry replied, 'that's half your trouble.' I do so like it when he uses my Christian name. He pretends that he'd like me to get out and about but really I know that he's just worried that I might be lonely. Silly man – what with my books and my diary and my medical programmes I've got everything I need.

In fact, it's a busy life – there's *Children's Hospital* and *Casualty* on a Monday and *Trauma* and the library on a Tuesday. I've read most of the health books now but they're getting me more from other libraries and all for the cost of a postcard and a stamp. Wednesday there's that lunchtime slot where a real doctor appears on the screen and you can phone him up and he'll answer your questions without frowning. Non-TV doctors aren't like that: they frown all the time.

I phoned up once. Honest I did. I asked if you could put on weight by smoothing aromatherapy oils on to your wrists. I mean, oil has a lot of calories per tablespoon. I was using a little lavender oil every day just like Mum did and Henry said 'You ought to watch it, Wendy. You're getting fat.' Well, what with the reading and the diary keeping I hardly have time to cook and just get by on some pasties from the Yesterday's Bakery beside the sweet shop. So I started wondering about absorbing all those calories from the oil. Not that Henry was being critical, you understand – it's just that he worries about my health. I suppose we both do. I wasn't at all well as a youngster: Mum was always keeping me off school.

But Mum's been in Oaksview Cemetery, Plot 3705, these past three years and now it's just me – and when he can get time off there's also Henry. When we're a proper family, he'll live here all the time. He likes a good meal, does Henry, so we can watch *Masterchef* and *Ready, Steady, Cook* and *You Do the Pudding*. I wonder if Melanie likes to cook. She's the kind of girl who would have teased me at school or just ignored me. I don't think that she'll ignore me now, especially when I'm saying, 'Pant harder' and 'One last push' as the baby's head comes out.

Thursday is *Watchdog*. They sometimes look at vitamin pills and compare different brands of baked beans. Some of them contain more sugar than a chocolate bar and a third put together. Then there's *Horizon* which is often about medical cover-ups: that's why I've skipped some of my talks with Dr Weeksley since Mum passed on by. He seems nice enough on the surface – though he's another of the ones who frown a lot – but he could be using me as an unwitting guinea pig and subjecting me to sinister clinical trials behind my back. I saw them doing bad things to Mel Gibson late one Sunday night. They piped evil thoughts through his phone and tried to change his thinking. Dr Weeksley might be making me eat all those coffee creams.

Toddlers should only eat cheese triangles and that special blackcurrant juice that is kind to teeth so I'll make sure that when Henry junior arrives I keep those sweets which the Ambassador serves to his guests locked in the basement. Dead bodies are also supposed to smell sweet and make tracker dogs start barking – that's why I rolled the big barrel down to the cellar and have been bringing down Mum's friend's bags of concrete powder ever since. He was planning to concrete over all of the grass out the front, was Mum's friend, when the Lord came and took him away without warning. Mum got rid of his photo and his cardigans but the big mixing barrel and the bags of powder stayed.

Say a person wanted rid of another person after she'd given birth. The first person would stab the second really hard then put their dead body, doubled up, into the barrel. Then they'd follow the instructions on the concrete mix and use a bucket to make up batch after batch. They'd pour it over the dead person and then that person would really and truly be missing, disappeared for life.

A life takes nine months to create. That means she'll be here for a month, the longest I've ever had a visitor. Henry only manages to stay for a couple of hours, they work him that hard.

He shows me he loves me and then he falls asleep and I lie there in the bed watching him breathing. Sometimes I wish that he'd never wake up, but he does. He looks at me in that funny way and says, 'Got to go.' His voice is all gruff at leaving. It's just like on the films only he doesn't whirl me around for five minutes on account of his bad back and weak left leg. I try to be brave because I know that his country needs him, but I can't help but cry.

I can't hear any cries from the living-room. That's good. Means the basement must be soundproof. I used to play down there with my nurse doll when Mum needed a rest. She said that there were no germs underground – not like in the shops and at school and all of the other dirty places. I put a Handy Andy over my nose when I go in the library nowadays.

I wonder if Melanie would like a proper handkerchief too? I left her three cheese and onion pasties and a glass of milk yesterday because phone-the-doc said that pregnant women needed the calcium in dairy products. I left her a brand new diary which I got for a pound on account of this being March. The chain around her ankle is a twenty-foot one so she can walk all the way across the cellar and back again. Pregnant women shouldn't overdo it but still need to take daily gentle exercise. I wouldn't have chained her up at all except that I sometimes watch *Prisoner Cell Block H* and know that women can be very bad to other women. And Henry would be shocked if I was bruised.

Henry knows what it's like to be bruised. He's seen unarmed combat and nuclear wars and he's also helped spy on the Russians. It's so lucky that I went for my library books at 10 a.m. that Wednesday. I usually go on a Tuesday after cashing my invalidity cheque but I'd just had another letter (date as postmark) about the importance of not missing any more hospital visits so stayed in to make Dr Weeksley think that I had one of my heads.

The library woman stepped back a little the way she always does when I approach the desk. I can tell she's worried about germs, but she needn't be because I have my Relax in a Radox Bath every morning. There was a man handing over his ticket so I smiled to reassure him that I was germ-free. Then I looked at his books: *Dad's Army* (based on the first series) and *The Spy Who Came in from the Cold*. 'Oh, you're a soldier,' I said.

He looked me up and down for a minute, the way they do on *EastEnders*, you know, then admitted, 'That's right, love.' He seemed pleased that I'd guessed.

'My dad was stationed in barracks,' I said. Mum told me that once but I was too young to know what it meant and I'm still not quite sure though I've watched *Land Girls* and the repeats of *Soldier, Soldier*.'

'You still live with him, like?' he asked.

'Oh no. He was sent abroad just after I was born. Then it was just me and Mum.'

'Just you and your mum.' He had his head to one side, was all thoughtful.

'But then she ... passed away with her pancreas. And now there's just me.'

'And you like soldiers, do you, love?' Looking back at it now, he was probably putting me through some sort of official test to see if I was suitable as an army girlfriend. Well, I suppose I can call myself a fiancée after today, now that I'm ready to bear him a child.

I nodded and the library woman came back and stamped his books. He left sharpish. Then she stamped mine and I walked through the doorway – to find him waiting in the vestibule. That's what they call that odd bit of space between one door and the next. You see it on *Home Interiors* and *Changing Rooms* and *Living Space*.

'I could kill for a cup of tea,' he said. 'Any idea where?' Well, I didn't. I mean, they sell such funny meals nowadays – soup made from du jours and la cartes. No pastries or stew. 'Being a soldier ... being sent to a new town every few weeks. It's not easy,' he continued. He was only about thirty but the stress had already made him lose most of his hair.

'Come back with me,' I said, tucking *Your Thyroid and You* more firmly under my right arm, 'I know how to warm the pot and let everything infuse properly.'

'I'll bet you do, darling,' he said. I knew then that he was going to be my friend, the way that Mum had had her friend.

And within a minute of finishing his Belgian biscuit he'd put his hand on my arm then slid it over to my breast. I went quite shaky, then, but he seemed to understand that I'd saved myself, said, 'Don't be nervous, love. It's Nature.' But he was shy himself and could hardly look at me as he undid all the buttons on my dress. That was almost three years ago. It's only right that we should be married. I can't phone him because the KGB has the army phones all tapped and I'd be at risk.

Then it occurred to me to check that Melanie wasn't at risk. It's at least a day since I showed her her new home and there's a lot that can go wrong with a first pregnancy. I don't know all of the names – you'd have to ask George Clooney. Anyway, I got a new knife from the cutlery drawer then went down to the basement to cheer Melanie up.

She was lying on the futon when I opened the door but she pushed herself back until her shoulders collided with the wall. 'Careful,' I said. 'You might harm the baby.' People always do that on television, tell you to think of someone else. Very thin girls are told to put on weight for their mums and drug addicts are told to think of their children. I think of Henry all the time – he's all I've got.

'I've brought you your lunch. It's still hot,' I said. I set the microwaved steak pie on my best plate at the end of the futon. Mum's social worker said that we should be eating hot food in the winter but we were always too busy keeping up with *Sunset Beach* and *Falcon Crest* to preheat the cooker so she got us the microwave.

'Why are you doing this?' Melanie asked in a little voice.

'Because you need to eat. Think of the baby.' I stayed near the door and kept the knife raised so that I could slash at her hand if she tried to grab my arm.

'No, I mean, why are you . . .?' She lifted the chain attached to her ankle and held it out to me.

'So that you'll stay here until the baby comes.'

'And then . . .?'

I must have glanced at the barrel and the bags of concrete mix in the corner because she sort of whined like the long-haired girls do in *The Boris Karloff Season* and began to rock back and forth.

Just then someone pounded on the door. It could be Henry. 'You keep quiet or else,' I said. They always say *or else*, especially on Channel 5 on a Saturday night. Sometimes they add, 'or you'll be sorry.' I said that bit too before I slammed the basement door.

I stood in the vestibule and called, 'Who is it?'

'Police.' I waited for them to kick the door down. 'Miss Lammar? We'd like to talk to you for a moment if we may.'

I put the chain on then peered out. A policeman and a policewoman stood there. He was holding a pen and pad.

'We've had a missing persons report.' I put my hands behind my back so that they couldn't steal my fingerprints and frame me for something else to improve their clear-up rate. 'Your next-door neighbour just came back from a business trip and he claims his wife has disappeared.'

'So, what's it do with me?' That's what the accused always say in *The Bill* though if it's a woman she usually has her hair in curlers. Mum always said we should be pleased with what the good Lord gave us so I've never seen the need for an artificial curl.

'Well, when did you last see her?' the policewoman said. Two minutes ago, I thought. I strained my ears and thought that I could hear a woman screaming.

'Do you have your TV on?' the man asked, turning his head to one side.

I noddingly lied yes and they stared some more. At this stage the accused usually turns to their loved one and says, 'I'll be back before dinner,' as they lead him or her away.

'My Henry will be worried if you take me down the cells,' I explained.

'Henry? He's . . .?' The policeman brandished his pen again and looked at me.

'Henry Smith,' I said, then added, 'But that's classified information,' remembering how reluctant Henry had been to tell me his second name.

'Classified?' The policeman licked his lips. The woman smiled at me really sweetly. If it hadn't been for Melanie screaming her head off in the basement I'd have invited them in for a coffee and a ginger snap.

'Exactly.' I tapped my nose.

It was then that the female police officer leaned closer. 'Mrs Lammar – '

'Miss – though I'm engaged to be married.'

'To Henry Smith?'

I nodded in case some bug was picking up my every word.

'So could Mr Smith have seen Melanie in the past two days?'

'No, he hasn't been able to get away since the first of August.'

'Because of his work?'

'It's a vocation,' I said. I mean, I watched *The Learning Zone* when the STV transmitter was down. I know the difference.

'So you just get by on postcards and phone calls?' the policewoman asked.

Again I felt sorry for my lonely man. 'No, I'm not on the phone and the enemy intercepts all his mail so we can't write to each other.'

The policeman was writing faster and faster. 'Miss Lammar, can you give us the name and address of your GP?'

I thought about saying no but that might be obstructing the peace or perverting the course of justice. So I told them and they wrote it down and went away.

They might come back and be undercover this time. I realised that I was going to have to look pregnant if I was to fool them. After all, I couldn't give birth to a baby in April if I'd not had a big stomach when they asked me questions in March. It was lucky that I'd put my chain on the door the first time round so that they could only see my face. Face it out – that's what Mum always said when the girls at school were laughing and pointing. So I got the spare pillow – Henry's pillow – from my keepsakes drawer and put it under my jumper and tied my apron back over the top.

Sometimes you have to be cruel to be kind so I went downstairs and slapped Melanie's face twice to stop her screaming. That never fails to work, especially if you add, 'And there'll be plenty more where that came from if you don't shape up.' She was still sort of breathing hard and whimpering and maybe sending messages to some tracker dog with specially good hearing. Made me wonder if that We Have Everything shop by the bus station sold proper gags.

Well, I thought I'd better get my strength back before going to the shop so I heated a vegetable bridie and a box of microwave chips, on account of vegetables being slimming and me wanting to fit into my wedding dress. Then I watched the first three episodes of *Jimmys* on video before going to fetch my coat.

I had one arm in one sleeve when the doorbell went again. This time there were three policemen and Dr Weeksley. I thought that they'd wanted my GP but maybe she was frowning too much to come along. 'Wendy, it's been a long time,' Dr Weeksley said and smiled really wide like Martians do on *The Twilight Zone*.

'I've been busy,' I said. 'You know – getting ready for the baby.'

The three policemen all looked at each other and then at Dr Weeksley and he said, 'Can we come in?'

I made a big show of standing back to protect my stomach before opening the door. Then I walked that sort of penguin way that a pregnant woman walks on GMTV when she's getting a makeover. 'How about we all have a nice chat at the kitchen table?' Dr Weeksley said.

Well, I've just got a scullery with a wee work surface so they had to settle for the living-room chairs. 'Can you give the man your full name, Wendy?' Dr Weeksley said. Honestly, that man is always asking stupid questions.

'Course I can,' I answered, turning to the man with the notebook. I even gave him both my middle names.

'And how old are you, Miss Lammar?' the writing man continued.

'I'm sixty,' I said.

He stopped writing then and sort of stared at my stomach. And Dr Weeksley frowned and then turned to them and said, 'You might want to look around.'

Two of them walked out and then Dr Weeksley asked how I'd been and if I'd been talking to Melanie, my missing neighbour. And I was just looking at his coat to see if he had a lie detector in his pocket when the police came back and said did I have the key to the locked room.

'What key?' I asked. At this stage they're supposed to say,

'You haven't heard the last of this,' but they didn't. They just drove me down to the police station (Women and Children's Unit) instead.

After that I claimed my Miranda rights and said I was taking the Fifth and that if they weren't going to think of me they should at least think of the baby. And Dr Weeksley asked me to lift my jumper and I saw that people behind enemy lines had stolen the baby and substituted a pillow instead. The social worker said didn't I realise the trauma I'd put poor Melanie through? I mean, I only ever spoke to her about the weather. And a tall man said that I was a danger to myself and to the public and sent me to a special place.

'Will the army let Henry see me now?' I ask the resident psychiatrist who I get to see for five minutes every single day.

'No, Henry took advantage of you when you were ill,' she says. 'If he came back he'd be facing criminal charges. He must realise he's done wrong because he didn't give you his real name and we've checked with the army and he isn't there.'

So Henry is missing too, roaming the streets night and day showing people my photograph. We were meant to be together so I'll have to escape and make my way back to the flat. Then the army will put us under the Witness Protection Programme and give us fake passports and big sun-glasses. Plus a foreign house with a slightly squint coconut tree.

I'll need to know what it's like being abroad, so I've started to watch *Wish You Were Here* and *The Travel Show* and *Holiday*. The psychiatrist says that armchair travel's broadening my horizons, that it's a very good sign. I also watch *Murder she Wrote* for tips on how to kill the security warden. The doc says that I'm over my medical obsessions, that I'm moving away from escapism towards real life.

Eileen Dewhurst

Over the last few years Eileen Dewhurst, who had in the past concentrated almost exclusively on writing novels, has produced a string of notable short stories. 'Three's Company' is a characteristically accomplished tale which tackles the 'missing person' theme obliquely but in compelling style. Readers who are familiar with Eileen's longer fiction may spot that one aspect of the story reminds them of a plot development in a novel she wrote a few years ago. The device is, however, used here in a different way and to different effect. Experienced crime writers do from time to time return to ideas that have especially appealed to them and relish the chance to approach them from a new angle (think of Agatha Christie's *Endless Night* as compared to *The Murder of Roger Ackroyd*); it is one of the pleasures of the craft.

THREE'S COMPANY

by Eileen Dewhurst

'You could come with me, you know,' she said, watching him. 'Why don't you? Once in a while at least. Peter and Emma are always telling me how much they'd like you to spend the night with them as well.'

Her husband yawned and stretched, smiling his pleasure at watching her as she dressed, and she turned away, shrugging, before his answer came.

'I'll join you one of these days, Alma, but it's a bit of a journey at the end of a working day, and it's not as if we don't see Peter and Emma at the golf club at weekends. Tell them thank you when you see them tonight, and I'll tell them myself on Saturday.'

'OK,' she said lightly. 'So long as you don't mind sleeping alone every Wednesday night.'

'I do mind. Come here . . .'

She moved over to the bed, but her air of imminent, unpostponable departure inhibited him from doing more than laying his hand on her arm and telling her she was working too hard.

'I only go this early when I'm at the Guildford office. It's time you were on the move too, by the way.'

He glanced at the bedside clock. 'By God, yes!' He was out of bed and rummaging around for his dressing-gown, his respect for routine taking over from his disappointment that she was on her way without the matutinal dalliance he so much enjoyed.

She kissed his cheek as he blundered past her, one leg into his y-fronts. 'See you tomorrow night, my darling. And I'll ring as usual tonight, of course.'

'Of course.' Oh, but he was blessed that this high-powered

and beautiful woman was his wife. 'I'll hang on the minutes, as usual.'

'I know you will. Bye-bye now, Jimmy dear.'

She was gone. He heard the rhythmic click of her feet on the stairs, then the various familiar sounds from the kitchen. She had a bowl of cereal before leaving, and there would just be time for him to get downstairs and kiss her again before she left. But he didn't feel like putting on a spurt. She would be turned off anyway, she'd been turned off when she said goodbye by the bed, and being Alma, she wouldn't turn herself on again until tomorrow night. When she did, though...

His mind a-glitter with erotic reminiscence, Jimmy Crowther ambled across the landing to the bathroom.

The out-of-town branch of the London firm of solicitors in which Alma was a partner offered more small frustrations than usual on this particular weekly visit, and by half-past five she had had enough. Emma was unlikely to be in, and Peter rarely got home before seven, but when her weekly overnight stays in Dorking became regular they had given her a key to their house. Actually it had been given to her and Jimmy, over Saturday lunch at the golf club and with a renewed invitation to Jimmy to extend their foursome to a Wednesday night. So far, though, he hadn't got round to it. Her husband had grown more middle-aged than she had, Alma reflected, not for the first time, as she entered Peter and Emma's driveway. Less and less inclined to undertake activity that called for any effort, or the least change of routine.

She parked outside the house, noting absently as she walked to the front door that Emma's garage was closed as usual, to disguise the absence of her car.

Unless she hadn't yet gone out...

But that would be highly unusual, and as soon as she entered the house and felt the totality of its silence, Alma knew it was empty. She took her small bag upstairs to the guest bedroom, smiling her approval of the weekly sophistication on Emma's part which had her removing the coverlet and turning the sheet down on Alma's side of the bed.

As usual, again, Alma took her best nightie out of her bag and placed it on her pillow, took her sponge bag through into the en suite bathroom, changed her blouse and her shoes. Then she went downstairs, helped herself to a drink from the cupboard in the corner of the snug, and sat down with it to read Emma's *Daily Mail*.

She heard Peter's car as she drained her glass, and set it down before going out to the hall to welcome him.

'Hi!'

'Hi! Oh, darling!'

As usual, they were instantly in each others' arms. As passionately glad to be together as they had been that first time almost three years ago. But passion that can be expressed only once a week has ample time to renew its intensity, and theirs was as intense as it had been at the start, that Wednesday night which had astounded them both when Emma had been called away to her sick mother.

'Peter! Oh, Peter! Every week seems longer than the last.'

'We have Saturdays.'

'We have Saturday torment. How do we manage not to give ourselves away?'

'We probably do, but Jimmy isn't looking.'

'No. Jimmy doesn't look at anything much beyond his navel. Where he's implanted a miniature of me smiling a wifely smile. God, darling, but Jimmy's pleased with himself and his limited little life.'

'Just as well.' Holding her by the waist he drew her back into the snug, kissed her again as he sat her in Emma's chair, then picked up her glass and went over to the corner cupboard. 'He's never likely to suspect.'

Watching her, he saw her shudder. 'No. He trusts me. He loves me. He's a good man.'

'Whom you married.' Glass in hand he dropped his long length to the floor by her chair and nestled his shoulders between her compliant legs. 'Good as he is, why did you marry him?'

'He was kind. Like he still is. And generous. And he loved me. And I was on the rebound.'

'Ah.'

'He was a friend and he helped me through it.'

'Not the best basis for marriage.'

'I don't find him repulsive.'

It was his turn to shudder. 'Don't tell me that!'

'You don't find Emma repulsive. I accept that. And Jimmy gave me William and Sue.'

'And trusts you blindly. Yes, I understand. And I'm fond of him too. Sometimes ... I feel badly every now and then that he's the odd one out, the only one of the four of us who doesn't know the way we live.'

'So do I. But ignorance is bliss for Jimmy, darling. And how can he ever lose it? Was there ever such a foolproof way of being unfaithful?'

'Never.' He twisted round between her knees, leaned up to kiss her. 'Emma's left us a new recipe. It sounds good.'

'It smells good too. Emma's ... all right, Peter?'

'I'd know if she wasn't.'

'Which means you and she are still OK.'

He twisted round again, to look steadily and seriously into her eyes. 'Yes.'

She managed not to flinch. 'And you're not living a lie. I envy you, Peter.'

'Jimmy's all right, you've just told me. And I see it for myself every Saturday.' He heaved himself to his feet. 'Another drink, darling?'

'I'm ahead of you, I'll wait for the wine.' Alma glanced at her watch. 'And ring Jimmy. It's his time.'

Jimmy took a while to answer, and when he did he sounded strange and uncertain.

'Oh ... Alma ...'

Alma's heart was suddenly squeezed very small by two swooping grasps of alarm. But she managed to tell him lightly that he didn't sound quite himself.

'Oh, I'm all right, darling. It's just that ... Well, I've got a visitor. Derek Wheatcroft, my new assistant – the cocky young chap I've been telling you about' – the parenthesis was a whisper – 'is here having a drink with me.' Alma wished her husband wasn't sounding so apologetic for so ridiculous a reason, it brought a quotation into her head, something about *a great gulf fixed* ...

'That's fine, darling, I'm glad you aren't on your own on a Wednesday night, for once.'

'I don't mind being on my own. He rather bulldozed me.' The whisper again. The fussy, hissing sound irritated Alma. 'I made the mistake of saying I was alone this evening, and he practically invited himself – '

She had to interrupt. 'So, that's flattering from the younger generation. Enjoy yourself, my love. I'm sorry there isn't enough supper for two.'

'I should say not!' her husband responded with swift indignation. 'I'll offer him a second drink – which he's bound to accept – and then he can be on his way.'

'He's not married, is he? You may have a job dislodging him.'

'We'll see.' He really shouldn't be sounding so grim about so trivial a task, Alma thought. But then, she shouldn't be so grimly anxious to bring her conversation with him to a close. 'What are you doing, darling?'

'Oh, chatting with Emma while she puts the finishing touches to one of her specials. Peter's working in the shed as usual, on his boat. Better let you go now, darling, and I'll see you tomorrow.'

'Oh, yes, darling. See you tomorrow!'

Peter turned round from the drinks cupboard as she switched off. 'So. Jimmy's entertaining?'

'Reluctantly. He's got his sidekick from the bank there for a drink. I think it's great, but he's obviously not happy. I just hope he isn't being too old-womanish, if the young man wants to be friends it can only be good for work relations.'

'Don't think about it tonight.' Peter crossed back to her chair, glanced at his watch, stood looking down at her. 'Emma said the food would be at its best at eight. It's seven now ... Shall we?'

Alma nodded without speaking, and he helped her to her feet. Still in silence, they climbed the stairs side by side and crossed the landing to the guest bedroom.

Jimmy didn't know how Derek Wheatcroft had contrived to get him where he now found himself. In the last place on earth, he told himself angrily, that he wanted to be. Derek had described the place over their drinks at home as the best club in the Home Counties, but Jimmy was finding the repetitive, minimalist music too insistent, and the light flickering through the semi-darkness disagreeably disturbing . . . And there was something about the women, and the men drinking with them at the few spaced tables in the gloom around him, that made him uneasy. Something baleful. Cold. Remote, even when he saw a woman at the nearest table put her hand on a man's arm. The movement had been too slow, too deliberate, to be any sort of warm or spontaneous gesture. Almost as if . . .

Alarm bells sounding, he started to get to his feet.

Now a hand was on *his* arm, but thank heaven it was only Derek's, and this gesture, at least, was unconsidered. 'What is it, Jimmy?' He didn't remember giving his subordinate permission to use his first name. 'Aren't you enjoying yourself?'

'These women . . .'

'Yes, if you wish.' Jimmy saw the young man's eyes gleam in the small globe of light in the centre of their table. 'But very high-class. Totally discreet. Some of them have to be for their own sakes, the middle-class housewives who need a safety valve. Shall we invite a couple of them for a drink? You don't have to carry it through.'

Jimmy shuddered. 'No, thank you. But don't let me inhibit *you*, Derek. I'll be on my way when I've finished my drink.' The one thing he had managed to insist on, thank God, was that he come in his own car. So he was free to leave when he was ready. And he had been ready from the moment he had stepped through the curtained door and been enveloped by this strange, cold, predatory atmosphere . . . He hadn't known he was so weak, so easily persuaded.

'Pity.' Derek Wheatcroft tapped the champagne bottle. 'There's a lot still in here.'

'All right, I'll stay for a fill-up.' He hadn't been weak, he'd been thinking about life at the bank if he refused to go for a drink with his assistant, that was what had had him reluctantly trailing Derek Wheatcroft through the Surrey lanes, his irritation increasing when he realised their destination was Dorking – as he'd been forced out for the evening anyhow he might as well have accepted Peter and Emma's invitation to join Alma at their house for the night, it would have been preferable to this nonsense . . .

He hadn't expected Derek's choice of place to be like this, but he mustn't turn tail, be so obviously chicken that the authority he had worked so steadily and hard for would be undermined. On a vision of sniggering youngsters and pitying looks, Jimmy Crowther smiled and raised his glass.

And over the rim of it saw something that made him clutch at his chest while his head seemed to explode in a cascade of fractured light.

'What is it, Jimmy?'

'Nothing. I just saw . . .' He'd played the hero's friend and confidant for years in the local dramatic society, for heaven's sake, he could still carry it off. His smile felt like a rictus, but he held it. 'I think I must just have been affected by those swirling lights.'

The young man chuckled. 'The strobes. You'd have to be careful in a disco, Jimmy. Now, shall we have a pair of ladies over?'

'No! No,' he repeated, less passionately. He had to be cunning. And the two glasses of champagne following the scotch he had had at home seemed to be sharpening him. 'Leave it for the moment, please, Derek. So far as I'm concerned, at least. If you want to – '

'No, no. I'm happy to take my time.' *And see more of my boss's sudden semi-capitulation.* Jimmy could see what Derek Wheatcroft was thinking, as clearly as if the lad's head had been made of glass.

'Good.' Jimmy took another mouthful of champagne, trying to sort out the whirl of implications in his head. Peter and Emma. Alma . . . He would sit there until the place closed if necessary. Or go back in when he'd managed to shake off Derek . . .

But after a queasy half-hour in which they finished the bottle of champagne, Derek told his boss there was a woman he rather wanted to be alone with. 'I haven't seen her here before' – Jimmy's heart leapt at the words, but sank again as Derek pointed the woman out – 'and I like what I see. Mind if I disappear sir?' Jimmy had to accept that the grin made the gentle mockery unexceptionable.

'Not at all.' A tall handsome woman was approaching their table, although Jimmy hadn't been aware of his companion making any sign. That was how it had been in his youth, he suddenly remembered, on a brief, bleak diminution of his rage: sitting in a public place with some workmates, noticing a pretty girl, and while he was wondering what he could do about it not realising that one of his companions had exchanged secret signs with her until he saw them moving towards one another . . . 'You go off, Derek my lad. I'll be on my way in a moment.'

'Shame.' But Derek, of course, didn't look surprised by Jimmy's announcement. Had he ever really expected his boss to disappear with one of these women?

The answer to that question didn't interest Jimmy. All that interested him was what he was going to do next, and he watched in relief as Derek and his choice disappeared behind the red curtain that hung across the far side of the room.

When they were out of sight he clicked his fingers at a waiter, a gesture he normally considered arrogant. 'I'll have a double scotch, please. And tell me: do the – ladies – have names?'

'Sure.' The waiter, who was young and friendly, smiled at him encouragingly. 'They have a table apiece, and the name goes with it. That one' – he nodded to the empty table nearest Jimmy's – 'they're known as Ringtime. On account of long fingers and lots of rings. You see the sort of thing?'

'Sure,' Jimmy echoed. 'And that one?'

The waiter gave him a swift keen look. 'That's Marilyn. I don't have to explain her name, do I?'

'No. That one?'

'Aah.' The boy nodded understandingly. 'General assessment of talent? That one's Wednesday. Only ever here on a Wednesday night.'

'I see. Thanks.'

If he hadn't been sitting down he'd have fallen to the floor. As it was, he had to hold on to the table as his head exploded for the second time. The music, the steady, soft, sinister beat, seemed to be happening inside him, tapping relentlessly at his breastbone. Wednesday. Wednesday after Wednesday after

Wednesday. *Emma in the kitchen preparing one of her specials ... Peter working outside on his boat ... Something nasty in the woodshed ...*

The waiter brought his drink, and he paid the outrageous price he was asked for it. There was a man at her table, he was anticipating a long wait. But after a few moments he saw her get to her feet, put a finger on the man's lips as he turned a suppliant face up to her, and set out across the room in the direction of the cloakrooms. Downing his scotch at a gulp, he got up and followed her.

She was just short of the women's room door when he caught up with her and took hold of her arm. He didn't know what he was going to say, but when she swung round, trying to shake her arm free, he heard his voice shout, 'Wednesday!'

Emma looked at him with amazement that turned to shock. Then, under his angry glare, she said, 'Oh, Jimmy!' and began to laugh.

'We've got to talk,' he said, tightening his grip on her arm. 'We'll go out to your car.'

'But I've got – '

'No you haven't, Emma, not tonight.' He had to have the worst, in so many words. 'Come on.'

When they were in her car she turned to him, smiling. 'So,' she said. 'You've caught up with the three of us at last, Jimmy. We've been sorry for you, the only one not in the know, we've felt really bad, but there didn't seem to be anything we could do. And now you've done it yourself. Peter and Alma will be as relieved as I am, we hated deceiving you ... Whatever is it?'

He was staring at her in horror. 'But I wasn't ... I didn't ... I was just brought here for a drink by my assistant, I had no idea ...' His voice cracked. 'Emma, for God's sake tell me ... Peter and Alma? Every Wednesday?'

'Oops!' she said. She had had quite a lot to drink. 'So it's still poor Jimmy!' And she started to laugh again.

The sun through the thin curtains of the guest bedroom woke Peter early. For a few moments he watched Alma as she continued to sleep, touching the hair to each side of her face so gently he didn't wake her. But soon he was unable to resist a kiss, and then she sighed and stretched and leaned up and took him yet again into her arms.

When they were eventually lying quietly side by side, smiling at one another, Peter said he would make tea, and got out of bed and padded over to the bathroom, where he filled the kettle. When he had put it on he went over to the window and drew back the curtains.

'It's a glorious morning. Set fair, I should say. Pity it's not Saturday and golf. I say!' He had brought his eyes down from the leafy horizon. 'Emma's car's in the drive. I didn't hear her come in.'

'Emma's the essence of discretion, darling.'

Of sophistication, too. Neither of them was the least bit disconcerted by her return. Just very slightly puzzled, because normally Alma saw Emma only on a Saturday, or when they made specific dates.

'I know. But – it's odd.'

Alma glanced at the bedside clock. 'It's barely seven. She's probably asleep.'

'Probably. But I think I'll just look in . . .' He was pulling on his dressing-gown as he spoke, and with a swift smile towards the bed he left the room.

He was back right away. 'Bed's not slept in. She must have just arrived and be still downstairs. I'll go and see . . .'

He stuck his feet into his slippers before leaving the room a second time. Feeling slightly put out by her lover's concern for his wife, Alma heard the flap of them on the stairs. Crossing the hall . . .

Then she heard a shout so hoarse and anguished she was out of bed on a reflex and struggling into her own dressing-gown as she followed Peter down the stairs. The continuing sounds – sunk now to a steady moaning – led her into the sitting-room.

Emma was sitting upright in her chair, and Peter was kneeling at her feet. The sitting-room curtains were heavier than the curtains in the guest bedroom, and through the gloom Alma couldn't think what was so upsetting Peter about his wife sitting at home in her usual chair. So she clicked on the overhead light, and then she too began to shout and then to moan.

Emma's face was mottled mauve and white, she was sticking her tongue out at Alma, and her eyes were wide and staring.

The police were hammering on the door before they had even got the binbag fastened.

Marjorie Eccles

Rather like Eileen Dewhurst, Marjorie Eccles is a well-established crime novelist who has of late turned to the short story with conspicuous success. Crucially, she cares about her characters; here, for instance, the relationship between Orlando and Sylvie is economically but convincingly portrayed. She is also skilled at evoking foreign locales; her contributions to the last two CWA anthologies were set in Armenia and South Africa respectively – now she provides us with a troubled outsider's perspective on Vienna.

THE SEARCH FOR OTTO WAGNER

by Marjorie Eccles

'Wagner?' she said. 'I thought he was a composer.'

'Otto, not Richard, my ignorant little love. Architect, not composer. Austrian, not German.'

'Oh, well, go if you must. But count me out. I shall go to Tenerife.' A pause. 'With Angela.' There was a world of meaning in that pause.

So, here he was, six weeks later, no Sylvie, and himself halfway through the first day of his first visit to Vienna. Distinctly underwhelmed by it at the moment, to be honest. A beautiful, cultured city, which for some reason had less to say to him than almost any other major city he'd ever visited, a circumstance that had put him out more than a little. Orlando expected the reality to come up to the expectation and was always annoyed when it didn't.

As a tourist, which he was for this morning only, he was in the sort of mood which made the city seem overcrowded and schmaltzy: he hadn't cared to visit the Spanish Riding School and disdained to view the sights vulgarly from a horse-drawn landau. St Stephen's cathedral seemed to him like the monkey house at the zoo, its glories obscured by too many people milling around. Tacky Mozart souvenirs met his eyes everywhere he turned – and the sachertorte with which he was now indulging himself was not wickedly rich, gooey and intensely chocolatey, as he'd been told it would be by everyone who knew he was coming here, but a tired, dry and crumbly affair, only edible by reason of the excellent coffee that washed it down. His interest in the Prater and its Ferris Wheel was minimal, he was already fed up with references to Harry Lime. And the smell of horse was overpowering.

As a professional... well. He'd known before he came that the city's architecture would contain too much grandiose imperialism for his taste; he had yet to encounter the art nouveau buildings which were the ostensible purpose of his visit. The florid, wedding cake public edifices imitating the past on the Ringstrasse filled him with dismay, though that could have been partly due to a restless night in an unfamiliar bed after having driven twice around the Ring in order to find the turning to the small family hotel Anton had booked for him – the woeful end of a lamentable journey, eleven hours at the wheel, most of it on the ruler-straight autobahn through mind-numbing, disciplined Germany, being hooted at by manic German drivers.

Plus time for that mind-shattering interlude at Melk, with the abbey shining in golden baroque splendour on its cliff above the sluggish river, while he heaved into the water the thing which had lain like an unexploded bomb in the boot until then. Where now, he hoped, it still lay, on the river bed. But possibly floating downstream towards the Danube, if the rocks he'd sought to weight it down with had torn through the plastic refuse sack he'd wrapped it in. Who could tell? All in all, it had been a nerve-wracking experience. He still felt unhinged.

But there was no going back, not now.

Orlando had some time ago decided that he disliked flying – or rather that he disliked airports, and the loss of individuality they brought, all that humanity being herded together like sheep. Also, he had known he was going to need his car at some point or other on the journey... a point which, in the event, had turned out to be Melk, a purely fortuitous stop, when he had seized his chance... But half-way through Germany, stalled in an accident tail-back for an hour, he'd have given much for a steadying glass of scotch and a comfortable seat with British Airways, rather than the sausages and stodge which was all the next services had to offer. His breakfast here in Vienna had been cold ham and sausage, too.

He endeavoured to pull himself together. He couldn't spend the rest of his life looking at the world through jaundiced eyes, missing Sylvie. He would have to accustom himself to being without her. What was done was done. Perhaps tomorrow, he'd feel different, when he'd had a good night's sleep and he'd seen the Karlsplatz and the Steinhof church for himself, and not merely in photographs . . .

It was unforgivable of Anton to be so late – if he'd ever had any intention of turning up, that is, of keeping his promise to show Orlando the delights of his wonderful native city.

He ordered another coffee while he gave Anton the benefit of a further half-hour, closing his eyes against the procession of plodding, weary old horses pulling open carriages filled with tourists, feeling the sun warm on his face as he sat at the small table outside the very café where the Secessionists were reputed to have met.

Otto Wagner . . . Orlando Williams . . . He had been entertained by the charming coincidence of them bearing the same initials, having already found so many other things to admire in the oeuvre of the Jugendstil architect whose work, he felt, had much to say to him. To have created a work of art out of a railway terminus, to have designed those twin pavilions of the Karlsplatz, to build them in white marble, moreover, embellishing them in green and gold, as unlike a London underground station as it was possible to imagine, seemed to Orlando nothing short of a marvel. He could barely wait to see them, and the church at Steinhof.

Anton, likewise, had professed to admire Wagner's work, though Orlando knew now that this was expediency rather than true admiration.

Orlando himself had originally thought of qualifying as an architect, but the long training had defeated his half-formed good intentions. Instead, he had found a niche in writing and lecturing about late nineteenth- and early twentieth-century architecture, a period which had a special appeal to him. A book and several articles on the art nouveau period had put him on the lecture circuit up and down the country, where he was very popular on account of his cherubic good looks and the throwaway humour he brought to his talks, and had proved reasonably profitable, so far. He wasn't sure how long this could go on. For one thing, he had begun to weary of the sinuous decadence, the lilies and languors of the art nouveau period proper. It was one of the reasons he'd warmed to the work of Otto Wagner, who was, so to speak, the last fling of the movement, and was less flamboyant and excessive than, say, Victor Horta, the Belgian, less outrageous than the exuberant Spaniard, Gaudi, but also less severely ascetic than Charles Rennie Mackintosh. Indeed, he seemed to Orlando to exemplify the concept of restrained decorative elegance, while embracing the doctrine of new artistic freedom equally as successfully as his friend, Gustav Klimt.

It was a Klimt design, an original but hitherto unknown mosaic panel in a copper frame, which had brought Orlando and Anton together, in London.

They had come across each other quite accidentally, or so it seemed at the time, a chance meeting at the Q Gallery where Sylvie worked – if work was the right word – one of life's little serendipities of the sort that was wont to lift Orlando's spirits. A remark from a stranger, both of them standing in admiration before the extremely valuable and recently acquired Klimt.

'But Otto Wagner, all the same,' Orlando had murmured, almost to himself, 'could never have been influenced by him.'

His overheard remark had an electric effect on the man standing next to him. 'Otto Wagner? You know his work?'

The man was foreign, that much was apparent. Given away not only by his accent, and the fact of his speaking to a stranger, but also by his long belted mackintosh.

'Not to say *know*,' replied Orlando. 'Only from drawings, photographs . . . his reputation, you understand.'

'Ah, but the real thing! Nothing can compensate for that.'

This was true, Orlando knew, and he immediately began addressing himself to the question of why he'd never before visited Vienna in pursuit of architecture, and resolving to bestir himself and make good the omission.

'So,' said his new acquaintance. 'I am Anton Drucker, from Vienna. An associate of Mr Quarmby.' He held out a manicured hand. A tall, handsome man with a fit, athletic body and narrow face, knowing eyes regarding him assessingly, a careless smile. 'You see the real thing,' he repeated,' – as no doubt the charming Miss Sylvie here would advise.'

'Sylvie?'

He should have known, even then. At the time he was too

preoccupied with trying not to laugh. Sylvie, who had only the vaguest smattering of knowledge about art and artists, and cared not at all. She was employed at the Q Gallery only to be decorative, to hover in the background and pass interested customers on to its owner, Jonathan Quarmby-Crump. Everyone, even the customers, recognised she was feather-brained, but when Sylvie smiled, no one minded. She and Orlando had lived together for nearly twelve months, which was a long time for both of them, especially in view of their differences.

He'd so far put up with her faults because she was the most beautiful creature he'd ever encountered, long-legged and slim, with her white, pearly skin and her damson-coloured hair. To possess such a wondrous being had at first seemed like winning the lottery twice over. But by and by, inevitably, custom had begun to stale her infinite variety. His self-indulgent existence was no longer his own. He was used to demanding perfection in every area of his life, and here was one in which he wasn't getting it. Her faults, he decided sorrowfully, were many. Out of bed, they had no common meeting ground: music, of the sort he listened to, sent her into cracking yawns; to her a book was a copy of *Vogue*; the pictures and works of art that surrounded her all day at the gallery might have been posters for all she knew or cared. His flat was no longer his own: bottles of dye, from whence the damson colour of her hair emerged, littered his hitherto pristine bathroom; her clothes nudged his out of the wardrobe. She was wildly untidy. He might have been prepared to put up with this, but in addition, food, a matter of the utmost importance to Orlando, who was as greedy for this as everything else in life, scarcely mattered at all to Sylvie. Her nails were so long she dared not prepare a meal, much less wash up after it, in case she broke one.

But for all their incompatibility, her flawed perfection, he saw now that he would miss her. He had loved her, as deeply as he was capable of loving anyone. Poor Sylvie. Shallow Sylvie, flitting from one job to the next, one man to another...

He wished, quite desperately for him, and now too late, that she was here.

He looked at his watch and faced the fact that Anton was not going to come either, no longer pretending to himself that he had ever expected he would, accepting that he had never intended to be in Vienna. He would just have to find some other way of meeting him, some other place where he could kill him. Unless Anton killed him first when he learned what he had done. He wasn't sure which would be preferable.

Meanwhile, Steinhof.

A few miles' drive took him to the City Psychiatric Clinic. There were guards at the gates but they let his car through without any trouble when he told them he wanted to visit the church. If you hadn't been told, you wouldn't have known this was a hospital, a psychiatric one at that. If, that is, you hadn't seen the bars on some of the windows of the purpose-designed buildings on the wooded hillside as the road wound upwards like a serpent, or passed groups of poor, lost souls being escorted between the trees.

At the summit, Wagner's white cruciform church crowned the hill like the cross on Calvary. Looking a little shabby now, nearly a hundred years having passed since its erection, verdigris from the once-gilded bronze bolts streaking its white marble facing slabs, its huge copper dome turned green, but still marvellous in its simplicity and elegance.

Inside, space and light. Light everywhere. White and gold and blue. The gilded angels on the golden dome over the altar glowing in the radiance of the sanctuary lamp. Light filtering through the stained glass windows on to white walls, while a woman played the piano to a small group of people gathered round her. Slow, haunting, discordant pieces. Schoenberg, who else? What other music could be more appropriate in this place designed to calm the unquiet, disturbed mind? Music that explored an interior world of violence, madness and despair.

He took his seat in a roomy, functionally designed pew, his eye drawn to the huge mosaic behind the altar with its elongated, haloed figures arising from convoluted curves that seemed to him to resemble the interstices of the human brain, while the atonal music dropped note by note into the hushed silence, into the concentrated listening of the people at the front of the church, and into his own consciousness. Its reverberations made him feel, for the first time, that he, too, must have been mad to do what he had done.

He was awed, and humbled, and profoundly affected by this place, one man's finest aspiration, conceived and executed nearly a hundred years ago. In the space of ten minutes he lived again the last few days, and the weeks that had led up to them, felt horror for the first time. It made him wish that he could go back and undo all that had been done, start his life again. Even now, he could not explain wherein had lain his motives. He had not given it thought; he had simply been propelled by a compulsion to do what he had done.

It had all stemmed from that first meeting with Anton, in the Q Gallery. Contrived, he knew now: Sylvie had asked him to meet her there as she finished work – knowing Anton would be there, too. That apparently spontaneous conversation – that casual invitation from Sylvie to Anton to join them for dinner ... Orlando hadn't objected, had in fact welcomed the chance to talk to someone who proved to be both intelligent and charming. More than charming to the impressionable Sylvie, it became apparent, as the friendship between the three of them grew, as Anton's visits to London became more frequent. Perhaps it was even then that Orlando had felt the first stirrings of anger against them both, sensing that she had begun to find him very dull by comparison with quick-witted Anton and the slight air of recklessness, the willingness to take risks that he projected: a spice of danger had always excited Sylvie. Perhaps Orlando's failure had been to refuse to admit this until after the event, to have ignored his own sense of impending doom.

Until he was getting ready to leave for Vienna, in fact.

It would never have occurred to Sylvie that cleaning out the flat before going on holiday was preferable to coming home and finding it stale and in chaos. That Orlando might feel otherwise, and clean out the fridge, empty the garbage. Especially that he would hoover the carpet, and find what she had hidden under their bed, along with two pairs of laddered tights, countless used tissues and a shoe bill for two hundred pounds.

What business did Sylvie have with a parcel like that, nearly two metres long, done up in bubble-wrap? Sylvie, who owned nothing in the world except clothes and make-up? Orlando had the answer to his own question immediately he saw it, without any need to undo the wrappings, but he opened it anyway. The story came back to him: the faulty burglar alarm at the Q Gallery which had gone off during the night some three weeks previously, the arrival of the police who had stemmed its clamour, put it out of action until it could be reset the following morning when the gallery opened. The discovery of the burglary which had subsequently taken place between the two times, without let or hindrance. The Klimt, found to have disappeared. Worth, what? A good deal, but it scarcely mattered how much. It wasn't going to set up Anton for life, but was probably only one in a long line of such acquisitions. It had been stolen, and that was all that mattered.

Everything else fell into place, doubts Orlando had shuffled to the back of his mind for weeks were answered. He knew Anton had engineered the whole thing, and Sylvie had obviously been involved in plans for the disposal of the Klimt, though not the actual theft, since she had indubitably been in bed with himself, Orlando, at the time. He wanted to believe that she had been inveigled into the scheme unwittingly, but even Sylvie couldn't have been so dim as to pretend not to know what it was all about.

He hadn't thought to query his own actions when he perceived the nature of the parcel. His only thought was anger at how he had been duped, and an overwhelming need for revenge. He did not like to be thwarted, or made a fool of, and both had happened to him.

Someone slid into the pew beside him. He raised his face and saw Anton, treacherous Anton, beside him, his narrow face concerned, but concerned only because he had decided that was how it ought to look.

Orlando refused to move until the music finished, and only then stood up. Together, they went outside.

'So, you found the place yourself, without assistance? I guessed you would be here – my apologies for being late. Where is Sylvie?' Anton asked, with a casualness that belied the urgency behind the question.

'In Tenerife with her friend, Angela.'

'Of course, of course. How could I have forgotten?'

How indeed? Their idea had been for them to allay suspicions by carrying on as planned, even to the point of Anton meeting him here, and Angela supposedly holiday-making in Tenerife.

There was a pause. Orlando imagined the questions racing through Anton's mind: why had Sylvie not contacted him, answered the telephone? What had happened to the Klimt?

He thought of the explanations he could give, if he were so minded, of the quick telephone call he himself had made to Angela which had confirmed what he had suspected, that Tenerife had never been on the agenda. Of how he'd gone to the hotel where Anton had a permanent reservation, with no doubt at all in his mind that Sylvie would be staying there, too. Found that Anton had already left for Vienna and then, having dealt with Sylvie –

But why should he tell Anton? Better to let him sweat, and not tempt fate by attempting to kill him, a fitter, more dangerous and far more ruthless man than he. He saw now that it had never been a serious option. He would have no idea how to go about deliberately planning a murder, never mind committing it.

Sylvie had been a different matter. A matter of rage, a moment's loss of control. Even now, some hapless chambermaid might well be opening the wardrobe door and finding her body . . .

He thought there was every chance he might get away with it. No one had seen him enter the hotel, or leave. He had known which room to go to, and Sylvie had answered the door. He would not easily forget her face when she had seen him, or forget his own sense of betrayal. She had lied, and cheated him in every possible way, and she deserved what she had got. Already, the high moral tone of his thoughts back there in the church was receding. He felt no remorse.

Only regret for the necessity of ridding himself of the work of art, which, in a moment of aberration, he had put in his car, intending to keep it until he could find the right moment to put it on the market. Coming to his senses on that long motorway journey, he had seen it as the one thing that would surely prove his undoing.

It had cost him, it had cost him dearly, to ditch the Klimt and leave it reposing at the bottom of a sluggish river somewhere in the Danube valley. He began to calculate.

Twice-wrapped, tightly, in polythene. Lowered into the scarcely moving water, at a spot he remembered well.

After a while, his spirits began to rise.

Martin Edwards

This story has distant origins in a newspaper account of a bizarre 'missing person' incident which occurred last December. As soon as I read the report, it struck me as providing intriguing material for a mystery, but whenever I tried to write it up, I felt dissatisfied. Eventually I realised that I needed to keep to my usual approach and avoid trying to fictionalise real life events. Once I had liberated my imagination from the fetters of fact, a fresh story came to me that almost wrote itself: an experience to be relished.

A STOLEN LIFE

by Martin Edwards

Tape 917, side A – Saturday, 31 July
A girl is missing in Cumbria. I know nothing about her beyond the bare details in a couple of newspaper paragraphs – yet the story makes me tremble. Is it foolish for me to be afraid? The girl's called Lucy Alpert; she's a student of twenty holidaying on her own. The smudged black and white photograph doesn't flatter her: nondescript features and a prominent chin. She didn't show up at the place where she was expected. It's something and nothing, scarcely a front page story. More than likely, she's just run off with someone who gave her a second glance. Yet for all the warmth of this summer day, I have begun to feel afraid.

Of course I'm being melodramatic. An occupational hazard in my profession. There have been false alarms before and nothing came of them. The commentators often remark on my flair for anticipating risks, then seizing the moment. The truth is simple: I have an instinct for danger. So far it has served me well.

Nothing much else to report. The Boss is still sunning himself in Antigua. The rumour mill is working overtime at present, and Benjamin called me this morning and suggested we might get together for a bite to eat. Interesting. But I made an excuse; I learned long ago to trust no one. It's a mistake to put yourself in someone else's power. Besides, I need to take a walk around the park to order my thoughts. It's an afternoon to cast one's mind back to the past.

In my first term at Oxford, even a girl as plain as Lucy Alpert would have seemed unattainable. Practically a goddess to a shy boy like myself. In those days, it was said that for every female student, there were ten young men. To have a girlfriend – any girlfriend – was to become an object of envy and admiration. No wonder Ramsey and I campaigned against the iniquities of sex discrimination.

Not that Ramsey had anything to worry about, of course. Girls flocked round him. It had been the same at school. We attended a small fee-paying place on the outskirts of Ravenglass, within an hour's drive of both our homes. Like most public schools at the time, it was single-sex, but that didn't stop Ramsey regaling us with tales of his holiday conquests in such unlikely settings for the apprentice Lothario as Barrow-in-Furness, Grange-over-Sands and Morecambe. He had something going with the school caretaker's daughter, to say nothing of a fling with the sister of our classmate Nigel Ashbrook. When we put on a joint production of *Death of a Salesman* with a girls' school, he played Willy Loman and had a brief affair with the pretty blonde stage manager. My job was to help paint the scenery. I used to watch him intently, trying to divine the secret of his success. In the end I persuaded myself that his regular features, thick wavy hair and rugby-firmed muscles were not the reasons why he managed to seduce any young lass who took his fancy. It was his casual self-confidence. He expected to charm the girls, he never believed that he could fail. And he did not fail.

I was so different that I wondered why he and I remained friends. We had interests in common, naturally. Politics, the theatre and football, for example. But whereas he played centre forward for the school team and fancied a career as a Labour cabinet minister, I was as clumsy with a ball at my feet as I was tongue-tied in debate. I saw my future as an academic, engaged in endless research at the Bodleian, far from the public eye. Fame was in Ramsey's stars, everyone agreed.

I would have died rather than let him know just how much I admired him. Merely by tagging along with him since we were both eleven, I'd avoided most of the bullying that might otherwise have driven me to despair. All the same, I had no confidence. The spectacles – I hadn't yet come to terms with contact lenses – didn't help, nor did the shyness so deeply ingrained that I felt sick even at the prospect of chatting up a stranger. Once during the holidays, when he was going out to a disco with Pauline Ashbrook, he arranged for a foursome: I was to pair up with Pauline's best friend, a girl called Zoe Gleave. It was a disaster. I doubt if Zoe and I exchanged a dozen sentences all evening and when Ramsey and Pauline disappeared off together, I paid for a taxi to take her home. She didn't even bother to say goodnight.

When I saw Ramsey the next day and told him the sad tale, he shrugged and said, 'Better luck next time, mate.'

I had already decided that there never would be a next time. I wasn't going to endure that kind of humiliation again. But I managed to stifle my embarrassment and ask – with a hapless attempt at a lascivious grin – how he had got on with Pauline.

'Mission accomplished,' he said. 'I won't be seeing her again, though, I don't think. She's far too clingy. Not my type, really, if you leave her tits out of it. So don't be downhearted. We're both in the same boat, you and me. Footloose and fancy free.'

I suppose he said it to make me feel better. But I did experience a pang of sympathy for Pauline, even though she was not the first girl he'd dumped. Nor would she be the last.

Oxford he regarded as a challenge, but within a week of our arrival, he was sleeping with a girl from Lady Margaret Hall. He'd met her on the first day of term, when we were all celebrating the re-election of Harold Wilson's government with a massively increased majority. She was passionate about politics, but her ardent feminist views were no protection against Ramsey's expert technique of seduction. For a month they went everywhere together, but then he met Leanne and instantly he was lost.

When he introduced me to Leanne, my immediate reaction was that she was the loveliest girl I'd ever seen. Her large dark eyes stared into mine with such intensity that for a wild instant I thought she was enraptured, until I realised that this was her nature. She gave everything her utmost concentration. When she spoke, which wasn't often, it was with a deliberation that invested even a commonplace remark about an essay crisis with a hint of unfathomable wisdom.

Usually Ramsey was wary of serious girls and preferred his women with a bit of flesh on them. Leanne was painfully thin, but even so she bowled him over. Perhaps it was because she didn't seem to be impressed by him. I've always believed that was the truth of it. He was accustomed to captivating people. Even those who didn't like him – and jealousy is, I have always reckoned, the commonest of all the deadly sins – found it hard to avoid coming under his spell and discovering that they had agreed to do his bidding. I often thought he would have made a wonderful hypnotist.

Conversely, I suppose, hypnotists should make the best politicians. Perhaps they already do.

Tape 917, side B – Sunday, 1 August
I scanned the pages of the newspapers with even more care than usual this morning. Nothing worthy of comment in the broadsheets, although Bill is doing his best to stir trouble between Shaun and Duncan again. He's fed a story to the Guardian *suggesting that Shaun's days are numbered. Because he's well known as a Chandler fan, it was headed 'Farewell, My Luvvy'. It's still blazing hot in Antigua, it seems. Before long the Boss will be reported as saying, 'Crisis, what crisis?' Ah well. It's not for me to bite the hand that feeds. Just to hope that it will feed me.*

More about Lucy Alpert, in a couple of the tabloids. According to the Express, *'fears are rising.' There was more information in the* Mail. *Mr and Mrs Alpert are in a distressed state. Lucy has never done anything like this before, it seems. The nature of the coverage suggests to me that the police have hinted to the journalists that they are genuinely concerned. Perhaps she hasn't simply bumped into Mr Right in a teashop at Hawes and decided to taste real life for the first time.*

I'm worried sick, even though I keep telling myself that everything will be all right. Lucy will turn up safe and sound. Perhaps she's simply changed her plans and decided to go off for a hike in the Yorkshire Dales. Yet I can't bank on it. Not every missing person is found again.

I enjoyed Leanne's company from the outset. With her, I never went in for long, intense conversations. She was interested in politics and when she talked about it, there was no denying that she had insight, although her views were scarcely radical. But one of the reasons why I liked her so much, quite apart from her waif-like good looks, was that she had a talent for the companionable silence. I never had the idea that I was under pressure to be witty or entertaining. Just as well, Ramsey might have said, in his familiar teasing fashion. But the more I came to know Leanne – and the three of us spent a great deal of time together during that first term – the more I became aware that Ramsey exhausted me. He was so vigorous, so full of the joys of being young. He could never stop *doing* things. Perhaps, as he said, that was what politics was all about. He'd even pinched a slogan from the Tories' feeble campaign back in '66, when we were both boys. '*Action, not words.*' But there are occasions, I began to think, when there may be something to be said for quiet reflection.

Just possibly, Leanne may have felt the same way. I never discussed it with her, during any of those long hours we spent in the Junior Common Room at college, leafing through the papers as we munched toast and drank bitter coffee. Yet there were odd moments when I would catch her eye at a time when Ramsey was in full flow and I'd see the faintest flicker of amusement in those earnest brown eyes. As if we were sharing a joke at his expense.

These brief platonic intimacies exhilarated me more than I can describe. It wasn't as though I disliked Ramsey. We were still the firmest of friends. Yet Leanne fascinated me, and I was flattered – pathetic as this may sound – by the way she treated me as an equal. It wasn't a familiar experience.

During the Christmas holidays, she came up to stay with Ramsey and his parents at their house in Ambleside. I saw plenty of the pair of them and it was during that week in January that I had the first sense that all was not well in the relationship.

Ramsey confided in me that she'd refused to share his bed. His parents had been quite relaxed about the couple sleeping together – Ramsey's father had made his money as an agent for a Liverpool pop group during the Mersey Beat era, his mother still sang in clubs when she got the chance and they were the least shockable over-forties I knew – but Leanne had decided that it wasn't right. I don't imagine for one second that moral scruples troubled her. Ramsey had already given me to understand that, when in the mood, she was like a wild creature at bedtime; he'd even taken off his shirt and showed me the marks where she'd clawed him at the moment of climax. But it was an opportunity for her to make it clear that, although she might not say much, she was no chattel. She made up her own mind.

'It's such a bloody waste,' he complained. 'You know something? She even locks her door. Anyone would think she was a timid little virgin.'

Ramsey became increasingly irritable. He wasn't used to being denied what he wanted. He told me that Leanne could be selfish; she wasn't sensitive to his needs. I muttered words of consolation, but privately my sympathies were with her. In fact, I could not resist a secret feeling of satisfaction. It would do my old friend good, I decided, to learn that none of us can have our own way all the time. Not, I must admit, that my reaction was entirely altruistic. Close as I was to Ramsey, I was only human; it was amusing to picture him in his lonely bed in the big house, gnashing his teeth in frustration.

Soon the holidays were over and the three of us were back at Oxford. I was reading History and I'd taken my examinations at the end of the Michaelmas term. But Ramsey was studying Jurisprudence – he'd deliberately opted not to read Politics, Philosophy and Economics, because he fancied earning some decent money at the Bar whilst he climbed the Labour Party's greasy pole – and Law Moderations took place at the end of Hilary term. Ramsey had won a scholarship and was regarded as far and away the outstanding member of the group of six young lawyers. But he had trouble with Roman Law; for him, Gaius and Justinian were dirty words and he didn't have much time for criminal law. He had no intention of working at the criminal Bar. 'The real money,' he told me more than once, 'is in the commercial field.' I suppose he saw it, too, as an opportunity to exploit his flair for drama.

I'd taken my own studies seriously, although I was beginning to wonder if Jurisprudence might have been more interesting, for Roman Law seemed to me to have more intellectual appeal than Ramsey would concede. But most of our friends concentrated on having a good time. Ramsey, though, was different. He had never known failure. The exams didn't matter; the results made no contribution to the final degree and he was confidently expected to get a First. But he was intent on making sure that he did well and the demands of the weekly essay meant that he began to see a little less of Leanne than in the past. From time to time when he was in the St Cross Building at a lecture or ploughing through the Institutes, she would come round to see me for tea and crumpets. Shades of *Brideshead*, I used to think to myself. Sometimes we talked about Ramsey, sometimes about politics, sometimes we speculated whether he might one day become Prime Minister. As often, we said little and simply listened to Dizzy Gillespie on my ageing turntable. I enjoyed those afternoons more than I can say. Naturally, I behaved myself. It was not simply a question of loyalty. I was quite sure in my own mind that, whatever tiffs Leanne and Ramsey might have from time to time, she felt no stirring of sexual desire where I was concerned. On the contrary, with me she felt safe. Whatever fantasies I might have entertained in the darkness of my cold little room in the small hours, I was content with what I had. I was determined, above all, not to exhibit any of my characteristic gaucherie. I would not make any move which might jeopardise my friendship with either Ramsey or Leanne.

As the examinations approached, Ramsey talked about the celebrations that would take place once they were over. He asked Leanne if she would come up to Cumbria again, but she told him that she was due to spend a month in Germany, returning to England just a few days before Trinity term. She had a long-standing pen-friend who lived in West Berlin, in a flat just across the way from the Wall.

'Amazing,' Ramsey said. 'Hey, can I come?'

Leanne frowned. 'I don't think so. Ute's not much interested in boys. She's quiet. A bit like Tim here, if you like. She's not much of a one for going out to the bars and clubs.'

'No problem. She doesn't have to be interested in me, does she? But I don't see why I can't tag along.'

'No, Ramsey,' she said quietly. 'It's not on.'

And that was that. Ramsey went into a sulk and the subject wasn't discussed again. Law Moderations came and went and he and I returned to the North-West for the vacation. I saw rather less of him than I had done at Christmas. My father was working on his latest book, the prime purpose of which was to establish that Crippen was innocent of everything other than stupidity and adultery, and he engaged me to undertake some of the legwork. I had to make a number of trips down to London, although I never did manage to convince myself that the death of Cora Crippen gave rise to one of the great miscarriages of justice.

With one thing and another, therefore, about ten days had elapsed since my last evening in a Keswick pub with Ramsey when a knock came on the door of our cottage.

'Will you get that?' my mother called from the cellar. 'Your dad's in his study, fretting about arsenic, and I'm unloading the tumble drier.'

I abandoned my perusal of *The Prince*, muttering some smart remark about sexual stereotyping, and went to answer the door. Outside on the step were two hefty men, both a few years older than myself. They were police officers, they said, and showed me their identification.

'Timothy Nicklin?'

'That's right.'

'May we come in?'

'What's this all about?' My mind was racing. Had my little fiddle over the rail ticket for my last trip to Euston been discovered?

'It's about Ramsey Gillott. He's a friend of yours, we understand.'

'Ramsey? Yes, of course. My best friend.' I stared at them. 'Why? What's happened?'

'I'm afraid,' said one of the detectives, who might easily have passed for an all-in wrestler, 'that he is missing, believed drowned.'

Tape 918 – side A, Monday, 2 August

Two days to go before the Boss leaves Antigua. He'll be making a couple of goodwill calls, one in Delhi, the other in Cape Town. He has developed a taste for the international stage, it has to be said. Perhaps it comes to all great leaders, to see themselves as they hope posterity will perceive them, as statesmen of stature.

Back at home, Benjamin gave an interview to the Independent *today. It wasn't exactly disloyal – but, well, it* was *very Benjamin. He called at midday and left a mesage on my answering machine. I think I'll leave it for the time being.*

As for the rest of the news, it's all silly season stuff. Except for the fact that Mr and Mrs Alpert have given a press conference, appealing for more information about Lucy's movements since she arrived in the Lake District. Things are not looking good. My heart can't sink much further (if that's not an unfortunate choice of metaphor). But what can I do? I feel so helpless.

Twenty-four hours after the police broke the news, I was still struggling to absorb it. Ramsey had been so full of life that I found it almost impossible to conceive of his death. He always had about him an air of invulnerability. To me, it was as if he had enjoyed a kind of immortality.

'There must be some mistake,' I said to Leanne. We were sitting in the corner of the lounge of a small pub in Keswick, a couple of miles from my home.

'I don't think so,' she whispered.

I had telephoned her as soon as the police left. Stunned by what I told her, she had announced an intention to travel north at once. She booked into a little bed and breakfast place down the road from where I lived. Ramsey's people had, as Leanne said, enough to cope with as they tried to come to terms with what had happened.

'Who telephoned the police?' she asked.

'They don't know. Someone dialled 999 at around eleven o'clock and said he'd seen a young man in the cove earlier that evening. It's a quiet place, not far from Grange. The beach had been deserted except for this one person, heading towards the sea. The description he gave fits Ramsey, by the way.

He watched as Ramsey undressed and left his clothes on the shore.'

'Folded?' Leanne asked sharply.

Despite everything, I laughed. I could guess what was going through her mind. A glimmer of suspicion, a flicker of hope. But I had to snuff it out. 'No, Ramsey wasn't about to break the habit of a lifetime and leave everything nice and tidy. They were left in a jumble at the water's edge. Then he walked into the waves – and simply disappeared from sight.'

She shivered and, instinctively, I put my arm around her. She snuggled closer and, in the chastest way, I held her close to me. We needed to comfort each other.

'What did this man do?'

'As far as I can gather, he was pretty horrified. Scared, too, I guess. The current there is notorious, so the police say. It was as if Ramsey deliberately set out to drown himself.'

'The clothes are his?'

'Oh yes. That's how the police got on to his identity so quickly. There was a massive search. Coastguards, air-sea rescue, you name it. But there's been no trace so far.'

We were both silent for a while. I was thinking of the damage that the sea water can do to the body of a human being. I couldn't help flinching. Somehow I guessed Leanne's mind was working on much the same lines.

She swallowed. 'And this man – the man who telephoned – he didn't give his name? Why would that be?'

'The police said that this cove is a haunt for courting couples. More than likely this chap's a Peeping Tom. But he saw something he didn't expect.'

'A suicide ...' she breathed. I could feel her body trembling against mine.

'We can't be sure he's dead.'

She shook her head. 'It's more than forty-eight hours since he went into the water, Tim. I know he can be theatrical, but he wasn't doing it for fun. How was he to know some creepy bloke would be out there snooping? He meant to die.'

I sighed. 'I suppose ... you may be right.'

'But why, Tim? Why would he do something like that?'

'God knows. The police asked the same question, of course.

And I've not stopped interrogating myself, ever since they left. I've had a word with his mum and dad. Naturally, they're shell-shocked. They do say he'd seemed a bit preoccupied, but they didn't realise there was anything to worry about. He'd mentioned that he was gloomy about his performance in Law Mods, but they didn't read anything into that. Ramsey has never failed an exam in his life.'

'And me?' The big brown eyes stared into mine. 'Did they say anything about Ramsey and me?'

I shifted my position, eased my arm away from her. To cover my embarrassment, I coughed several times.

'Well?' she demanded. 'Did they? Did they?'

I took a breath. 'He'd been a bit pissed off, according to his mother. Apparently he'd been expecting a card from you in West Berlin.'

She closed her eyes. 'I never wrote to him.'

'I'd asked him how you were getting on with your pen-pal,' I said quickly, mortified to see her cheeks crimsoning with guilt. 'He said all right, or words to that effect. He never let slip to me that he was bothered that you hadn't been in touch.'

'Well, he wouldn't, would he?' she demanded. 'Ramsey's always revelled in the limelight. And in being hero-worshipped by you, Tim. Sorry, that sounds mean. But it's true, isn't it? He likes to lord it over you. Glamorous Ramsey. The supreme over-achiever.'

There was a cynicism in her tone which shocked me. 'I'm not sure . . .' I began.

'Listen,' she said, 'he wouldn't want you to think that things had cooled between him and me.'

I frowned. 'Had they?'

She bent her head. In a muffled voice, she said, 'We'd been going through a sticky patch, you might say. I suppose most couples do at some stage. I'm not the easiest person in the world to get on with, I'm the first to admit that. I'd kind of hinted to him at the end of term that perhaps we ought to ease off. Maybe not think of ourselves as a couple. We're still young, it's good to have a bit of space. I said all that, but he didn't seem to take it in.'

'I see,' I said after a pause.

'Oh God,' she said, as tears started to edge down her cheeks. 'Don't look at me like that, Tim. You make me feel like a murderess.'

'Sorry,' I said and put my arm back around her. She didn't resist.

Later, I walked her back to the place where she was staying. She had a late night key. To my astonishment, when I said goodbye, she murmured, 'Would you like to come in for a bit?'

I didn't know what to say. She was looking at the ground, not at me. As I tried to make sense of her question, it struck me that if I made an excuse and left, she would never ask again. This was an extraordinary night. We had both suffered a bereavement; it was a shared loss. We needed each other.

'Well . . .' I hesitated. 'If you don't mind.'

Without another word, she unlocked the door and led me upstairs. As if in a dream, I followed her up the uncarpeted stairs, afraid that the sound of my nervous footsteps would awake the landlady.

Later, when Leanne screamed, I did not know whether it was out of pleasure or pain.

Tape 918, side B – Tuesday, 3 August

If the papers are to be believed, Shaun is finished. The rumour mill is in full swing. Apparently, there's a story doing the rounds in Fleet Street. Nothing to do with women, this time. It's money, and it's serious. I ought to be cock-a-hoop, but somehow I don't feel able to concentrate on anything. Except the fate of Lucy Alpert.

There's been a sighting. A week ago, she was seen by a family of Japanese tourists who had been visiting Keswick. On a trip to the stone circle at Castlerigg, they came across her and asked if she would use their camera to take a photograph of them. They exchanged pleasantries with her, it seems, and she said something about staying in the town for a day or two. The police have announced they are going to concentrate their enquiries in the area. Oh God, oh God, oh God. It's as bad as it could be.

*

When we met again the next day, we were both subdued. We'd arranged to have a bite of lunch in a small cafeteria near the shops, but it was like a conversation between distant acquaintances. I suppose that both of us had an acute awareness that we had betrayed Ramsey. Her lover, my friend. Yet I could not feel regret. I had been initiated and life would never be the same again. The virginity which had hung around my neck like an albatross was gone for ever. I was a man.

As for Leanne, her thoughts were impossible to read. We talked about inconsequential things. Ramsey was scarcely mentioned. The following Thursday we were due back at Oxford, but it didn't seem right to discuss the forthcoming term. So much lay ahead of us that had now been denied to Ramsey.

When I'd paid the bill, Leanne said, 'I suppose I'd better think about getting back home. There's nothing more I can do here. I never hit it off with his parents and I think they blame me for . . . for what happened.'

'That's barmy!'

'It's only natural,' she said. 'I didn't realise how much he cared. Maybe if I did, I'd have spent the last few weeks here, not in Germany.'

I gritted my teeth. Ridiculous though it might be, I felt a sudden spurt of jealousy. Even in death, even after what we had shared the previous evening, she still belonged to him. Suddenly, I was seized by the urge to forget about Ramsey. He was dead now. Gone. I had to get along without him. The same was true of Leanne. Who could tell what the future held for us? But one thing was for sure. I mustn't let Ramsey's ghost come between us.

'When are you leaving?'

'I'm setting off in an hour. My luggage is all packed.'

'You could stay with us,' I said urgently. I didn't want to lose her. I was afraid that, once she left, I would never be able to rekindle the flame that had burned between us the night before.

She shook her head. 'No, Tim. You already know, I'm someone who needs a bit of space. But don't worry. I'll see you soon.'

'Leanne...'

She touched my hand. 'Don't worry, Tim. I won't – forget.'

With that, I had to be content. The rest of the day passed in a blur. So much had happened so quickly. I still found it difficult to understand Ramsey's reckless act of self-destruction, but I told myself that there was no point in trying to understand it. What is done can never be undone. I must look forward, not back. And the simple truth was that Leanne had liberated me. I felt free, for the first time in my life. I was exhilarated, even though I never even stopped to ask myself, 'Free of *what*?'

That evening, I went to bed early. My parents were solicitous. They knew that my life had always revolved around Ramsey's and were inclined to treat me as an invalid. It wasn't an uncongenial experience, being waited on hand and foot. I couldn't get to sleep, though. My mind was too active. I was anticipating Oxford in Trinity, daring to hope that Leanne was telling the truth when she promised that she would not forget. Imagining a term spent with her, morning, noon and night.

A sound roused me from my pleasurable, drowsy imaginings. It was rather like something from a child's Enid Blyton thriller, when gravel is thrown against a window to attract attention. I got out of bed and peered down into the back garden. Someone was standing there, waving at me. A familiar figure, yet now a wholly unexpected visitor.

'Yes!' Ramsey hissed. 'It's me!'

Tape 919, side A – Wednesday, 4 August

The Boss returns on the late flight this evening. The speculation about the reshuffle is now unbearable. I've stopped taking calls from journalists. If anyone asks, I have to take refuge in anodyne phrases about willingness to serve in whatever capacity where one might be thought able to help.

In any event, I'm too preoccupied to give a thought to my future prospects. Well, that's something I never expected to say and yet, at this most crucial moment, it happens to be true. Extraordinary.

Another witness has come forward. Someone who saw Lucy Alpert camping out near Derwent Water. She left her tent there without any explanation. I fear that the explanation is obvious. What happens next is equally easy to predict.

'Coming down?' Ramsey hissed. 'I don't want anyone else to see me.'

My thoughts were in disarray, but I stumbled into some clothes and hurried downstairs as quickly as I could. My parents had already gone to bed. They both took sleeping pills, so there wasn't much danger of disturbing them, but even so I tiptoed down the steps, feeling like a criminal in my own home.

Ramsey was lounging against the wooden toolshed at the side of the patio. 'Surprised to see me?' he asked as I approached.

'What on earth . . .?'

He stepped over a spade that my father had carelessly left outside the shed. 'Sorry if I frightened you, mate. But it had to be done. I simply couldn't take anyone into my confidence. Not that I didn't trust you. But I wanted you to react as if I really had decided to top myself.'

'I don't understand.'

'I called the police myself, of course. I've never dialled 999 before. Gave me quite a buzz, actually. Even though the report of my death was somewhat exaggerated.'

'But they had the air-sea rescue out,' I said, trying in vain to make sense of it all.

'Yeah, pretty dramatic, eh?'

'You'll be prosecuted! What about the waste of police time? All the cost?'

He shook his head. 'OK, it was a bit naughty, I suppose. But it was a good hoax, all the same.'

'But why? Why did you do this – this crazy thing?'

Ramsey tapped the side of his nose. 'Take it from me, Tim. Faint heart never won fair lady.'

'I don't know what you're talking about.'

'Leanne, of course. The lovely Leanne. See, it's like this. She's been slipping away from me. I wanted her to realise how much she means to me. Oh, I know I've had my share of women in the past. But this is different, believe me. With Leanne, it's for keeps. Yet she didn't seem able to cotton on to that. I've given her a shock now. She must realise I can't live without her. My idea is, I'm going to propose the next time I see her. Don't expect an answer right away, of course. You'd better be around yourself, mate. Handy with the smelling salts. But my bet is, when she comes round, she'll say yes. Would you like to be my best man?'

For a moment I stared at him. At this distance of time, I can't be sure exactly what went through my mind. Something to do with the loss of Leanne – and I saw that, despite everything, I was about to lose her to him. Something to do with the loss of my own life. It had taken me so long to escape his shadow. Now he wanted to consign me to the darkness again.

I wasn't thinking rationally, that much is for certain. There was no careful calculation of percentages. The most deterrent penal regime in the world would have had no effect on what I did next. It was instinct. Sheer bloody instinct.

I picked up my father's spade, lifted it as if endowed with unnatural strength and smashed it against Ramsey's skull. Once, twice, three times. To make sure.

Tape 919, side B – Thursday, 5 August
My name is in all the papers this morning. I'm the hot tip for promotion. Shaun is finished, everyone can see that. It's the day I've dreamed of, worked towards for so many years. Hence my taped diaries, so patiently compiled for the benefit of future biographers.

And yet all I can think of is the search for Lucy Alpert. Will they find her body quickly? Or will the scuba divers first discover whatever remains of Ramsey Gillott?

I can't remember much about what happened afterwards. I was functioning on autopilot, whatever subconscious motivating force which helps us to protect ourselves in times of the gravest crisis. I had an old banger which was barely roadworthy and, once I'd wrapped Ramsey's bloody corpse in sacking and weighted it with stones I'd taken from a pile in the garden, I drove to the quiet spot where Father kept a little boat moored. I lugged my cargo along the grassy path and dumped it into the boat, then rowed out to the middle of the lake before tossing my friend into the cold unforgiving water.

Tape 920, side A – Friday, 6 August
The call came five minutes ago. Would I be able to call at Number 10 at eleven o'clock? I mumbled something which no doubt was taken as gratified assent.

I shan't be there, of course. It would be quite wrong. It ought to be Ramsey Gillott who is appointed as Home Secretary, not me. Leanne should be by his side in Whitehall, not mine. We're in enough trouble already for saying one thing and doing another. Even the Boss would struggle to explain it away when the minister responsible for criminal justice was charged with the murder of the poor bastard who has just – it was on the news moments after the latest on the reshuffle – been dredged up from the bottom of Derwent Water.

I think I'll opt for the old-fashioned way out. Doing the decent thing. It's gone out of vogue lately, but I really can't see myself being rehabilitated after a brief spell of purdah on the back benches. Even if the Boss commends the dignity of my departure from office and sympathises with my one unfortunate lapse of judgement. No, I fear it's the glass of whisky in the study and, since I don't possess a pearl-handled revolver, a suitably conclusive overdose of paracetamol.

I owe it to Ramsey. The time's come for the debt to be paid. After all, I stole more than his wife. I stole his life.

John Hall

John Hall is an expert on matters Sherlockian and contributes to that excellent publication *Sherlock Holmes: The Detective Magazine*. With this story, though, he offers a pastiche of the work of Conan Doyle's brother-in-law, E. W. Hornung. Much of Hornung's work is today forgotten, but the creation of A. J. Raffles, the amateur cracksman, was a stroke of genius. Raffles is a character who has become embedded in the collective consciousness and this is a story which Hornung himself would not, I think, be ashamed to have written.

RAFFLES AND MISS MORRIS

by John Hall

'Work?' asked A. J. Raffles incredulously.

'I only suggest it as – '

'My dear Bunny, your own literary efforts, enchanting, vivacious, and so on, as they may very well be, have singularly failed to earn the recognition they indubitably deserve. As for my own poor abilities – well, when you say "work" to me, Bunny, it means only one thing!'

'Oh, Lord!' I gazed at him miserably. Raffles shrugged his shoulders, and looked out of the window of his flat in the Albany. It was early spring, but the balmy days, the feathery green plumes on the plane trees, the girls in their new dresses, all these were wasted upon us just then. The proceeds of the Morgan jewel robbery had long been spent, and we were having, in Raffles' own words, 'to think again'.

'Anyway,' said he, turning back to me, 'come along and I'll buy you lunch.'

'Can't, I'm afraid, though I appreciate the offer. I promised to have a drink with a chap. Come along with me, if you like?'

Raffles shook his head. 'I need to do some heavy thinking, Bunny, and I know how your glass or two at lunchtime can so easily degenerate into a debauch worthy of Tiberius or Caligula.'

I left him still staring out of the window, and a feeling of foreboding crept over me, for I knew well enough what sort of heavy thinking he would be doing.

It does not matter just where I went, or what the name of my friend might have been, but what does matter is a remark that friend made as we stood together at the bar. We were both bemoaning the parlous state of our finances, and he laughed and said, 'I could wish that I had some skill as a detective, you know!'

'And why's that?' I asked, spilling my drink – for my conscience makes me extravagantly sensitive to any mention of police or detectives or anything of that kind.

'Oh,' he said, 'I hear that old Morris is looking for a discreet agent to investigate the disappearance of his daughter.'

'Gustav Morris? Mildred Morris?' This Morris, I hardly need remind you, was the founder, sole proprietor, and general presiding genius of Morris & Co., the gigantic department store in Knightsbridge. Mildred, his only child, was an attractive but, by all accounts, a scatterbrained girl whose portrait appeared regularly in the illustrated papers. 'Has she disappeared, then? I hadn't heard anything of the kind.'

'It hasn't been made public, of course.'

'Then how do you know about it?' I wondered.

'Some of the chaps were talking.'

'Oh, if it's only gossip – !'

'More than gossip, old man, more than gossip,' my friend assured me earnestly. 'You know what the newspapers say – "we are reliably informed", that kind of thing. Apparently old Morris is frothing at the mouth. Offered a huge reward.'

'Oh?'

'Yes, hundreds. Thousands, very likely.'

'But you don't have a precise figure?' I asked sceptically.

'No,' said he very seriously, 'as I told you, it hasn't been officially announced, so to speak. But it stands to reason, doesn't it? A chap like that, rich as Croesus, only daughter, and what have you? Bound to offer a reward. Attractive girl, too,' he added, producing the latest issue of the *Strand* magazine and turning to the 'Society Beauties' page.

'I have seen her picture more than once,' said I, glancing at the page. An idea, or the germ of an idea, at any rate, was starting to form somewhere at the back of my mind. 'Look here,' I said, waving the paper, 'd'you mind if I borrow this?'

'Oh, keep it,' he said.

'Thanks, and I'll see you later.'

'Oh, are you off?' and he stared after me as I practically ran from the place and set off back to the Albany.

I found Raffles still contemplating the view from his window, and smoking his Sullivans. I told him what I had been told, and showed him the *Strand*. 'Well?' I demanded.

'Very nice, Bunny.'

'Yes, she's an attractive girl. But what about – '

'Not the girl, Bunny, though she is, as you say, not too hard to look upon. No, I was meaning those,' and he tapped a finger against the diamonds which circled the neck of Miss Mildred Morris.

'Raffles, how can you think of jewels at a time like this?'

'It's my trade, Bunny, and you must allow a man to be proud of his trade. Did Jack Falstaff not say something of the sort? But you're right, my Bunny. The father must be worried if the daughter has indeed vanished. A reward, you say?'

'So Rumour has it.'

'Ah, Rumour of a Thousand Tongues! Well, it would be only natural, would it not? I must say, the whole business has been kept very quiet, assuming for a moment that Rumour mistakes not the truth. It might be fun to play the policeman's part for once, might it not, Bunny? Yes, here's another of those "Sherlock Holmes" stories in the *Strand*.' He glanced at the paper again, and laughed. 'Not that I think he'll last, Bunny! Too much the inspired amateur for my taste. No, I don't think you or I would have anything to fear from Mr Holmes.' He took his stick and coat from the rack. 'Pass my hat, would you, there's a good chap.'

'Shall we see Mr Morris, then?'

'We shall indeed.' Raffles took the latest *Who's Who*, the Bible of his 'trade,' from his shelf, and consulted it. 'Fashionable town address, of course. Come along, Bunny.'

Mr Morris's town address was in the most fashionable part of Mayfair, and I quailed at the basilisk gaze of the butler who admitted us and took our cards. But Raffles never turned a hair, and greeted Mr Morris, who came out to see us, with a cheery 'Hullo!' and a firm handshake.

Morris was somewhat under the middle height, perhaps fifty years of age, but his hair was still untouched by grey, and his eyes were wonderfully penetrating. He showed some signs of fatigue, which made me suspect that the rumours were not far short of the mark. His first words confirmed this. 'Mr Raffles, I have heard of you, of course. And your friend,' he added with a rather patronising nod in my general direction. 'But you must excuse me, sir, for I am rather busy just at the moment. I would not like to be unhospitable, but pray be brief.'

'It is about your daughter, sir.'

Quite unexpectedly, Morris's attitude changed. His face darkened, and he took a step towards Raffles. 'If you're a friend of that damned rascal – ' he began.

The butler hastily moved to block his master's way; I stood in front of Raffles, bleating, 'I say!' or something equally ineffectual.

Raffles himself never moved or spoke until things had calmed down a little, then he raised a hand, and told Morris, 'I assure you, sir, that my motives in coming here are purely to lend you whatever assistance I might. I know nothing of this matter save what gossip tells me.'

Morris subsided a little at this. He dismissed the butler with a nod, and waved us into what was evidently his study. 'I suppose it was only to be expected that word of this would get out,' he said, helping himself to brandy with an unsteady hand. 'Would you care for anything?' he asked as an afterthought, waving the decanter.

'A brandy would be very acceptable!' I said.

Raffles frowned at me. 'Nothing for either of us, thank you,' he said firmly. 'We wish to keep clear heads for this very serious matter.'

'Of course.' Morris hesitated. 'I hardly know where to begin,' he said ruefully.

'Well, to begin with, has your daughter disappeared?' asked Raffles.

'Not inasmuch as I know, in broad terms, where she is. And with whom,' Morris added gloomily.

'Has she been abducted, then?' I asked.

'Not in the conventional sense, sir.'

'Run off, then?'

Morris winced at my words. 'You put the matter very badly, sir, but you are not far from the truth.' He swigged his brandy, shuddered, and went on, 'Last year, my daughter took a holiday at Biarritz. Business commitments meant that I could not go with her, but I made sure that she was accompanied by a most respectable lady who acted as a chaperone. My daughter is, I regret to say, somewhat headstrong. She eluded the watchful eye of her guardian more than once and, as she puts it, "had some fun" on her own account. On one of these pleasurable and illicit excursions, she made the acquaintance of a man whom I personally would not care to know, a man named Pargetter, if that indeed is his real name. A glib and good-looking rogue. A gigolo, if you want the plain word, gentlemen.

'Well, she had to return to London, of course, and this fellow stayed over there. But then, three weeks ago, no more, he turns up here in London, having apparently taken a house somewhere in the city, though I do not know the exact address. Now, I have told you what happened – or what I assume happened – but I was myself in ignorance of all this until the occasion, three weeks back, when this fellow turned up here! Then, of course, my daughter had to tell me some of what had gone on, though I had to read between the lines quite considerably.' He paused, and took a more measured pull at his brandy.

'I take it that you were not favourably impressed by the young man?' Raffles asked.

Morris snorted. 'I was not, sir! Indeed, once I saw what was going on, I forbade him to come here again. My daughter, who is, as I told you, of a temperamental nature, flared up at this, said she would not be treated like a child, the usual things. And then, two days ago, she left me a note saying she was going to stay with this fellow until they can get a licence and be married!'

'I say!' I gasped.

Morris waved a hand. 'It is not quite so bad as it might sound, for there are servants in the house, a housekeeper who is, I trust, quite respectable, and who can chaperone my daughter. But still, the situation is far from satisfactory.'

'Your objection to this man is a personal one?' asked Raffles.

'Personal, sir. And financial.'

'Ah!'

'My late wife was a wealthy woman in her own right. When she died some eight years ago, she left a fortune in trust for

Mildred. When my daughter should come of age, she was to have the income from the money, and she has drawn that income now for two years, for she is now three-and-twenty. But if she married, being of age, she was to have the entire capital as well.'

'I see. A fortune, you say?'

'A positive fortune, sir. I have no financial interest myself, of course, since I have a claim neither to interest nor to capital. But I should hate to see this ruffian get his hands on the money.' If ever I heard a man speak the truth, it was then. Morris was evidently one of those men who derive pleasure not merely from the accumulation of wealth for themselves but from the denying of it to others. Although, to be honest, I could see that he had a point in the present instance.

Raffles was saying, 'I may be able to help.'

'I should, of course, be most grateful.' Morris hesitated. 'A modest reward, some slight recompense, would not be altogether inappropriate. A hundred, shall we say?'

'A hundred? To have your daughter back, out of the hands of an unscrupulous rogue?' It was wrong of me, I know, but I could not keep the words back.

Morris flushed. 'Five hundred, then! I'm damned if I'll haggle! Five hundred, when my daughter is returned to me.'

'With no questions asked?' said Raffles.

'No questions asked. I don't care how you do it.'

'Agreed.'

A flurry of handshakes sealed the bargain, and before I knew it Raffles and I were outside in the street.

'What a charming fellow, Raffles!'

'He is not too prepossessing, is he, Bunny? But one must make allowances.'

'And have you a plan?'

'A vague idea only. The first problem is to find where the lady is staying.'

'It could be anywhere, though!'

'Hardly, Bunny. If this fellow is in effect a confidence trickster, then he must act in a fashion calculated to build his victim's confidence, must he not? That means a decent house in a stylish location. It should not be too difficult to find out if anyone arrived from Biarritz three weeks ago and took such a property.'

He was right, as always. At the third house agents we tried, we found the address we sought, and went there at once. It was, just as Raffles had predicted, a large house in a reasonably desirable neighbourhood. We kept watch from a convenient doorway opposite, avoiding the glance of a passing policeman, and were rewarded by the sight of two young people who emerged, escorted by a large and fierce-looking woman, towards the hour when honest folk are setting off for their dinner. Miss Morris was even lovelier than her picture; her male companion was a year or so older than her, and good-looking in what I must call a coarse sort of way. All did not seem sweetness and light, though; as they climbed into the carriage I heard Miss Morris speak rather sharply to Pargetter, and he tried to laugh it off and made but a poor show of it.

'His face is his fortune, Bunny,' said Raffles, echoing my unspoken thoughts. 'Though I expect he'll go to seed once he reaches thirty, as all these fellows do.'

Something was nagging at me. 'You know, Raffles, I could swear I've seen that fellow somewhere before.'

'A common enough type, Bunny. So, they're off to their dinner. Now, I wonder? Should we go to ours, or should we act tonight?'

'Tonight?'

'This very night, Bunny. The problem, you see, is one of time, or the lack thereof. This fellow wants to get his hands on the money, and to do that he has to marry the lady. So he'll want to do that as soon as possible, and that means he'll be wanting a special licence, or whatever it's called. And there seemed a slight difference of opinion there, did you notice? If the lady is having second thoughts, Pargetter will want the ring on her finger as soon as possible, so that it's too late for her to change her mind.'

A horrid thought struck me. 'Suppose they're married already?'

'H'mm. I rather think not. If they were, then Mr Morris would have heard from the gentleman's solicitors regarding the cash. And besides, would they go out to dinner on their wedding night? And if they did, would they bother with a chaperone?'

'And your plan?'

'Ah, my plan. It involves our providing ourselves with masks and revolvers, and getting into that house.'

'Raffles!'

'Nothing like that, Bunny, I do assure you.'

'Raffles, I've spoken harshly to you more than once about your secretive nature. Will you tell me what you propose?'

He regarded me for a while, then laughed. 'You are right,' he said. 'Very well then, Bunny. It's no good our taking the lady from the house and returning her to her father by force. She's of age, she would simply go back to her lover. Nor is it any use trying to tell her what sort of a man he is, for she wouldn't listen. Her father has already tried, and she didn't listen to him, so why would she listen to us?'

'He – '

Raffles held up a hand. 'The only thing to be done, the only thing that has a ghost of a chance of working the trick, is to show her what sort of a man he is. To make him reveal his true nature. And that's what I intend to do.'

'Raffles – '

'Does that satisfy you? Any points on which you would desire further clarification?'

'No, that's fine, as far as it goes. But Raffles, what I was trying to say was, suppose he isn't a villain, after all? Suppose old Mr Morris is seeing things through a father's eyes, quite understandably, of course, but blinkered, so to speak? Suppose this Pargetter's intentions are honourable, after all?'

'I confess, Bunny, that the prospect had not occurred to me. But now you mention it, my little plan should allow for that too. Yes, Bunny, we'll see this fellow in his true colours tonight, and if those colours are clear and – oh, be damned to this metaphor, for I don't even know if it is artistic or nautical! If he's a regular chap, we'll find that out tonight, Bunny, and there's an end to it!'

We secured the masks and our revolvers, though we did not load these, Raffles saying that the precaution was unnecessary. We returned to the house, donned our masks, and entered via a rear window, one of those absurdly ineffectively fastened and so very convenient rear windows which make the burglar's task so easy. We made our way to the drawing-room and concealed ourselves behind the heavy curtains.

'Now, Bunny,' Raffles whispered, 'I suspect they'll come in here, but if not we shall track them down. If they do come in here, I'll do what's necessary, and you will remain under cover until I call you.'

'As usual!'

'Bunny, how often must I tell you how important is your task? If I am not much mistaken, then we have to deal with a thorough-going villain, and I may be in very real danger tonight, danger from which I rely upon you to extricate me.' And with that, unsatisfactory though it was, I had to be content.

We lurked behind those curtains for an hour, two hours, three, then Raffles gripped my arm. 'Ready, Bunny?'

I heard the door open and the sound of lamps being lit. Raffles had his eye to the slit of the curtains, but I had to be satisfied with listening to events unfold in the drawing-room.

'Here we are!' The voice of the man, Pargetter. Educated, or pretending to be educated? It was hard to tell. There was a sort of subdued giggle, presumably from Miss Morris, then Pargetter said, 'Thank you, Mrs Green, that will be all.' I took it that Mrs Green was the companion, or housekeeper, or something, who had accompanied them. Whoever she might have been, she was evidently in no hurry to leave, perhaps feeling that it was not entirely proper to leave the two of them alone in there, a sentiment with which I heartily concurred – I mean, I would have concurred with it had that been Mrs Green's sentiment, if you follow me.

It was not until a young woman, presumably Miss Morris, said, 'It will be fine, dear Mrs Green,' that an older woman's voice said, 'Goodnight, miss,' adding reluctantly as it seemed to me, 'Sir,' and there were sounds of footsteps leaving the room and the door closing.

'Well, here we are,' said Pargetter again. 'Just the two of us.'

'Not quite.' It was Raffles who spoke, in his best East End accent, as he stepped out into the room, waving his revolver in an easygoing fashion. 'Don't make no noise, lady, and nobody'll get 'urt,' he added. 'It's them sparklers I'm 'ere for, nothink else.'

I was now able to shift myself a foot or so towards the slit in the curtains, and could now see, as well as hear, what was happening.

'You cur!' It was Pargetter who said it, and in a surprisingly firm voice, as he stepped between Raffles and Miss Morris. 'If you want that necklace, you'll have to deal with me first!'

'I will,' promised Raffles. 'Move yourself, or so 'elp me, I'll shoot!'

'You won't shoot!' Pargetter's words had the ring of certainty. 'You haven't got the nerve. Clear off, before I thrash you! And where's your pal, come to that? I know there must be another of you somewhere, you haven't the courage to work alone.'

I shuddered. Had Pargetter, or one of his creatures, seen us enter the house? Was he so very confident because he knew he faced an empty pistol? It seemed rankly impossible that he should know, but yet I could not account for his attitude in any other way. Unless he were braver than any man I have ever known, brave to the point of foolhardiness.

Raffles was facing the two young people, and his back was to the door. But from my hiding place I commanded a view of the entire room, with only a slight movement of my eyes, and to my horror I saw the door being opened, slowly and carefully. Miss Morris and Pargetter saw it too, I could tell that. Miss Morris gasped, but Raffles must have taken that as being part of her general distress, and ignored it. Pargetter never turned a hair, to do him credit, but remained as cool as Raffles himself.

What could I do? Raffles had told me to remain in hiding until he needed me. And it certainly seemed as if he might need me, for two men, masked like Raffles and myself, armed with revolvers like Raffles and myself, made their way into the room!

Raffles, of course, was still watching Pargetter, who was talking in the same blustering fashion, calling Raffles all sorts of a coward, and daring him to do his worst. The first Raffles knew of the two newcomers was when one of them shoved his pistol into Raffles' ribs, and said hoarsely, 'Stick 'em up!'

Raffles did not move for a moment, then he laid is revolver on a little table.

Pargetter's reaction was odd. It was true that he asked, 'Just what is going on?' but I swear he was unafraid, almost as if he knew exactly what was happening. He sounded almost, were it not ridiculous to think it, amused by the turn events had taken!

The burglar who had his gun in Raffles' ribs said, 'Yus, what the— is going on?'

'I dunno,' said Raffles, still in character. 'Nothink to do wiv me, these two geezers.' He jerked a thumb at the newcomers.

Pargetter's face never changed as he said, 'You mean – what do you mean? Two gangs of crooks?' Again, that odd note was in his voice, a note which betokened some special knowledge, or I missed my guess.

I stepped out from the curtains. In my best Limehouse tones I said, 'I don't know what they mean, but I mean to shoot the first one as moves! Put them guns down, you two!'

Raffles gave me as grateful a look as any man can manage who is wearing a black silk mask, as he recovered his own weapon and took the pistols from the two burglars, who were clearly puzzled. 'This is a pretty kettle o' fish, I must say!' he told me.

'Yus, what they calls a "cow inside ants", I think.'

His look of gratitude was replaced by something less sympathetic. 'Coincidence be damned!' he said. 'Somethink's wrong 'ere, and I want to find out what.' He jerked the barrel of his revolver in a menacing fashion at the nearest burglar, who flinched.

'Don't shoot! I'll tell yer!'

'Go on, then,' urged Raffles.

'It was 'im, wasn't it?'

''Im?'

''Im.' The burglar indicated Pargetter, whose face had changed – indeed, he was now looking positively unwell. ''E told us you'd be 'ere. Paid us to stick you up, and then to fake a burglary, like, and run off when 'e defended the lady 'ere.'

'You unspeakable wretch!' It was neither Raffles nor I who said it, but Miss Morris.

'But why'd 'e do that?' asked Raffles.

'Oh, I can tell you that!' said Miss Morris. 'This villain persuaded me to leave my home and my father and fly with him! I confess I was not entirely unwilling, but then some doubts crept in, doubts as to the advisability of my actions, and doubts, I will be blunt, as to this man's ultimate intentions. He sensed that, and has concocted this ridiculous scheme to convince me that I should marry him! Well, it has failed, sir,' she told Pargetter, who slumped into a chair. 'If these – gentlemen,' she indicated Raffles and myself, and the pause was barely perceptible, 'will be so kind as to escort me home, then I shall leave you to settle accounts with your hirelings there.'

'O' course, lady. Just get yer coat an' 'at, won't yer, and we'll be orf.' And whilst Miss Morris made her preparations, Raffles took the two supposed 'burglars' to one side, and tore off their masks. 'Now,' he told them, 'you don't know me, but I knows you! An' if ever you mentions this little affair . . .' and he waved his revolver in a menacing fashion.

We escorted Miss Morris back home. It was no great distance, I am pleased to say, for Raffles and I dared not take a cab or yet remove our masks, so we had to walk. Fortunately Miss Morris was so angry with her former paramour that she did not remark upon our informal progress, nor yet our odd costume. We left her at the gate, and she flounced up the drive, with her thanks unspoken.

'There's gratitude for you!' said Raffles. 'And I didn't even take her necklace! By the way, Bunny, what the devil was your accent supposed to be?'

'East End, Raffles! I was rather proud of it.'

'East End? More like the West Riding of Yorkshire!'

'Well, yours was nothing special! It would never 'ave passed in 'Oxton, guv'nor!'

'I assure you, Bunny, I have made a careful study of phonetics! But I rue not taking that necklace, old chap!'

'There's always the reward,' I told him. 'We could hardly claim that had we lifted the necklace! And Morris knows us, remember, he'd be sure to want the blasted thing back.'

'Ah, yes, the reward, to be sure.' And Raffles laughed out loud as he removed his mask.

We were at the Morris house next morning bright and early, but Mr Morris did not rush to receive us. On the contrary, he kept us waiting a full half-hour before we were shown into his study. Raffles did not seem at all put out by this, but strolled casually about the drawing-room whilst we waited, staring out into the street, or studying the bell pull. At last, the butler escorted us into Morris's presence. Our host did not seem over-eager to see us, and his bearing, too, was not quite what one might have hoped for. 'Well?' was his greeting.

Raffles raised an eyebrow. 'Your daughter is safe and well, I trust?'

'She is, sir. And what of it?'

'We had an agreement, as I recall. A matter of five hundred pounds, and no questions asked – '

Morris snorted. 'I don't know how you know she's back,' he told us, 'but I don't see what it has to do with you? My daughter has told me what occurred last night,' he went on, 'and it is clear that you had no hand in the matter. You can hardly claim the credit for the fact that two common criminals showed some spark of decency!'

'Can I not?' Raffles seemed puzzled.

'Can you?'

I have seldom seen Raffles at a loss for words, but I saw it then. 'No,' he agreed reluctantly, 'I cannot.'

'Then there's no more to be said. You know the way out.'

I stood upon the pavement, furious. 'Nothing irritates a man like being slung out on his ear, Raffles!' I said angrily. 'And just lately, it seems to be becoming a habit! Can you beat that for sheer nerve, though? Fancy his refusing us the reward like that!'

'Bunny, Bunny, calm yourself, dear chap! I never thought he would pay up, you know.'

'You didn't?'

'A mean man, Bunny, mean of spirit as well as in the conventional sense. It would naturally, have been very nice if he had paid up, a bonus, so to speak, but I did not expect it. No, dear Bunny, 'twas not the reward I sought.'

'Wasn't it? Then – '

'Bunny, Bunny! I wanted to see the layout of the house, of

course! You have probably been so busy studying the pictures of the daughter that you have not noticed any mention of the father's little hobby. He collects gems, Bunny. Not any gems, mark you, but antique carved gems. *Multum in parvo*, if I remember the tag correctly. A lot of value, in a small compass. And he keeps them in the house! You noticed the safe, of course? In his study, behind that large painting of the well-nourished and entirely shameless young lady?'

'Oh, so that was it!'

We returned to the Albany, and sat in silence for a while, Raffles smoking his Sullivan. Then a thought struck me. 'Raffles?'

'Yes, Bunny?'

'How long have you had your eye on his gemstone collection?'

'Oh, some time now.'

'Some considerable time?'

'A year or so.'

A few minutes passed in silence. 'Raffles?'

'Yes?'

'Weren't you in Biarritz last year?'

'Was I?'

'Yes, you were! I say, Raffles?'

'Well?'

'This whole business wasn't some elaborate scheme of yours, was it? Designed expressly to give you an excuse to get into Morris's house?'

'Upon my soul, Bunny!' Raffles laughed, and threw the end of his Sullivan into the fire. 'You give me more credit than I deserve, old chap.'

'Yes, but it might have been.'

'Oh, anything might have been – '

'Yes,' I went on, warming to my hypothesis, 'I thought I'd seen that fellow before! I said as much, Raffles! I've seen him with you, or I'm much mistaken!'

'Most of my friends look very similar.'

'And the scheme to show him up, get Miss Morris to show her gratitude, ask us into the house – '

'Well, then,' he interrupted scornfully, 'why should I need the second lot of supposed burglars? They were redundant, Bunny.'

'Yes, that's true enough – no! Of course, it would look far more impressive if there were three men, in two separate gangs, and Pargetter, or whatever his real name is, seemed full of bravado and then broke down as he did! Yes, the contrast would be that much more pointed! And it would be a most curious coincidence had you both come up with the same scheme, your staging a fake robbery to show him up for a coward, and then his staging another one to prove himself a hero! A bit much to swallow, Raffles, even for me!'

Raffles lit another Sullivan. 'There is yet another possibility, Bunny.'

'Is there?'

'Well, suppose for one moment that I had, as you suggest, engineered an elaborate scheme, asked a – friend – to gain the lady's affections and what not. What – just "what", Bunny, nothing more – what if the man upon whom I had relied had decided to double-cross me, to bring in his own men, to cut me out, prove himself to the lady, and thereby get his hands upon her entire fortune, instead of being content with the miserable pittance I had – might have – paid him? What then? Why,' he went on as I floundered for words, 'who could I ultimately rely upon but my little Bunny, lurking as always behind the arras?'

I put a hand to my head, which was swirling. 'But – is that what it was? But, Raffles – if those two crooks were Pargetter's men, and if they expected to have to deal with you . . .'

'Yes, Bunny?'

'Their guns were very probably loaded! And mine was empty!' I sat down rather heavily.

'Ah, but if matters were as we have postulated, they wouldn't expect you, would they, Bunny? They might have been told that I was effectively unarmed, but they would have to work on the assumption that you were not. They would very probably assume that I had taken the same sort of elementary precaution which they themselves would take. And Pargetter could hardly tell them that you were harmless – for one thing, he could not be sure, and for another, it would give the game away to Miss Morris. Once we had their weapons, of course, all was well in any event.'

'Even so!'

Raffles shook his head. 'Let's just say it worked out rather well, shall we? Yes, I mean to have those gems, Bunny.'

And he did too, though that, as they say, is another story altogether.

Edward D. Hoch

Who could resist a story with a title as cheekily punning as 'The Laddie Vanishes'? Not me, especially when the author is the world's leading exponent of the short crime story. I have long admired Ed Hoch's work, but we did not meet until 1995, and then only in the unexpected and challenging environment of a crime fiction quiz based on the TV programme *Mastermind*, at the World Mystery Convention, or Bouchercon. When we finally escaped from the dreaded black chair, it was good to have the chance to chat to him. I did not dream then that one day I would have the chance to invite him to contribute to the anthology of the CWA, of which he is a long-standing overseas member. His contribution to last year's collection, 'Past Crimes', was set in Britain and this time around he has again ventured to the UK, with a story whose railway setting owes much to the Hitchcock film (based on a novel by Ethel Lina White) which no doubt inspired it.

THE LADDIE VANISHES

by Edward D. Hoch

Felicity Sloane's first impression of PC Derek Chamberlain was that he seemed too young to be a police constable. His photo on the laminated Edinburgh police ID he held up for her inspection made him appear even younger, showing a sly smile that went well with his coal-black hair and deep brown eyes. 'Police officer, ma'am,' he said as the London to Edinburgh express sped north through the night.

'What have I done?' she asked playfully. He was in plain clothes, after all, and lacked the instant intimidation of a uniformed officer.

The sly smile danced about his full lips. 'Nothing, I hope. I'm searching the train for a young, dark-haired Scotsman with a port-wine birthmark on his left cheek near his ear.' He indicated the area on his own face. 'Have you seen anything of him?'

She shook her head. 'No. What's he done?'

'Killed a bloke last winter in Edinburgh, then fled to the Continent. Customs spotted him when he re-entered the country at Dover a few days ago. I'm returning him to Scotland for trial.'

'And he got away from you?'

'Not far. He went to the loo and somehow slipped out when I wasn't looking. But he certainly didn't jump off a train travelling at a hundred kilometres an hour. He's on here somewhere. I've got the guard searching from the front of the train. I wonder if you could come with me and help search from the rear.'

'All right,' she agreed readily enough. The overnight express to Scotland was a dull journey at best, with nothing to be seen out of the windows for seven hours but the reflection of one's own face. This, at least, promised to be something of an adventure.

'I may need you to check the loos for me,' he explained as they headed toward the rear of the train. 'By the way, what's your name?'

'Felicity Sloane. I'm a fashion illustrator in London.'

'You're going the wrong way.'

She smiled. 'Up to Scotland to visit my parents for the long weekend.' Then, 'Have you ever lost a prisoner before?'

'No, ma'am, and I never will again, if I have to go to the loo with them. I only looked away from that door for an instant, when the guard came through, but that must have been all the time he needed.'

'Didn't anyone else in your carriage notice him?'

'They were mostly asleep. And of course Angus Selkirk meant nothing to them. He was just another passenger.'

'Angus Selkirk.' She repeated the name as they moved into the next carriage. 'Do you think he's dangerous?'

'Any man who kills another human being is dangerous.'

'No, I mean do you think he's dangerous now? Will he resist arrest?'

'I believe he will.'

'Are you armed?'

Chamberlain shook his head. 'We were escorted to the train and we're being met at the other end. The theory is that an express train is like one long tunnel. While it's moving there's no escape. The prisoner is only handcuffed to me when we're entering or leaving the train. While on board, a weapon might only cause casualties if it fell into the prisoner's hands.'

They had covered half the train when they came upon the guard, a grim-faced man named Mortimer. 'Any luck?' the constable asked.

The guard shook his head. 'I found four passengers who remembered seeing the man with the birthmark on his face, but there's no sign of him now.'

'I'd like to speak to them.' Then, remembering her presence, he added, 'This is Felicity Sloane. She's helping with the search.'

The guard acknowledged her presence with a nod. 'Follow me, please.'

Mortimer led them toward the front of the train. 'This is where we were seated,' PC Chamberlain said, indicating two empty seats facing the loo.

'I remember you,' a middle-aged woman across the aisle said. The white haired man accompanying her nodded his agreement. 'And the laddie with the birthmark on his face.'

'He was a prisoner I was escorting back to Scotland,' Chamberlain explained. 'He went to the loo and seems to have disappeared. Did you see him alone, without me?'

Both travellers shook their heads. 'We might have been dozing,' the man admitted.

The memory of a young woman in the seat behind them was much the same. She remembered the man with the birthmark but hadn't noticed where he went. A teenage boy a few seats back had also noticed Angus Selkirk, but he'd been reading a homework assignment, on his way back to school after visiting his father in London for the weekend. 'I'll keep an eye out,' the guard promised, moving on about his business.

'He could have jumped from the train,' Felicity suggested.

Chamberlain shook his head. 'Selkirk isn't the suicidal type.'

'What type is he?'

The constable shrugged. 'Twenty years old, a minor criminal record until last February when he assaulted a bloke at an automatic teller machine. He stole the man's money and car, and the victim died of his injuries the following day. The car was recovered with Selkirk's fingerprints on it. He's not the smartest criminal in the world. But by that time he'd used some of the stolen money to buy a plane ticket to Paris. The French police weren't able to trace him after he landed, but we knew the money would run out and we were betting he'd head back here to continue his life of crime. All customs stations have been watching for him for several months. They caught him at Dover, the most likely crossing point.'

'What about his parents?'

'They're still in Edinburgh, but he's been on his own about three years now. There's a sister too, though he never sees her.'

Felicity pondered the life of this young man who'd been fleeing for so long. 'I suppose it was the birthmark that made him such an outcast.'

He shook his head. 'I don't buy that excuse. Plenty of people have overcome deformities a lot worse than his. And there's laser treatment for such things these days.' They sat for a moment in one of the empty seats, and when his jacket sleeve slid up a bit she noticed a small tattooed word – *taureau* – above his right wrist. She was about to suggest that police constables might wish to have tattoos removed in the same manner, but then decided it was none of her business. Such things were not uncommon among young people these days.

In the middle of the night the restaurant car was empty, but the adjoining buffet bar still had a few customers, including a nun in a traditional wimple who was seated alone eating a toffee bar of some sort. In a first-class carriage was a young man with a bandaged face. She gripped Derek Chamberlain's arm. 'What about him? The bandage could be covering his birthmark.'

He shook his head. 'The guard mentioned him right off, but he's been on the train since London.'

'Forgetting the bandage, does the rest of him look like Selkirk?'

'Not really. His clothes are different. And his hair is longer than Selkirk's.

'The clothes might have been changed and the hair could be a wig. I saw an old movie once where a woman vanished on a train and they hid her by having her all bandaged up.'

'Who did?'

'The bad guys, of course! Come on.' She was warming to the chase.

The youth with the bandaged face glanced up as they paused by his seat.

Chamberlain said to the older woman sitting opposite the youth, 'I'm searching for an escaped criminal, ma'am. Could I see some identification for yourself and the young man?'

'He's my son. He's had a bit of plastic surgery in London and we're returning home.' She showed them her driver's licence.

Chamberlain studied it and handed it back. 'Thank you, Mrs ... Elfin. And your son is . . .?'

'I'm Robert,' he said with a noticeable Scottish accent.

The constable studied his face and eyes for only a moment. 'Thank you, both of you. Sorry to have bothered you.'

Back in the corridor he told Felicity, 'That's not him. When I got a closer look I knew right away it wasn't.'

He knocked on the loo door at the end of the carriage and a woman's voice answered. 'Occupied!'

'Sorry, ma'am. This is the police. If you'll unlock the door a female will glance inside. We're searching for an escaped prisoner.'

They heard the bolt slide open and the door opened barely an inch. 'Show me some ID,' the woman said. Chamberlain produced his card and the door opened enough for Felicity to peek inside.

'Check behind the door,' the constable instructed. She did but there was no one hiding.

Felicity thanked the woman and they moved on. 'She looked a bit ill. Maybe train travel doesn't agree with her.'

'After tonight it doesn't agree with me, either. Unless I find Selkirk I'll be back directing traffic on Princes Street.'

They reached the front of the train without finding the missing prisoner. 'Look,' Felicity said, 'we have to go about this in a more organised manner. Somehow he might have got by us as we searched the train, and then doubled back to the rear.'

They found Mortimer, the guard, again and he agreed to come through behind them in case Selkirk revealed himself. Once more everything was checked. When they reached the other end of the train and Mortimer caught up with them, he said simply, 'The man you describe is not on this train.'

'But he was on it!' Chamberlain argued. 'You heard those witnesses. They saw me with him.'

'Wait a minute,' said Felicity. 'The witnesses really saw nothing but that birthmark. Suppose it was a fake?'

He shook his head. 'No chance. I've seen mug shots of him from the time of his first arrest. The birthmark was always there.'

'Then he covered it up somehow.'

'We already checked the laddie with the bandaged face,' he reminded her. 'No other person on this train has his face covered.'

'No other man,' she corrected.

'What?'

'There was a nun wearing a wimple when we passed through earlier. That wimple could have covered most of Angus Selkirk's birthmark.'

'But he would have needed an accomplice on the train for that, someone to supply the nun's habit. No one could have known which train we'd be on.'

'The trains to Edinburgh and the east coast of Scotland leave from King's Cross, don't they?'

'Well, yes,' he admitted.

'An accomplice could easily guess you'd be returning Selkirk to Scotland today or tomorrow. Someone could have waited at the station with the nun's habit in a bag until they saw him, then simply followed the two of you on board, waiting for him to give you the slip.'

'I suppose so.' Chamberlain sighed. 'We'd better go and check her out. But you'll have to do that.'

The nun was still seated in the same compartment, and she smiled as they entered. Her name was Sister Benedict. 'I've been to London for the computer show,' she explained. 'Our convent is purchasing several and I have to decide which model is best for our needs. There are plenty of people in Edinburgh to advise us, but I wanted to know about the very latest advances.'

PC Chamberlain smiled and showed his identification. 'I have to ask you a great favour, Sister Benedict, and I trust you won't feel it is too much of an imposition. While I wait in the corridor, could you remove your wimple for Miss Sloane here? We're searching for an escaped criminal and I – '

'It's no problem,' she assured them. 'I often go without it these days, but Mother Superior thought it might be safer to wear it travelling to London. It does garner a certain degree of respect.'

Felicity knew before the uncovering took place that this was truly a woman, but she went through with it while Chamberlain paced the corridor outside. 'You're very beautiful,' she said, staring at Sister Benedict's unmarked cheeks. 'Thank you so much for helping us.'

'It was no trouble at all.'

'There are eight carriages on this train,' Felicity told Derek Chamberlain, 'and we've been through them all. Your man is nowhere on this train. He must have slipped out of the loo, opened the door and jumped. There's no other possibility.'

'Someone would have seen him!' the constable protested.

'You didn't see him leave the loo and you were awake. Most of the other passengers were dozing.'

'I suppose you have a point,' he conceded. 'Any other ideas?'

She thought about it. 'What's at the front of the train? Is there a luggage compartment?'

He chuckled at the idea. 'You've been seeing too many old movies.'

They sought out Mortimer once more. He verified that the train carried sacks of mail in the carriage behind the engine. 'But it's locked,' he informed them. 'No one goes in there.'

'You must have a key in case of emergencies.'

He conceded that there was an emergency key. 'It's locked up in the guard's van. But you can't go in there.'

Chamberlain brought out his badge and ID again. His photo was beginning to curl a bit at one corner. 'This badge gives me the right to go there or anywhere else in the investigation of a crime! I'm not going to touch your mailbags. I just want to check for any possible hiding place.'

Felicity trailed along as they walked through the first-class coach to the locked door. Mortimer turned the key and the metal door swung open. The overhead lights were turned on, revealing tan sacks of woven plastic, each bearing the bold letters 'Royal Mail'. They were secured at the top and though each was about a metre in height they could not have hidden even a small man. On this trip, at least, there was no place in the mail coach for Angus Selkirk or anyone else to have hidden.

PC Chamberlain seemed at a loss as to his next move. They left the mail coach and the guard relocked it. 'What's the next stop?' Chamberlain asked Mortimer as they returned to the guard's van.

'There's no scheduled stop until Edinburgh in the morning.'

'You could stop at Newcastle.'

The grim-faced Mortimer shook his head. 'Only in emergencies. This is the Edinburgh express.'

'This is an emergency, damn it! I need to contact the authorities and begin a search of the track area. I'm beginning to think my laddie must have jumped after all.'

'If he jumped from this train when it was moving at top speed you can stop worrying about him getting away. He'll be right there waiting for you. As for contacting the authorities, you can use a telephone here on the train.'

'No, I can't. Anyone can listen in on a cellular phone if they have the right equipment, and Selkirk has lots of friends in the underworld. I need a secure ground line to Edinburgh and Scotland Yard. If he's off this train and still alive we need to find him before they do.'

The guard thought about it and then picked up a telephone that connected him to the driver. He identified himself and said, 'We have a passenger on board, PC Derek Chamberlain. A prisoner he was escorting gave him the slip and apparently jumped off the train. He's requesting to be dropped off at Newcastle so he can report to his superiors over a safe phone line.' Mortimer listened and glanced at his watch. 'I'll tell him.'

'Will he do it?' the constable asked.

Mortimer nodded. 'We pass through Newcastle in thirty-four minutes. Be ready to get off. He can only stop for a few seconds.'

'That's good enough.'

Felicity followed him to a seat near a door. 'I'm sorry I couldn't be of more help.'

He shrugged. 'We did what we could. We certainly established he's nowhere on the train.'

'Will you have to spend the rest of the night searching for the body?'

'I hope not. There are others to do that.'

Felicity turned to stare out at the darkness. 'Did you grow up in Edinburgh?'

'That I did. I'm a home boy. Never been farther away than London until this trip to Dover. The way it turned out I should have stayed at home.'

'Don't blame yourself.'

'Who else is there to blame?'

Occasionally they passed through a town where a few lights broke the darkness, but it was not until the train reached the outskirts of Newcastle that the night began to brighten. 'I'll be leaving now,' he said as the train rumbled across the bridge over the Tyne. 'Thanks for your help.'

The train was slowing for its brief stop at the station. He held out his hand to shake hers as the guard came forward to open the door. 'Derek . . .?' she said as she took it.

'What?'

'I have one more solution.'

'After the bandaged face and the nun and the luggage compartment?' His eyes were laughing at her now.

'Yes. One place I never thought to look.'

'Come on if you're coming!' the guard bellowed as the train slowed to a stop.

'Where's that?' Chamberlain asked her.

'Right here, right before my eyes. You are Angus Selkirk, and it was PC Chamberlain who was thrown from the train.'

He would have been wiser to have laughed at her and walked away. As it was, her words so panicked him that he pushed her aside in the aisle and bolted for the door. Mortimer grabbed at him, but the effect was to throw the fleeing man off balance. He fell to the station platform and a uniformed officer hurried over to assist him.

'I'm PC Chamberlain,' he tried to say, holding up his badge and photo ID for the last time.

But now Felicity was on him. 'That's not true!' she shouted to the officer. 'He's an escaped murderer named Selkirk!' And to prove it she grabbed at the laminated identification card and peeled off his photograph, revealing an entirely different photo underneath, that of a slightly older man with a birthmark on his cheek.

The officer's face hardened. 'You'd better come along with me, sir. Impersonating a policeman is a serious offence. And you too, miss.'

It was some time later, as dawn was breaking over the city of Newcastle, that Felicity got to tell her story to an inspector named Rollings. 'When did you first become suspicious of this man, Miss Sloane?' he asked pleasantly.

'Well, he showed his ID to someone and I noticed one corner of his photo was beginning to curl. But the thing was laminated, don't you see, and the photo should have been under the lamination, not on top of it. I think PC Chamberlain probably went into the loo with Selkirk and somehow Selkirk managed to overpower him and kill him there. With the passengers dozing or asleep it wasn't difficult for him to hoist Chamberlain's body a few feet and open the train door. The constable was gone into the night and Selkirk now had his badge and identification. He must have been carrying an extra passport photo for emergencies like this. He cut it down to size and stuck it over Chamberlain's photo on the ID.'

'Stuck it with what?'

'Anything sticky! A bit of softened toffee from the buffet bar would have done the trick. Now only one problem remained for him. He had to get the train to stop somewhere before the Edinburgh station, where the police would be waiting for their prisoner and would be sure to recognise him. He went about this in a clever manner. First he persuaded me that he was a constable escorting a prisoner and then he described Chamberlain's birthmarked face as being that of the prisoner Selkirk. We spent over an hour searching the train, aided by the guard, before he decided he had to get off and organise a search party for the body. Once he was free in Newcastle, of course, he'd have been on his way.'

Inspector Rollings was amazed. 'All that from a curled-up photo?'

'There was one other thing,' she admitted. 'When he put out his hand to shake mine as he was leaving the train, I caught another glimpse of the word *taureau* tattooed above his right wrist. It's a French word but he said he'd never been further away than Dover. Selkirk had just come back from France, and the word *taureau* means bull in French. I've been to Paris several times doing my fashion illustrations and I know the language.'

'Bull?'

Felicity nodded. 'Selkirk's first name is Angus, remember, as in Black Angus cattle. I imagine he got the tattoo over there to impress the French ladies.'

Bill Kirton

Bill Kirton is a relatively recent arrival on the crime fiction scene who has not previously contributed to a CWA anthology. His name may not, perhaps, be familiar to some readers, but 'Missing' will, I believe, prompt a good many people to search for his other work. It is a marvellous, gripping story which addresses the 'missing person' concept head on. Quite simply, it demanded to be included in this book from the moment I first read the manuscript.

MISSING

by Bill Kirton

Mum died. That's what started it. Terrible, isn't it? Two syllables, seven letters and it's enough to hollow out the universe. Think I'm exaggerating? Your mum's obviously still alive. One minute you're flipping a peanut in the air and catching it in your mouth as you reach to answer the phone, the next, your sister's voice, quiet, apologetic, just saying, 'Bad news. It's Mum.' And all the comfortable stuff around you – your furniture, the pictures on your walls, your ornaments – suddenly belongs to somebody else. Because the person you were, the person that bought it all, arranged it, lived with it, has been catapulted away out of reach. And this new you is just left there, crying, knowing that crying isn't enough, desperate to go and kneel in one of the churches to weep on the shoulder of a god you stopped believing in years ago. Funnily enough, it's like being born. One minute, you're snug inside your space, the next, you're in a gaping new place, with no values, no sense to it, no structure. And the person who's always been there approving of you, keeping you straight, isn't around.

I don't want to dwell on it but I warn you now, it's never far away from me. She was the most precious lady in the world. I don't say that easily. I'm not a guy that misses people. When my wife, Christine, took off with an English teacher because she'd had enough of the irregular hours I worked, I was jealous for about a week then realised that I was having a great time leaving my clothes over the backs of chairs, eating in front of the telly, coming and going when I pleased without the worms of guilt turning in my head. I was suddenly grateful to the teacher and knew that I never wanted to live with anyone again. People make demands, even when they don't mean to, and I like the way I live too much to start compromising. So, you see, when I say I don't miss people, it's true.

But I miss Mum.

Not that I ever saw much of her. She lived in Edinburgh and I've been in Aberdeen for ages. We phoned one another now and again, but not regularly, not every week even. I used to drive down once in a while but I wasn't what you'd call a dutiful son. I took her for granted, I suppose. She was only wee, not much over five feet, and there was no fat on her, not to speak of, but the vacuum she's left . . .

Anyway, as I said, I'm sure that's what started it. I was working on a missing person enquiry and my sister's phone call and the emptiness of the days after it redefined the whole idea of being missing. It's too easy to treat it as a statistic. Not that I was doing that. I was already semi-obsessed with the case. It was one of those where you know exactly who's guilty but can't find enough evidence to take to the procurator fiscal. Cindy Armstrong hadn't come home from a holiday trip to Cornwall. She'd driven down on her own at the beginning of the month and, when she wasn't back by the fifteenth, her husband, Donald, got in touch with us. This is the same Donald Armstrong who, just over two years ago, walked into headquarters in Queen Street, confessed to killing his first wife and was acquitted by the jury in Aberdeen's High Court. It's also the same Donald Armstrong whose company has ridden out the occasional lows of the oil industry by judicious staff pruning; not so much downsizing as annihilation. He drives a Mercedes CLK430 coupé, which he imported from the States for some reason, and lives in a detached architect's special out at Milltimber, not far off the North Deeside Road. He made his money from designing a plug that operators use to seal off offshore oil and gas pipes while they're working on them. I found out about that when I was investigating the death of wife number one. He may be a complete pillock but he's some engineer. You just slip this plug down the line, hit a couple of buttons and the hydraulics squeeze these seals out against the pipe wall so that not even high pressure gas can get through. It's made him rich enough to be able to treat people like . . . I almost said shit, but I'll settle for commodities.

I'd just been made up to detective inspector and was the duty officer when he arrived that first time. It was six in the morning when they called me in. Right from the start, I disliked him. He's sitting there in the interview room, all Paul Smith suit and Nicole Farhi shirt, calmly telling us he's had a fight with his wife and that he's strangled her. He's quiet, keeps his eyes down, but there's no emotion coming off him. It's as if he's there to report a lost bike. At first, with that sort of thing, you're gentle, you take it easy, trying to help them tell the full story. But with him, sympathy was out. He didn't want it, I couldn't give it. Something was going on. It wasn't a hunch or anything like that; the guy was just emotionally cold. His words, his voice, the actual sounds he was making – none of them fitted the context.

His story was that he and his wife, Elspeth, had been for a meal in Les Amis, then gone on to the Amadeus night-club down at the beach. By two in the morning, they were both very drunk and she started accusing him of chatting up some of the young women there. They got a taxi home, arguing all the way, and, when they got inside, the row became a real fight. Elspeth started screaming all sorts of stuff at him, saying he was a sick bastard, a pervert, slapping and scratching him. (He showed us the evidence – deep parallel gouges down the side of his neck and on his left cheek.) He shouted back but didn't touch her until she started calling him a poof. Yeah, one minute she's accusing him of chatting up women, the next he's a poof. You tell me. Anyway, she went on about that, said that he'd never given her a decent fuck, was pathetic, limp-dicked and that she'd make sure that all his pals knew about it.

He couldn't take much of that. ('Well, could you?' he asked us.) Started slapping her back. That made her worse and, in the end, he found himself kneeling on the bed with his hands round her neck, squeezing to shut her up.

As soon as he realised what he was doing, he got up and went out to cool down.

'Where did you go?' I asked him.

'Just around the garden. Out on to the road. Just walking. Trying to get my head together. Not many places to go in Milltimber that time of night.'

'How long did you stay out?'

He shook his head. 'Don't know. But when I went back, she was still there. On the bed. Where I'd left her.'

'So what did you do?'

'Shouted at her. Tried to wake her up. Checked her pulse. Felt her neck. She was cold. I got a taxi straight here.'

'You didn't phone for an ambulance?'

'No point. I thought you wanted scenes of crime to be undisturbed.'

You see, that was weird, wasn't it? He's sitting there with us, his wife's lying dead at home, and he's more concerned with leaving the clues intact than with trying to save her. Talk about helping the police with their enquiries.

When we'd finished the first run-through, I left him making his statement and went straight out to his place with the scene of crime boys. It was like a film set. The bedroom's all plum-coloured walls and velvet drapes. There's rugs and parquet flooring, table lights on all over the place. And there, on the king-size bed with its black sheets and duvet, is Mrs Armstrong, curled up as if she's just decided to take a nap. There were bruises on her face and neck from the fight but, apart from that, no signs of a struggle. Not one. All the rooms were the same. If they'd had the sort of fight he'd described to us, it should have been chaotic. But there was nothing broken, nothing overturned. Maybe rich folks are genteel when they argue. But whatever had gone on in the house, everything was tidy and spotless. There weren't even any creases in the sheets or the duvet she was lying on. He couldn't possibly have knelt on that bed. He must have hovered above it.

When I asked him about that later, he said I'd made a mistake. He insisted that he'd knelt with his legs either side of her, pushing her head hard into the bed. It had been a real fight and there were bound to be signs of it. He even suggested we should look again.

In the end, the tidiness was one of the things which helped him to get away with it. You see, it wasn't the strangling that killed her, it was booze. That was what the medic said. Alcohol poisoning. Armstrong sat there listening to this, saying nothing. He just shook his head once or twice. Like he couldn't believe what he was hearing. I'm not surprised. The stuff his lawyer spouted was all bloody fiction. He reckoned that, when Armstrong left the house, his wife was semi-conscious, from drink more than from the attempt to throttle her. At last, she got up, drank some more and tidied the place up while she was waiting for him to come back.

The jury bought it. There was plenty in his favour – the fact that he'd given himself up right away, the evidence, from several of his friends, that Elspeth had a real drink problem and, most of all, the tidiness of the house, which proved that she was still alive when he left and so he couldn't possibly be responsible for her death. It never seemed to occur to anyone that he could have forced the booze down her, made the strangulation marks after she'd died and tidied the place up himself before coming to us with his fairy-tale. No pathologist could pick up the fact that the strangling was post-mortem if it more or less coincided with her dying. Confessing was a risky strategy, but in the end it worked for him.

He killed her. There's no doubt in my mind of that. It wasn't the first time we'd had to call him in. He beat up two prostitutes one time, left one of them with a broken thumb and blind in one eye. When it came to it, though, they wouldn't press charges. Combination of being afraid of him and getting a fat backhander to keep quiet. It's part of the way he does things. The world has to be shaped his way. If individuals stray from the paths he's made for them, they become ... inconvenient, and they disappear, either by dying or, at work, by getting the boot.

And then, of course, wife number two goes AWOL. Surprise, surprise.

I thought it was ironic for him to say she was missing. He doesn't know what a missing person is. To understand that, you have to acknowledge that they have their own personal place in the world, accept their separateness, their independence of you and everyone else. None of the people connected with Armstrong has that. They don't go missing; they just stop being who they were supposed to be in his scheme of things. In my book, anyone with that sort of attitude has got serious problems.

I went out to his place to get the details. Again, there was no emotion in him. The same, flat voice, as if he was bored by it all. He didn't even try to pretend to be upset. I think he knew what I thought of him and reckoned I wasn't worth trying to convince.

The interview was short and very frustrating. He didn't know where she'd intended staying. Cornwall, that was all. She'd decided to hire a car but he didn't know where from. He hadn't heard from her at all since she'd left. And so on, and so on. I was getting fed up with the grunting and the monosyllables. Tried to provoke him a bit. Asked him whether they'd had a row before she left. He knew what I meant but he just said no. He poured himself a drink. I noticed it was a fifteen-year-old malt. He didn't offer me one.

When I'd finished and was at the door putting on my raincoat, he lifted his hand and felt the material briefly.

'Police pay still lousy, I see,' he said.

'Serving the public is its own reward,' I said.

'Just as well,' he replied.

I'd meant to be sarcastic but it was a feeble effort. Still, the alternative was to punch him in the face, so it was a small victory.

We did all the usual checks. None of the local or national hire firms had any record of Cindy Armstrong hiring a car. She hadn't used an assumed name either; we contacted all the female customers the companies had listed around the relevant dates and they all checked out. None of her friends knew where she'd intended going or even that she was planning a holiday. In fact, two of them, who claimed to be her closest friends, were surprised to hear that she was driving such a long way in her condition. Apparently, she was pregnant. She'd had a miscarriage just eight months before and they knew she was anxious not to do anything that might trigger another. When I heard that, I went to see the two of them myself. They were receptionists for DEFAB, an engineering company specialising in decommissioning offshore structures. I didn't stay long with them because our conversation was interrupted every minute or so by the switchboard beeping and one of them picking up the phone and reciting, 'Good afternoon. DEFAB. How can I help you?' in a grooved, singsong tone well removed from normal speech. My trip was worth it, though.

'I don't know why she wanted to have a kid of his in the first place,' said Hayley, a blonde twenty-something with cropped hair and eyes whose green probably came from contact lenses. It was as well that they were so fascinating, otherwise I wouldn't have been able to keep my own away from her incredible breasts.

'You're not a fan of his, then?' I said.

'You met him?' was all she replied.

'What did he think about the baby?'

'Wanted her to get rid of it. They started arguing about it the minute she told him.'

'Did they argue a lot?'

Hayley and her friend, Midge, looked at one another, nodding.

'Even before they got married,' said Midge.

When I heard her speak, I guessed where her name came from. I know midges don't make a noise but if they did, her voice is what they would sound like.

'He's a bastard,' she added.

'In what way?' I asked.

'Every way. Treated her like shit. We've seen her with bruises all over, haven't we, Hayle?'

Hayley nodded.

They were happy to slag Armstrong off as long as I wanted but it started to get repetitive and none of it gave me any evidence to work with. I asked about Cindy again and, the more we talked about her, the less likely it seemed that she would just drive off to Cornwall without telling them and everyone else she knew. In the end, I was glad to get away from Midge's voice, but sorry to be deprived of Hayley's breasts.

That evening, I got my sister's call.

It cut me adrift. Left me insecure, feeling I was in a wide open, empty, empty space. No walls, no points of reference. Lost.

I was no use to anyone for the best part of two days. I never cry but all the tears I'd kept back over the years came out then.

Day and night. Hour after hour. I kept saying 'Mum' over and over again. I've never been lower. It wasn't just that there was a hole in my life, there was a hole all around it and through it.

I forced myself back to work on the Thursday. All the guys made the right, quiet noises but I needed not to be reminded. I needed to get back into the Armstrong stuff. While I'd been off, Jim Ross, one of my sergeants, had found out that Armstrong's company had been granted a special landfill licence to dispose of some pipes and equipment at their yard which had been contaminated by LSA scale. That's radioactive stuff that gets precipitated from some downhole fluids. It's low level but still nasty. They'd concreted them into an underground chamber and sealed the lot with tons more concrete. And guess when that had happened? Yeah, that's right. Beginning of the month. It was all so obvious, wasn't it? We'd need cast-iron evidence against him before we could get the go-ahead (and the funds) to dig up the pipes. It would be a massive operation and there was bound to be a risk of exposure to radiation.

When I heard that, I felt angry, but there was misery, too. Another person lost. Another gap. In my head, it was as if Armstrong was connected with Mum's death. I know, I know, that's stupid, but it was just the way that, for me, a precious, precious person had disappeared and drained everything out of my life with her, while he'd wiped out somebody he must have loved once, just to keep his life easy. And he'd done it before. It made the investigation personal.

We had no body, but I wanted him. I decided to try to upset him again, so asked him to come to the station to answer some questions. He tried telling me he was too busy, but I didn't give him any options. He knew he had to come. I told him to bring his solicitor, too. I wanted him unsettled.

When he arrived, I took him down to interview room two. I started the tape and identified the people in the room – myself, Armstrong, his solicitor Ballater, and Detective Sergeant Ross. I made it clear that no accusations were being made but that it was important for us to have everything on record because the evidence suggested that this could be a serious crime.

'What evidence?' asked Ballater.

I just looked at him. He should have known better.

We went through all the stuff Armstrong had already told us – the hire car, the planning of the trip, the silence and his eventual anxiety.

'Yes, that's something that puzzles me,' I said. 'Were you happy about your wife driving all that way?'

'Sure,' said Armstrong. 'She was a big girl.'

I noticed the tense but didn't pick up on it then.

'And about to get bigger,' I said.

He said nothing but his eyes locked on to mine and he was wary.

'That's what I mean, really,' I went on. 'Driving to Cornwall when she's pregnant. Especially after the miscarriage.'

He still said nothing.

'Didn't that worry you?' I asked.

'No.'

'Why not?'

'She was a big girl,' he repeated.

'But surely you didn't want to risk losing a second baby?'

'The kid was Cindy's idea, not mine. She knew what I thought about it.'

Ballater must have caught the aggression in his tone.

'May I ask the relevance of these questions?' he asked, as much to distract attention from Armstrong as to make a point.

'I don't know yet,' I said, then turned back to Armstrong.

'The pregnancy was a source of friction then, was it?' I asked.

'I don't have time for kids.'

'But Mrs Armstrong does.'

He looked hard at me again.

'Ask her,' he said.

His sneering, his disregard for people really got to me. I can usually handle it, but I nearly reached across and punched him. Vulnerable, see? Because of Mum. I waited a bit, looking at the various notes I'd brought with me. One of the sheets of paper was a report on Cindy Armstrong's admission to Aberdeen Royal Infirmary when she'd miscarried.

'Tell me about the miscarriage,' I said.

Ballater started another protest but I shut him up.

'What's to tell?' said Armstrong, sitting back as if he was describing a total non-event. 'She threw up a few times, bled all over the bed and that was that.'

'Any idea what caused it?'

'What am I, a fucking gynaecologist?'

Charmer, eh?

'According to the report,' I said, 'there was a fair bit of bruising around her abdomen. How did that happen?'

I didn't expect to get away with it and Ballater was quick to jump in.

'Inspector, this is very irregular. I'm afraid I'm going to have to ask you to – '

I ignored him.

'Somebody else you needed to get out of the way, Mr Armstrong? The baby, I mean? Another bit of rescheduling?'

Armstrong and Ballater both stood up. I felt Jim Ross's hand on my arm but I was launched. It was the equivalent of punching him.

'And then it happens again, so this time you dump the baby and the woman who keeps threatening to produce them. Bit of a habit with you, disposing of people, isn't it?'

'Fuck you,' said Armstrong.

Ballater was calm. There was even a smile on his face.

'I want a transcript of that tape and I want your superiors to hear it,' he said.

Jim said, 'Interview suspended at two thirty-seven,' switched off the machine and took out the tape. Ballater and Armstrong were already out of the room.

'What the hell are you doing, boss?' said Jim and went out after them.

And I just started crying again. I went home. Spent the rest of the day there looking at photos of me as a kid.

But I wasn't about to let him get away with it again. I had an interview with the Chief Constable, of course, and he chewed my balls off and threatened suspension, but I didn't let it get in the way of digging for more information. There was plenty of it. Armstrong and his wife were always rowing in public; there were plenty of people, friends of hers and colleagues of his, who confirmed it. Apparently, after she'd married him, she'd become what the shrinks call a depressive. Did irrational things. Her friends said it was because he was always with other women, his friends said that he only went with the other women to get away from her demands. They said she was obsessional and hysterical.

The thing that really got to me, though, was the transcript of an interview we did with him about the two prostitutes he beat up. He denied any knowledge of them but Danny Ritchie, who was interviewing him, was sharp enough to get him talking about prostitutes in general, not just the two involved.

'I don't see the problem,' said Armstrong. 'They're in it for profit. Same as me with engineering solutions. If I don't deliver, I expect to suffer. It's a market place. Dog eat dog.'

'Nobody beats you up, though,' said Danny.

'I'm in engineering, not flesh,' said Armstrong. 'Occupational hazard for them, isn't it?'

'They should be able to choose, though, shouldn't they?' said Danny. He was clever. Talking to Armstrong as if they were in a pub, just having a quiet chat over a bevvy.

'Choose? They've made their fucking choice,' said Armstrong. 'They put their bums and tits up for sale. What do they expect? Know what that makes them? Stock items on the inventory. The sad buggers who go to them are just buying substitutes for their wives, spare parts, replacements. If a spare part's no good, what do you do? Chuck it away. Simple as that.'

There was more of the same. He was so bloody sure of himself, so dismissive of the women, so empty of anything like understanding or compassion. The seventeen-year-old in the hospital with her thumb in a splint and bandages over the empty socket of her left eye was discounted. For him, she had no more significance or value than a restaurant menu.

The next time I questioned him, I'd brought all this together and was determined to stay calm and gradually pile the information up until its weight began to affect him. He'd killed two wives (as well as two babies) and he knew that I knew it. I just wanted to show him that he wasn't going to get away with it. I actually started this time with his first wife. I think it took him by surprise, but I was careful with it and there were no complaints. When I brought up the two prostitutes, he was wary, didn't say much, but just listened. Again, though, I kept it low key, kept my cool and just let the facts come out. I didn't accuse him of anything. I did repeat some of the words he'd used in his interview with Danny, but I didn't really accuse him of anything. In a way, I was giving him the chance to . . . what's the word? . . . redeem himself. Yes, that's it.

'You see, you reported your wife as missing, but I'm not sure what you think that means,' I said.

'It means she's gone. Not here any more. What the hell could it mean?'

'But is she missing in the same way that, say, the people you've made redundant are missing?'

His face showed that he didn't know what I was on about.

'Pieces of jigsaw puzzles, they go missing,' I said. 'You see, it means something . . . well, definite, really. Means something's not complete. Being dead, for instance; that's not really being missing, is it?'

'Who says she's dead?' he asked, wary again.

'No, I mean generally speaking. Dead is natural. It's complete. Missing's sort of different. Means the balance is wrong, something's gone from the equation.'

'What's this got to do with – ?'

I didn't let him finish.

'I think it would help you in all sorts of ways to learn what being missing means,' I said. 'Change your values a bit.'

'OK,' he said. 'That's enough fucking me about. I've got a business to run. It's time we – '

I hit him. A quick, short swing with my right hand, the one holding the Browning .25. It's only a small gun but it adds beef to a punch. I didn't quite connect with his jaw. The punch was too high and his nose started squirting blood. It didn't matter. I didn't want to knock him out, just stun him, disorientate him, so that I could get on with it.

Course, I didn't tell you, did I? It was a Sunday and I'd fetched him from his house and brought him to his engineering yard. That was what the Browning was for. So that he wouldn't argue. We were in the pipe storage area. We'd had to raise our voices to speak over the din of a generator that ran permanently to supply the site with independent power.

He'd fallen back and was leaning on one elbow, slowly shaking his head. I looped a length of cable over him and pulled him up, locking his arms to his sides then tying his wrists together at the front.

I bent, slung him over my shoulder in a fireman's lift and carried him to a rack of 36-inch diameter pipes at the furthest end of the yard. They were stacked with one end hard against the yard wall. When we got to them, I turned and slid his feet into one at about shoulder height, then pushed until he was lying inside it, with his head just at the opening. I tell you, it was a relief to get him off me. I stretched and straightened a bit.

'You're a heavy bugger,' I said. 'You want to watch what you're eating. Still, I might be able to help you with that.'

He was still too groggy to do anything and, if he tried to wriggle out of the pipe, he'd only fall on his head. He was beginning to take notice, though.

'Now then,' I said, 'you know what I think? I think you got rid of your wife – Cindy, I mean, we know you got rid of the first one – and I think you slipped her into one of the pipes you buried over in the contamination area.'

'I didn't – ' he said, his words slurring as if he'd had a few.

'And you reported her as missing, but she's not. She's dead. And we've agreed that that's not the same thing.'

'Honest to God,' he said. 'I'm telling you it's not – '

'No, no, listen,' I said. 'This is important. She'd only be missing if she was in the pipe and still alive. Dead doesn't count. Just think about that a minute.'

From the look in his eyes, he'd already started thinking about it and he didn't like what he was imagining. I left him to it while I went across to a stack of his sealing plugs. Beside them was a diesel trolley with blocks and pulleys on it to lift individual plugs on to lorries for transport. I started it up, hooked up a 36-inch diameter plug, hauled on the chains to get it clear of the stack and put the trolley in gear to guide it back to where Armstrong was lying. Even if he hadn't cottoned on before, there wasn't much doubt in him when I switched off the diesel, with the plug swinging just a couple of feet away from his face.

'Now then,' I said. 'About your wife. Cindy. Where is she?'

He shook his head. Little spots of blood dripped from his nose on to the inside wall of the pipe.

'You're not making this very easy,' I said. I put my hands on his shoulders and began to push him further in. The pipes are about twelve metres long so there was plenty of room inside. He started to struggle but there was nothing he could do.

'Last chance,' I said.

He was crying now. And terrified. Well, wouldn't you be?

'OK, OK,' he said. 'Bastard, bastard, bastard. Let me out. I'll tell you.'

'No, no. Tell me first.'

He was quiet apart from the sobs, still not willing to admit to anything. I gave another little push to remind him. His reaction was a shout.

'Yes. I killed her, all right? I killed her. She was trying to – '

'No, no,' I said. 'That's all I wanted to hear. I don't need the details. You buried her with the pipes, right?'

'Yes,' he said.

It gave me no satisfaction to be proved right. I just looked at him for a while, then pushed him further into the pipe. As I did it, I was thinking about his wives, the two girls he'd battered and, of course, about mum. She wouldn't have approved of what I was doing but she'd have understood it.

I had to get inside the pipe myself to make sure that he was well along it. I pushed him almost to the end which was up against the wall. I checked the cable holding him and loosened it so that he'd soon be able to work it free. He watched me, whimpering and crying, not managing any words. He was lying on his side, his knees pulled up to his chest and his hands bent in front of his face. I crawled out and hauled on the chains again to get the plug in position. It had two solid rubber seals set back inside its profile. Before I slid it home, I hacked at them with a Stanley knife. I didn't want the pipe to be airtight. Didn't want him to suffocate.

When I did force it inside the end of the pipe, I could tell right away what a good piece of design it was. He'd been screaming on and off since he'd realised what I was up to. It was bloody loud. Echoed a lot. But the minute the end of the pipe was covered, I couldn't hear a thing. Just the whine of the generator. I rammed the plug further in, crawling behind it, heaving against it with my shoulders. It was polished steel. The surface slid very easily along the pipe wall. I didn't stop until I was just about exhausted. By then, it was far enough inside the pipe to be invisible to anyone in the yard. I reckon the section Armstrong was in was about three metres long.

There was just enough room for me to wriggle into position to operate the buttons which set the seals. I heard them hiss into place, gave a few more shoves against the plug to make sure it was set, crawled back out into the light and drove home.

It wasn't a mature thing to do. It made me no better than Armstrong. But I couldn't help myself. I really needed to do it. It wasn't about the law. It was about justice. People. It was about love. And mum.

Armstrong was reported missing at the end of that week. That was over a month ago.

They still haven't found him.

Janet Laurence

Janet Laurence was such a hard-working and energetic chairman of the CWA that it was remarkable she found any time for writing at all during her recently ended term of office, let alone to produce a story as neat and appealing as 'A Small Problem at the Gallery'. I much valued Janet's enthusiastic support for the anthology and I was delighted that she was willing to contribute to it in the best and most direct way of all, with a short piece that suits the theme of this book in more ways than one.

A SMALL PROBLEM AT THE GALLERY

by Janet Laurence

'Missing?' asked a bemused chairman of the gallery governors.

'Missing,' I reluctantly conceded.

'A case of missing persons,' said Mark Scott, the junior curator, with what I considered unwarranted flippancy.

'The loss of *Three Persons in the Park* is a disaster of major proportions,' Sir William said severely. 'It's as well our benefactor is dead, otherwise the bequest could be rescinded.'

I waited for Mark to point out that a bequest wasn't the sort of gift that could be taken back. Along with a volatile attitude to life that encompassed such foolish activities as gambling, fast cars and the pursuit of beautiful women, he delighted in proving others wrong. He had, though, a wonderful eye for a painting.

'Forgive me, Sir William, I am as upset about this as you are.'

'When was the last time the sketch was seen?' pursued the chairman.

'After the Impressionist exhibition two years ago,' I said.

'Ah, yes, the Impressionists. You did a fine job there, Morton.'

'Thank you, Sir William.' The old fool hadn't deigned to congratulate me at the time. Perhaps he thought the praise trumpeted by the media had been sufficient.

We had been incredibly fortunate. A high profile entrepreneur and art collector had wandered into the gallery one day. I'd immediately steered him in front of our little collection of French Impressionist and neo-Impressionist painters, amongst them a small Renoir, a nice Whistler and two really fine paintings by Manet and Seurat.

He'd been impressed. 'I'd never have thought a provincial gallery could have such treasures.' Then he'd offered to lend us his Impressionists for an exhibition.

It was only when I visited his Elizabethan house, tastefully modernised, that I realised just how fortunate we were. I gazed at the painting of three people negligently posed in a park, at the pointillist brush strokes in blues, greens and pinks that had the softness of nature.

'I think we have something in our store room that will interest you, Mr Maxton,' I said, my mouth dry with excitement.

It was the first time ever that the preliminary sketch for *Three Persons in a Park* had been shown together with the final painting. The media had descended like greedy seagulls.

Paul Maxton had tried to buy the sketch. He'd given me a wry smile when told it wasn't for sale, 'Can't say I blame you, it's an enchanting piece.'

Three weeks ago he'd died. A heart attack the obituaries said, victim of his high pressure lifestyle. Today Sir William had told us he'd left the gallery *Three Persons in a Park*. Then he'd asked to see the sketch.

'After the exhibition we returned it to storage,' I said, a little jerkily despite my efforts to appear calm. 'As you know, in itself it isn't much to display.'

'When was the last time either of you saw the sketch?' Sir William asked testily.

I looked at Mark.

'Not since Helen returned it to the basement,' he said defensively.

'Ah, yes,' said Sir William with a glint in his eye. 'Helen Watts, is it not?'

Helen was my assistant. Grace Kelly looks, a figure to match and a knowledge of the history of art that almost rivalled my own. There had been a time when I'd thought we might have a future together but Mark, his youth and rakish good looks had won out.

'Helen wrote the catalogue,' I said thoughtfully. A catalogue that had included a lyrical description of the sketch and pointed out how the finished painting had lost the fluidity of the figures, the charm of the colours and the tension between the two men and the woman.

'Maxton's left us *Three Persons in the Park*?' Helen cried incredulously when told. Then, 'And you say the preparatory sketch is missing?'

'Perhaps it got put back in the wrong place?' Mark suggested with the air of a man producing the solution.

'You'd better look through everything,' Sir William said urgently.

We spent hours going through the stacks of paintings, drawings and sketches, carefully stored on end in special holders in a temperature-controlled vault in the basement. Hardly visited since I'd finished cataloguing its contents, it was filled with Victorian monstrosities that were now back in fashion, doubtful Renaissance drawings donated when their owners had discovered they weren't by Michaelangelo or Leonardo da Vinci, turn of the century watercolours that didn't match the quality of those on display, a few North European interiors unattributable to any known artists, plus prints and engravings by the hundred.

The sketch was not more than eighteen inches by twelve; it took a long time to establish it hadn't slipped in somewhere it shouldn't have.

Eventually I reported to Sir William it couldn't be found and suggested the police were sent for.

'The police? Is that necessary?'

'Sir William, now that the gallery owns the finished painting, that preparatory sketch is worth much, much more than our previous estimate.'

'You think it has been stolen, then?'

'I cannot see any other possibility.'

The police were thorough, I'll say that for them. They established there was no sign of a forced entry nor did the gallery's sophisticated alarm system appear to have been tampered with. They announced what I had been sure of from the first – it must have been an inside job.

Mark emerged from his interview without his insouciance. 'Bastards,' he said viciously. 'As if I'd steal the damn thing, I didn't even like it!'

Helen came out red-eyed and desperate.

'I'm sure you didn't have anything to do with its disappearance,' I said, hoping I didn't sound doubtful.

My own interview was gruelling but I was able to suggest a possible motive to the police. 'After all the publicity, the sketch is too well known to sell on the open market. It will have been stolen, if indeed it has been stolen, to order, for someone to enjoy in secret.'

'And would any of the staff here know of anyone wanting to acquire this work?'

I shrugged my shoulders. 'That, Inspector, I am quite unable to say.'

The police didn't leave it there, of course. They looked into all our backgrounds, obtained warrants and searched each of our homes. Nothing.

Finally they announced that the Art Loss register had been notified and said that the case would remain open.

The day of my retirement drew near. The question of who was to take over exercised everyone. The governors had left the decision to me and it was obvious it had to be either Mark or Helen. Tension grew.

One day I found them rowing. 'I know you made the police suspect me,' shouted Helen, her lovely face scrunched into ugliness.

'You mean it was you who told them I needed some quick funds,' Mark raged back at her, his open handsomeness quite destroyed by the spite in his face.

'And how did you find the cash?' she spat at him.

'A lucky win on the horses,' he shot back.

Then they saw me and returned to their work.

I could understand their tension. Both were ambitious and to be curator could set either of them on the path to great things. I had come late to the job, one of them would be luckier.

That night I went home, drew the curtains, switched on all the lights and poured a glass of excellent claret.

Above the mantelpiece was an attractive watercolour of the Newlyn school, fisherwives with baskets on a rainy day. I'd constructed the frame myself. A little elaborate perhaps for this painting but essential for the other. A moment's fiddling and the top slid off. I laid the Newlyn frame down and sat sipping my wine and relishing my possession. Such intensity of vision, so wonderfully realised in the sketch and so lacking in the final work.

I didn't realise the door had opened until Helen was suddenly standing there.

'Ah, you still have your key,' I said after a moment.

Yes, there had been a time I'd given her the freedom of my house.

She nodded, her huge blue eyes riveted on the sketch. 'The missing *Persons*, I knew it,' she breathed.

'What are you going to do?'

'Why, nothing. That is, nothing if you make me your successor.'

'Ah!'

Her eyes fixed themselves on me, 'I might even renew our former relationship from time to time,' she added.

'Mark lost his charms?'

She made an impatient gesture, 'A callow youth with no depth.'

She'd taken long enough to discover that.

'Where have you put the others?'

'Others?'

'Don't play games, you know what I mean. The other paintings and sketches you've stolen from the gallery.' She enumerated a couple.

She couldn't know the whole and I was amazed she'd found out those two were missing. She'd be a worthy successor.

'Sold,' I said. 'You have to admit the job doesn't pay well and I'm looking forward to a comfortable retirement.'

I looked again at the sketch. 'One too many, perhaps, but the best of all. I thought by the time anyone realised, I would have been long gone. Then Maxton had to die and leave us the finished picture,' I added bitterly. 'And Sir William didn't give me a chance to return the sketch.'

I appointed Helen as my successor, of course. We enjoyed several delightful evenings before my retirement, and I began to feel we had a future together after all.

It was, I'm afraid, the lunacy of a foolish old man. Tonight

Helen is coming for what I sense will be the last time. Knowing what she does, I cannot allow her to leave. I still have keys to the gallery and the store room is the perfect place to hide a body. She will be another missing person and I will continue to enjoy *Three Persons in a Park*.

Peter Lewis

I have never visited Mauritius, but I imagine it as the sort of place that industrious cabinet ministers visit regularly on important fact-finding missions or as an idyllic holiday refuge from critical headlines. Peter Lewis, thankfully, is not a politician, but rather an author and academic who – together with his wife Margaret, a fellow member of the CWA – has evidently fallen in love with the island. Peter tells me he is currently at work on a novel set in Mauritius with a 'missing persons' plot, but that, other than the locale, it has no resemblance to 'After the Sega', which he dedicates to former CWA chairman Susan Moody.

AFTER THE SEGA

by Peter Lewis

It was Saturday night, Sega Night, at the Hotel Josephine. Sega Night was the busiest night of the week, and since coming to Mauritius from Durban Miranda had usually been on duty on Saturdays. She was nearing the end of her stay after a few months' work experience as part of her hotel management training in South Africa. The previous Sega Show had to be cancelled because of a severe storm warning, so for almost all the hotel guests this was their first one. For Miranda it was the last Sega Show she would ever see without a flicker of foreboding, the shadow of a dark memory. It wasn't the Show itself, but what happened after – not that she or anyone else ever found out what did happen after. Not for sure. But must every mystery have a solution? Does there have to be an answer to every question? First one person disappeared, then a second, then . . .

Among recent arrivals were a couple from South Africa, Hendrik and Constance, who were conspicuous for their conspicuousness. This was not difficult given the hotel's clientèle, but Hen and Con, as Miranda dubbed them, did it in style. Miranda hadn't been long at the Josephine when she told a receptionist that glamour was in such short supply among the guests that you'd need an electron microscope to see it. Many of the holiday-makers were overweight, middle-aged, well-to-do couples from Europe. Miranda wondered whether sufficiently long tape measures were available to circumnavigate the waists of the Germans. The French smoked as though acquiring lung cancer was a national priority. The Brits soaked up the sun as though acquiring melanoma was a national priority.

Enter Hendrik and Constance. Initially Miranda didn't much like the look of Hen, an Afrikaner from the toes peeping out of his sandals to the top of his shaven head, but at least he was something to look at. Hen spoke Afrikaans with Con and turned to Miranda for information because she was the only staff member who knew the language. Tall, broad-shouldered and muscular, he was perhaps a little old to be a member of the South African rugby team now, but she could see him in green and gold battering his way through the opposition. He might also have belonged to one of those police units of the Apartheid era with a tendency to lean rather carelessly on black detainees looking out of open windows at the top of high buildings.

Some years younger than Hen, Con was pretty rather than beautiful, but the cascade of red curls did not come out of a bottle and Miranda acknowledged that her figure and legs would turn many an envying woman's head, let alone any red-blooded man's. If Hen was a prime exhibit of Afrikanerdom, Con was an out-and-out exhibitionist.

Apart from the French, few female guests went topless on the beach or around the pool. Mauritians didn't on principle. Middle-aged Germans didn't, for which everyone was grateful. Italians and South Africans usually didn't out of some kind of modesty. Miranda didn't because she had no intention of revealing how little she had to reveal. Brits sometimes did if no one was likely to look. But Con did most of the time, and the more who looked the better.

Yet Con nearly naked did not compare with Con dressed. Clothes certainly made this woman, and she had no end of clothes. She converted the main public area into a catwalk for her one-model fashion show. During the day, there were various tarty outfits, from tiny skin-tight shorts and peekabo bustiers to skirts slashed almost to the waist on one side or both and transparent voile tops. For dinner, she might appear in a long, flowing, backless dress or a short deconstructed one with holes of different sizes cut in tantalising places.

The Sega Show took place after dinner on a hot Saturday

night. Six female dancers in their bright costumes and with flowers in their hair glided into the performing area followed by male musicians and singers chanting the harsh, raw music of the Sega. All were barefoot, and the men wore floral shirts open to the waist and tight white breeches to just below the knee. After some explanations by the leader about its origins as a slave dance, the Show continued with demonstrations of the Sega by the women in their frilly halter tops and long, swirly skirts.

At first sight there didn't seem to be much to the Sega. The foot movements were shuffles, supposedly because the slaves danced with ankle chains, although the performers incorporated spins and twirls. The dynamics of the dance were all in hip rotations and pelvic thrusts. It was only when Miranda tried it during her first Sega Night that she appreciated how difficult it was. She had no trouble doing the foot shuffles and the hip movements separately, but combining them successfully was another matter.

But as well as the predominantly vertical part of the Sega, there was a horizontal component. The women kneeled down with their legs slightly apart and then leaned back until their heads touched the ground, all the time swivelling their hips and pushing their pelvises up. It seemed like an invitation to copulate. The leading male singer crouched on all fours over the body of a dancer who gyrated rhythmically while he continued to sing.

As usual the Show ended with the hotel guests being invited to join in. Hen and Con were quick to have a go. Hen couldn't co-ordinate his feet and hips, but Con, a born dancer, had no difficulty. Hen gave up and began to return to the bar, pulling Con by the hand. She resisted. She was obviously enjoying the challenge of a new dance and wanted to continue. Watching them, Miranda thought for a moment that Hen was going to hit Con, but he let her go and barged his way to the bar. He always behaved possessively towards Con, but Miranda hadn't seen him thwarted before.

One of the singers homed in on the partnerless Con, urging her down into the horizontal position until her body was arched back, her pelvis rotating, and her skirt up to her crotch.

AFTER THE SEGA

As the other dancers formed a circle around Con and the singer, Miranda noticed Hen at the bar looking sulkily furious. From the look on his face it was clear that there were limits and that Con was going too far this time. Then the singer went down on his hands and knees over Con, simulating copulation while she continued to rotate orgasmically. Miranda had never seen anything remotely like this at a Sega Show and was becoming extremely apprehensive about how it would end. Hen looked on the point of erupting, but instead marched off, though not before sweeping all the glasses from the bar on to the ground.

Con had been a focus of attention since arriving at the Josephine, but now she had virtually the entire hotel spellbound. She looked triumphant. A few minutes later, as she and the singer returned to the vertical, the Sega show was over. Miranda watched Con looking around for Hen. It might, she thought, be better if Con didn't find him.

On Sunday morning Miranda noticed that the table used by Hen and Con remained empty during breakfast. Odd. They usually appeared every morning at about the same time. Could they have dived in first thing before catching a tour bus? Or hired a car for the day and made an early start? Or gone deep-sea fishing? Or perhaps ...

While organising various activities during the day, Miranda kept an eye open for Hen and Con but without catching a glimpse of either of them. There was still no sign at dinner, and although a few guests went to local restaurants, Hen and Con were on half-board and had seemed perfectly content to stay put.

As Miranda strolled through the grounds before turning in, she concluded that the suspicions she'd been harbouring since breakfast were correct. Hen, in a fury, must have set about Con when she returned to their room. He'd probably given her a black eye, if not two, and they were lying low. Con wouldn't want to be seen as though she'd just done fifteen rounds in the ring with a heavyweight champion, and for Hen to appear on his own would have aroused curiosity about her.

Yet if Miranda was right, how could they possibly have spent the day together in their room? Without killing each other, that is. Then in the moonlight Miranda saw a figure entering the hotel grounds from the beach in what she called *the sneaky way* – through the gate beside the boatman's hut, where she heard a security guard saying 'Goodnight' to someone. It was too dark and shadowy to see who it was, but the height and shape were unmistakable. Hendrik. Only Hen would produce that silhouette. At least he was alive. And then he was gone.

Miranda and the deputy manager had to attend a meeting about tourism in the capital Port Louis on Monday morning, but before setting off, she dropped by the restaurant to see if Con and Hen were there. They weren't. But that didn't mean anything. It was still early. Back in the hotel in the afternoon, the receptionist told Miranda there'd been a call from Hendrik for her, but there was no reply when she rang Con and Hen's room. Or when she tried again every so often.

In the evening, Miranda's pager summoned her to a phone. It was Hen from the village asking her to meet him. Urgently. Somewhere quiet. He sounded on edge, not his usual self at all. She suggested the fish-landing station near the hotel since there wouldn't be anyone there. Apprehensive rather than frightened, she hoped Hen wasn't going to ask her how to dispose of a body in Mauritius.

'Sorry about this, Miranda, but you're the only South African working here, so the best person to help.' As usual he spoke in Afrikaans. 'Con's gone. Vanished. She just took off. What to do? Go to the police?'

'After the Sega, I suppose.' He nodded. 'What happened? Did you have a row?'

'You could call it that,' he said. 'I was mad at her – you know why, you were there. And I slapped her a bit. No punches or anything. Just slaps.' She tried to imagine what a slap from someone with paws the size of Hen's would feel like. One slap, all your teeth fall out. Two slaps, your head drops off.

'What did she do then?' she asked, thinking that Con, with her head on one side of the room and the rest of her on the other with her teeth scattered all around, wasn't capable of doing much.

'She left.'

'As she was? Just with the clothes she was wearing?'

'No. She shoved stuff in a case.'

Hen sounded genuine, but Miranda didn't know how much to believe. If he were a policeman he'd know how to cover his tracks. What if he'd killed Con, not intentionally perhaps, but with a slap too far? Men like Hen didn't know their own strength. Could he have spent the early hours of Sunday morning getting rid of her body in the ocean? Not as difficult as it might seem for someone like Hen on a moonlit night, since once he had her in the water – and their room was only metres from the high-tide mark – he could have towed her beyond the reef in a few minutes and then swum out a good distance. In a matter of days he'd be back in South Africa, and if her body ever did turn up, it would probably be impossible to find out how she died. So was he now establishing an innocent explanation about her running off to account for her disappearance?

He said, 'It's not the first time she's walked out. There's a disagreement and she goes walkabout for a few days. But then tempers cool down and we get back together.'

'That's OK back home, but where would she go in Mauritius?'

'That's why I've been expecting her back. Could she have gone with the Sega dancers?'

'Highly unlikely.'

'There are some people from home she knows, staying at the Pirogue just along the coast.'

'More likely. Have you been in touch with them?'

'No. I didn't know how to ask them. If she wasn't there, they'd wonder how I'd mislaid her.' And if she was there, thought Miranda, with two black eyes and no teeth, it would be even more embarrassing to ask.

'I thought they'd get in touch with me if Con was with them' he said, 'but they haven't. That's why I'm wondering whether she's in trouble or done something silly.'

'If she's not with your South African friends, she probably got a taxi to take her somewhere to hole up for a couple of days. Or the airport to try for another flight. Did she have her passport and ticket?'

'Yes. She's very independent is Con.'

'Before we start talking about her as a missing person, I'll do some discreet checking with the Sega troupe and our hotel taxi drivers. Your friends, too, if you give me their names. Con doesn't hide her light under a bushel, does she? She wouldn't have any trouble getting someone to help a damsel in distress. Someone will have seen her and know where she is. I'm sure there's nothing to worry about. But it'll be tomorrow before I can talk to some of them, so you'll have to be patient. Best I can do, I'm afraid. And I'm on duty now, so I'll have to go.'

Miranda had no luck that evening. The only taxi driver available knew Con by sight, but hadn't taken her anywhere on Saturday night. The South Africans at the Pirogue had gone out for dinner. She didn't even bother to try the Sega troupe since she knew they would be performing.

The next morning, Tuesday, Miranda had to drive to the north of the island to represent the Josephine at the opening of a tourism exhibition in the national Conference Centre, but when she returned to the hotel she managed to contact the leader of the Sega troupe, who certainly remembered Con but hadn't seen her since. Miranda found a different taxi driver in the car-park, but he too had no information. The South Africans were out for the day fishing for marlin. She'd try them again later, but concluded that if Con was not providing nourishment for sharks, she would appear at the airport in a couple of days for the return flight with Hen unless she'd already departed. Miranda couldn't find Hen but left him a message saying that so far she'd drawn a blank but would keep trying. He wasn't to worry unduly because, whatever had happened, Con wouldn't miss the flight home.

Later that night, he called her from the Pirogue. He'd taken a taxi there on the off-chance of finding Con's South African friends, but if they knew anything about her, they weren't letting on. It was high time, he believed, to summon the police, although Miranda told him they wouldn't do anything unless she failed to join her flight. *That* would look serious, but until then it appeared to be no more than a lovers' tiff.

On Wednesday morning Miranda didn't go out of her way to find Hen although she expected him to contact her. He didn't. There was a police station not far from the hotel in the village and he wouldn't need Miranda's help to report a missing person if that was what he'd decided to do.

But why would he? Assuming he'd killed Con, Miranda's solution was that it would look much better if he officially reported her missing before leaving Mauritius than if he left without a word, only for her body to turn up days, weeks or months later. That would look very suspicious indeed. Therefore his eagerness to involve the police was primarily a matter of self-interest although it looked like concern for her. Of course, if Con had simply run off to get away from him, it was understandable that after a couple of days he would be anxious and turn to the police for help.

Miranda was playing the armchair detective when she was urgently summoned to the boathouse. The glass-bottomed boat had just returned from its afternoon trip to view the coral reef, and an English woman on board, Joan, was in a state because she thought she'd seen part of a body wedged under rocks and coral. The boatmen hadn't seen anything suspicious, nor had anyone else on board, so they didn't take Joan seriously. Miranda was not quite so dismissive. What if . . .

When she talked to Joan she found her genuinely shaken, and whatever Joan had seen had disturbed her. Miranda told her that there were many curious sights along the reef and that it was not uncommon for visitors to mistake unfamiliar shapes for something else. Joan accepted this. She had probably been seeing things, imagining things. It must have been some tropical oddity. But as she left Joan, Miranda wondered whether in seeing things Joan might actually have been seeing a corpse.

On Miranda's next visit to the desk, the receptionist asked her whether she'd seen Hendrik that day.

'No,' said Miranda. 'Why?'

'There's been a woman calling him. About every hour.

Sounds South African. Always asks for him, not Constance. She hasn't left a name or a message.'

'Probably one of his South African friends at the Pirogue.'

'There's something else about Hendrik and Constance. The maid mentioned that when she did their room this afternoon it looked as though it had been vacated, although they don't leave until tomorrow.'

There were a few more calls for Hen but no Hen. Before dinner, Miranda asked waiters and barmen if they could remember seeing him that day, but no one had. She mounted a search of her own throughout the grounds and even down the beach without success. As she went to bed she kept her fingers crossed that both Hen and Con would turn up at the airport tomorrow.

Phone calls for Hen from an unidentified South African woman began at breakfast time on Thursday morning, but he was not to be found. The telephonist passed the second call to Miranda in the hope that she could elicit some information, but the caller hung up. Miranda herself went to Hen and Con's room with the cleaning supervisor and found it as the maid had left it the previous day. No one had spent the night there. The last Miranda had heard from Hen was the call from the Pirogue on Tuesday night, and as far as she could tell he hadn't put in an appearance at the Josephine on Wednesday. As for Con ... who could say? But if this came out, the Josephine would acquire a reputation for being singularly careless about its South Africans. First one, now two.

It seemed clear that neither Hen nor Con would be back before their scheduled flight. Miranda was deciding what to do next when one of the security guards brought her a letter that had just been delivered by a messenger from the Pirogue. The envelope was addressed to her with a note in English: IMPORTANT. TO BE DELIVERED THURSDAY MORNING. The letter itself was in Afrikaans and was undated. It was from Hen.

Dear Miranda,

I want to thank you so much for your help during the last couple of days. I haven't told you the full story about

Con, but now that we have reached the end, I should fill it out a little before departing. So these are my exit lines to you.

For us, the holiday in Mauritius was a last chance. We've been on-off, on-off for some time, since my first marriage broke up. My wife was very different from Con – a straight Afrikaner girl from a farm in northern Transvaal. You know the type. Dutch Reformed Church and all that. Reliable but prudish. Steady but could never let her hair down. I thought she would change. She didn't. If I hadn't been travelling round the Republic so much with my job, it might have worked eventually, but I met different sorts of women who opened my eyes. Especially Con. She knew how to let her hair down. It was seldom anything else. Reliable she wasn't, but fun she was. For someone like me, she was a fantasy come true.

But she was wayward and wilful. Very independent. Flirtatious. So there'd be a bust-up and we'd separate, then get together again, then have another bust-up. She could be violent, too. It wasn't just me. She knew where to kick a man and she did. She also knew how to use her long, sharp nails. We seemed to be at the end of the road, but I couldn't bring myself to give her up. For some reason she was the same. She tormented me, drove me mad sometimes, but part of her still clung to me.

I suggested a holiday in Mauritius since neither of us knew it. Honeymoon island for South Africans. Paradise. So we'd have a final attempt to sort things out in the Garden of Eden. I should have known better. You saw for yourself what she was like here. Somehow Mauritius brought out the worst in her, the non-stop show-off performance for men. She just couldn't help herself somehow. The Sega Night was the last straw. You can call me possessive, but how many men would put up with that?

So that's it. She made my life fizz for a while, but there's nothing left now. I feel empty, hollow. And what sort of future do we face in the new South Africa? The ANC go on about Reconciliation, but there's going to be revenge someday, a backlash. A blacklash, we call it where I come from. But I don't have to lecture you about the new South Africa.

That's enough of this. I won't see you again so thanks once more. All the best for your future and goodbye.

Hendrik

Miranda read it through a few times looking for a subtext. Was this letter of farewell also a confession? Whenever he referred to Con he used the past tense, but did that necessarily mean she was dead? It might indicate that he had now drawn a line and that Con belonged to his past.

So was that the end of the story? Miranda supposed it was, unless Con turned up dead somewhere. Then what? Hen would presumably be back in South Africa and the police would descend on the hotel. It was better to keep her fingers crossed than think where that might lead. Fortunately, perhaps, she herself would soon be back in Durban.

When the coach collecting people for the airport arrived at the Josephine, Miranda sent a message to the courier that two South African passengers had already left. Nothing unusual about that. Many people preferred going by taxi. Miranda was toying with the idea of phoning the airline later to check that Hen and Con had caught their flight, but intensely curious as she was, she concluded that this might backfire on her if something was wrong. She would almost be implicating herself in whatever had happened. Miranda was half expecting an enquiry about Hen and Con on Friday but nobody contacted the Josephine, which Miranda interpreted as a sign that all was well.

It was Saturday again, Sega time, but Miranda wasn't looking forward to the evening Show. In the late morning a waiter informed her that something unusual was going on at the fish-landing station, but he didn't know what. She walked along the beach to find out, and saw a group of people, mainly fishermen, talking to a local policeman she was friendly with. As she approached, she noticed something like a roll of carpet on the ground behind the fishermen, but then the policeman turned towards her.

'Hello, Miranda,' he said. 'You should go back to the hotel. Please.'

'Why? What's the matter? Is anything wrong? What's that over there?'

'There's a problem. It's better if you leave us to deal with this now. I'll talk to you later. They'll be here in a minute.'

As they were speaking, a police car and an ambulance arrived and the policeman went to meet them. Miranda turned to the fishermen to find out what had happened. One of them told her that they'd recovered a body outside the reef. They'd wrapped it in some pieces of plastic as best they could and were now waiting for the police to collect it for investigation. But there was something odd about it.

It was going to be Con, she knew. It had to be. The woman in the glass-bottomed boat hadn't been seeing things, after all. Or rather, what she'd seen was what she thought she'd seen. As the plastic blew around in the breeze, she looked more closely. What did people look like after being in water for a few days? Were they all chewed up by crabs and fish? She couldn't see much because of the plastic but she did notice handcuffs on the wrists in front of the corpse. There also seemed to be a length of heavy chain wrapped around it, the type of chain used for anchoring boats. A drowning accident this most certainly wasn't. This was murder, OK. What else?

But something wasn't right. What? She could see very little of the body, but it seemed too big for Con. But then weren't corpses supposed to swell and become bloated when immersed?

As one of the fishermen moved a piece of plastic from the head with his foot, the policeman she knew, who was coming back with a group of others, shouted, 'Miranda. I thought I told you to go back to the hotel.'

'Sorry, going,' she said, but first she looked down at the head the fisherman had exposed. She took a couple of steps back, felt her gorge rise, turned around, and threw up.

The policeman put an arm around her shoulder and led her

away. 'I warned you, Miranda. You should have listened. Are you all right?'

'Yes, sorry,' she gargled, walking off. The head was swollen, distorted, lacerated, gouged. But it was recognisable. It was Hen.

What the hell had happened? Various scenarios followed one another through her mind. It looked as though someone had murdered Hen, but if there'd been any killing, surely he was the guilty one. Who could possibly have killed him? Who and what army? If Con were still alive and feeling murderous, she would have needed a contingent of Mauritian coastguards to help her dispose of Hen. What about the chain and handcuffs? The chain must have come from one of the many boats moored near the hotel. Anybody could have taken that, including Hen. The handcuffs fitted Miranda's sense that Hen might have been a policeman at some time, but if they were his, he hadn't brought them on holiday to play cops and robbers, now had he? Not unless that was one of his bondage games with Con.

Miranda reread Hen's letter. And then it clicked. She'd taken it at face value as a letter of farewell, but now she saw it as a possible suicide note, obliquely written to a virtual stranger: 'reached the end ... before departing ... my exit lines ... the end of the road ... a final attempt ... the last straw ... there's nothing left now ... I feel empty, hollow ... I won't see you again ... goodbye.' Without Con, there was nothing for him, especially in a South Africa he felt alienated from, so suicide made sense. Doubly so, if he'd killed Con.

After seeing the body, Miranda assumed that Hen must have been handcuffed by someone else before being bludgeoned to death and wrapped in the chain to weigh his body down. Considering Hen's size and weight, it would have taken some doing but wasn't impossible. But what if Hen had drowned himself, first putting on the handcuffs to prevent himself swimming and then draping the chain around his body to help keep him under? He was strong enough to achieve this.

Miranda wasn't sure whether to award herself the Miss Marple Award for brilliant detection or to tell herself to stop indulging in loony speculation. But if she was right, Con was probably still out there somewhere. Wherever she was, the police were bound to be all over the hotel once they'd identified Hen, questioning everyone about what they knew, and Miranda recognised that she could easily find herself in a difficult situation.

What would a Mauritian police investigation be like? Not as bad as a South African one, for sure, but even so she'd rather not find out. With the suspicious death of a tourist, which at first sight would look to them like murder, they'd sniff her out before long and want to know all sorts of things. Why hadn't she reported Con's disappearance as soon as she'd discovered it? Why had she been covering for Hen? She didn't know what to do about Hen's letter. Destroy it? But what if it could help her explain things? She had only one week left in Mauritius, but if she were caught up in a murder investigation as a material witness, could they keep her here for weeks or even months?

She wanted out, fast. Depending how efficient they were, it would take the police a few days at least to establish Hen's identity and begin putting the narrative together. If she made herself scarce, the police would have enough to do without becoming interested in a visiting trainee who had recently gone home. Wouldn't they? Or would that look suspicious? No matter, she wanted out, fast. She phoned her best friend in South Africa and shouted *Help*.

Within a couple of hours, messages by phone, fax and e-mail arrived at the Josephine from South Africa requesting Miranda to phone at once and return home urgently because of a family crisis. The manager was sympathetic, especially as she only had a week to go and was due a few days off in any case. She should fly as soon as possible. There was a flight to Johannesburg the next day with a few seats available.

Miranda still had to cope with her last Sega Night, but she made sure she was so busy during the rest of Saturday that she didn't have much opportunity to think. There was some chat and speculation among the hotel staff about whoever it was who had drowned, but she turned a deaf ear to this. It was obvious from what was said that no one else had seen or knew anything.

And then she was off. On the way to the airport she wouldn't have been surprised if a police car had pulled her over. How about Passport control? Would they call her aside? When the wheels of the plane finally left the runway she began to sob and weep. The Afrikaner woman next to her, jumping to the conclusion that she was broken-hearted because a holiday romance had ended, said all sorts of reassuring but totally inappropriate things.

Two days later, Miranda noticed a brief newspaper report about a South African who had not returned as expected from a holiday in Mauritius. It was Hen, all right. There were fears that the as-yet unidentified body of a man who had drowned in the ocean was that of the missing South African since the body had been recovered not far from the hotel where he was staying. Somewhat to her surprise there was no hint of a second missing South African.

There was a fuller report a couple of days later stating that a positive identification of the corpse had now been made. This confirmed fears that the missing South African was indeed the dead man, but the only explanation of his death was that there were some dangerous spots along that stretch of coast, and he must have got into difficulties. Still nothing about Con.

So Hen's death was being presented as a tragic accident. There was no hint of suspicious circumstances, and certainly no mention of the chain or handcuffs. It occurred to Miranda that there might have been pressure from somewhere to sanitise the death, to ensure that it came over as a 'tragic accident' rather than anything more sinister. Mauritius depended so heavily on its paradise-island image and its appeal to wealthy tourists that it would want to avoid any bad publicity if at all possible.

She combed the papers for the next few days expecting to find further information, but found nothing. And then she was brought up short by a headline as she did her daily skim: DANCING THE SEGA. She looked at the two photographs accompanying the article. Could it be? Of course it was Con. One picture was of Con in an abbreviated version of the

Mauritian Sega costume. In the other she was in the horizontal Sega position with a muscle-bound hunk in only a posing pouch kneeling between her wide-open legs.

The article was about the popular exotic dancer Sukki Coxx, just back from Mauritius where she had learned the local erotic dance and was incorporating it in her new performance at one of Jo'burg's leading night spots. Reading the piece about Con made Miranda want to throw up. There wasn't the slightest hint of Hen's existence. Mauritius had been 'the holiday of a lifetime' for Con, 'living up to its reputation as paradise on earth.' If she 'ever got round to a honeymoon, this would be the only place.' She'd 'danced with the local villagers and had discovered the most sensual dance in the southern hemisphere.'

As she read about Con, images of Hen's body focused in Miranda's mind. The distorted features, the bloated torso, the chain, the handcuffs. Alive he seemed the epitome of strength and power. Dead he was human flotsam, helpless and pitiful. She hadn't liked Hen at first because he struck her as a typical Afrikaner bully boy, tough and insensitive. It was hard to think of someone like him as a victim, but underneath he had proved to be extremely vulnerable. She hadn't realised how vulnerable until he was dead. In fact she hadn't realised how vulnerable until now when she discovered that Con was still alive.

Could she have done more to help him, to save him? Looking back to Mauritius, Miranda felt guilty about jumping to the conclusion that Hen had killed Con. She had assumed Con to be the victim. How wrong can you be? Miranda had allowed her prejudices about unsophisticated Afrikaner men to sway her, and although she had become aware that Hen was in torment, she had failed to read the situation correctly. She couldn't be blamed, but neither did she feel altogether blameless.

No doubt Hen had family to grieve for him, but she owed him something, at least a gesture of mourning. Since her schooldays she had lapsed badly as a Catholic. If she ever went to confession again, she'd either have to do it as a six-part serial or request an ensuite confessional for comfort breaks. But something propelled her towards her local church. Miranda no longer knew what it meant to pray for the souls of the dead, or how to do it properly, but kneeling in front of the altar in the deserted church she began to work her way through her store of remembered prayers, even a couple in Latin from her schooldays. She began as always, 'Hail Mary . . .'

Phil Lovesey

Peter Lovesey is not only one of our most distinguished mystery writers but also a past editor of the CWA anthology. It therefore gives me special pleasure to include a story this year by his son Phil, who is already carving himself a distinct reputation. Phil first made his name in the genre with short fiction; in the past couple of years he has turned to writing novels with considerable success. *Death Duties* was to my mind one of the best crime débuts of 1998 and it has had a strong follow-up with *Ploughing Potter's Field*. Phil's work is quite different from his father's, but it is easy to predict that he too will enjoy much acclaim in the years that lie ahead since, as 'Trust Me' demonstrates, he has the sure touch of a born storyteller.

TRUST ME

by Phil Lovesey

'Fifty thousand is a hell of a lot of money,' the DI said cautiously.

The worried father bit back. 'Christ's sakes, we realise that! But anything's better than just sitting here!'

The DI looked at the three strained faces in the gloomy council house lounge, battle-weary, ashen, red-eyed from lack of sleep. 'All I'm saying, Mr Rogers, is that when rewards are offered so publicly, well, it can attract the wrong kind of help.'

The father sat next to his wife, tried to hold her hand which she quickly withdrew. 'We don't care any more, don't you see that? We just want her back. Someone's got to know something.'

'And we're doing all we can. The television appeal, for instance, brought several new leads . . .'

The mother's tired eyes met his. 'But they haven't brought us Claire, have they? She's two years old. She could be anywhere. She could be . . .'

The older woman, grandmother to the missing infant, took her daughter's hand. The experienced DI noticed how the mother was happier with the maternal comfort, trusting, and he understood why her husband's similar gesture had been rejected – he was the one, after all, who had left the child outside the newsagent's in the pushchair as he bought cigarettes inside. To her mind, he was responsible for losing their daughter on that windy Sunday morning just four days previously.

The DI tried tact and reason. 'Mr and Mrs Rogers, I understand your concerns, but—'

'But what?' the grandmother cut in icily.

'Offering that sort of money can attract a lot of cranks. I've got over thirty officers working on Claire's disappearance, sifting through mountains of material. A reward of fifty thousand's going to attract every nutter in the area. We could be snowed under, interviewing and taking statements for weeks. And in the meantime, we get no closer to Claire.'

She narrowed her eyes, hands still clasped around her sobbing daughter's. 'I've always thought money concentrates the mind, Inspector,' she said deliberately. 'Especially the memory. Please try to understand, we simply can't sit by and wait any longer. It's tearing what little there's left of this family apart.'

'I appreciate that, Mrs . . .'

'Hymes,' she snapped back, rising from the tattered sofa. 'A word in private, if I may?'

The DI followed her into the small kitchen.

Mrs Hymes closed the door on the distraught couple, then gestured to the small plastic bowl of cornflakes on the kitchen table and lowered her voice. 'Every morning, Inspector, my daughter puts out breakfast for Claire. Then lunch, finally supper. We all sit around in silence, trying our best to eat, ignore the uneaten meal. It's . . .'

The DI held up both hands in genuine empathy. 'All I'm saying, is that a reward isn't necessarily the way. It could really clog things up, attract the wrong type of person.'

'You think we'll lose the money as well?'

He said nothing, the implication clear.

'It's not important if we do, Inspector. Besides, it's my money. Something I can contribute. And let's face it, what do I need it for? I'm a widow, well provided for by my late husband. This way I can really feel as if I'm helping.'

'You're helping by simply being here.'

She shook her head. 'No. We've all talked long and hard about it.' She paused, and for an instant the DI suspected she might be about to cry. 'Even if Claire's no longer with us . . . well, we need to find her body. And if my money can make the difference between some piece of filth informing on another one, it will have been well spent.'

There was nothing more to say. The DI could sense desperation driving a process all his professional advice had no chance of countering. Besides, it was their money, their daughter, her granddaughter, their collective hell they sought to buy a way out from.

'What are you going to do next?' he asked.

'Call the local television stations,' the woman replied. 'Arrange another press conference. Make the offer. Then wait.'

It was his turn to whisper. 'Please. Think again. It could blow the whole thing.'

Mrs Hymes looked him in the eye again. 'But it could get her back, couldn't it?'

He had no reply.

They returned from the second television appeal later that evening, ears ringing with promises by the station's producer to phone them the minute the promised reward trawled in a positive response.

As Mrs Hymes had suspected, the cynical DI hadn't turned up at the recording, leaving just the three of them to make their tearful appeal.

And now, once again, they all stood aimlessly in the small lounge, waiting.

It was her daughter Amy who broke the uncomfortable silence. 'Must see to Claire's clothes for the morning,' she said with eerie brightness. 'Playgroup on Thursday mornings. Coming, Mum?'

'Upstairs?' Mrs Hymes asked, caught between complicity and practicality. She was so tired, and hardly had the strength to carry on the tragic play-acting which seemed the only way her daughter was coping.

'No, silly,' Amy smiled. 'Tomorrow.'

'Oh. Probably.'

Paul Rogers slumped on the sofa and lit up. Mrs Hymes watched her daughter disappear upstairs. Then she too sat and watched her son-in-law.

'She's cracking up,' he said softly, drained.

'It's her way.'

There was a long awkward silence during which Mrs Hymes saw the young man begin to sob.

'Listen,' he said, 'I know you've never approved of me—'

'Now's not the time, Paul.' But he was right. She'd disliked him from the moment Amy brought him home to meet her, a garage mechanic, oil in the creases of his hands, no prospects. Common, her dear departed Fred would have called him. And to her mind, he was. But, as is the way in matrimonial matters, the parents had little say, any objections merely serving to strengthen Amy's defiance. It didn't matter that Mrs Hymes had tried her best to warn her away from the man, her mind was made up. She'd chosen her bed, and now was the time to lie in it.

But this dreadful business, Claire's abduction, who could have foreseen that?

'She blames me, you know,' he said simply.

'She's not herself, Paul.'

'I blame me.'

'What could you have done?'

He shook his head sadly. 'So many things. Not taken Claire for a walk. Not left her outside that bloody shop. Not been a smoker. Not—'

'But you did,' Mrs Hymes replied, feeling a nugget of genuine sympathy for the wrecked man opposite. 'We have to look forward, not back.'

'Ain't that easy, though, is it?'

'No.'

'But I want to say, that the moment Claire comes back, I'll graft every goddamned hour to repay you your money. Every bloody hour, I promise you.'

'There's no need.'

He stubbed out the cigarette as Amy returned downstairs. 'Just running Claire's bath. Bring her up in a minute, will you, love?' she asked.

'Amy—' Paul tried.

'And her pyjamas. They're drying on the kitchen rail.'

He stood unsteadily, swallowed hard. 'She's not here, Amy. Claire's not here.'

'Nonsense. Little pixie's probably hiding, that's all. You know how she hates going to bed.'

Paul ran stubby fingers through his short cropped hair. 'For God's sake, Amy, Claire's missing! When are you going to—'

'Not now,' Mrs Hymes nervously advised.

'There's not going to be any bath, Amy!' Paul shouted, moving towards his shocked wife, taking her by the shoulders. 'She's missing. Not hiding. Missing!'

A change of mood gradually clouded Amy Rogers' optimistic face. The eyes narrowed, lips tightened, jaw clenched. 'You!' she spat back. 'It's all your stupid bloody fault! You lost her! You useless bloody bastard! You lost my baby!' She began wriggling from his grasp, then viciously kicked out.

Paul winced in pain and shock, stunned for a terrifying moment. Mrs Hymes began to cry. He made for the front door.

'That's it!' Amy shouted after him. 'Run away and hide! It's all you ever do, isn't it? You lost my baby, and I hate you for it!'

Forty minutes later, Paul lit up another cigarette. 'Happy to see your dad, then?' he asked the little girl wriggling on his lap.

Claire Rogers responded with a beaming smile.

He turned to the other figure in the room. 'What about you? Just as glad to see me?'

Susan Morgan nodded, hating the way he smoked in front of the child. 'Thought you'd never come, to be honest,' she replied, wishing she could pull the girl from the stinking smoke which fast enveloped her.

'Had trouble getting away, darling. Got to judge it, know what I mean? Do us a favour, get us a cold beer, will you?'

Susan obediently went to the fridge.

'See us on the telly, then, did you?'

She handed him the cold lager. 'How do you do that?' she asked. 'Cry on cue?'

He sat the tot on the floor. 'Jesus,' he said, pulling Susan on to his lap. 'For fifty thou, I could do a lot more than turn on the bloody waterworks, don't you worry.'

She pulled away, watching him drink thirstily from the dark blue can. 'It's not been easy, today, you know. She gets bored cooped up in here. We both do. She cries.'

He laughed. 'Christ on a bike, you think your day's been hard! You've got the easy end of all this, believe me.'

'Yes. Maybe.' Susan knew better than to disagree. Not that he'd ever got rough with her, never even had cross words – no, there was simply something *in* Paul, a hidden brooding menace, almost, which made her cautious. Though, initially, it was this same unseen power which had attracted her to the fast-talking Romeo she'd met at the wine bar. Something about the danger in the ice-blue eyes which both intrigued and repelled at the same erotically charged instant. Unfortunately for Susan, intrigue won the night.

The affair had continued for five months, an erratic pattern of Paul visiting her flat seemingly whenever it suited, or occasionally meeting in some out-of-the-way pub, where he'd spend a couple of hours detailing the misery of his marriage.

He was using her, but as she figured, only because she allowed him to. In some ways it suited her. She was only twenty-one, single, bored, lonely. He was thirty, a rogue, sexually adventurous and never around to see her stretch-marks in the morning. So she couldn't complain, could she?

Though quite how he'd managed to persuade her to get so deeply involved in his latest scam was almost beyond her. Almost – because late the previous night, as she and Claire had sat reading together, she realised that once again she'd allowed Paul to convince her. That perhaps these few snatched days with someone else's child would go some way to compensating for something which nature had so cruelly taken from her.

Perhaps.

'Please,' she asked quietly. 'I'm getting lost in all this. I'm not sure I can go on, Paul.'

A frown clouded the mechanic's face. 'Can't go on?'

'It's so wrong.'

'It's our start. Fifty grand in the bin, so's we can sod off and start over somewhere new.' He crushed the empty beer can in his fist. 'Jesus, don't give up now, girl! Not now we're this close.'

'How much longer?'

'Five days. Monday night, eight exactly, you take Claire

round to the green in front of the off-licence on Dudley Road. You know it?'

She nodded, familiar with the little parade of shops on the other side of town. A twenty-minute walk, probably. Twenty-five with the pushchair. And though it would be a massive relief to hand the child back, part of her knew she was going to dread every step. 'I get so confused,' she said quietly. 'I don't understand how it's all going to work out.'

Paul stubbed out the cigarette, gritting his teeth. 'Body of a model, brains of a bloody rocking horse.'

'I'm sorry.'

He lifted the gurgling toddler on to Susan's lap, glad they seemed so happy in each other's company. It had been one of his biggest concerns, that Claire would scream the place down, day and night. Which is why he'd spent so much time finding the flat, a top-storey attic conversion with the nearest tenant living in the basement. Two weeks it had taken, simply finding the right place, just one tiny piece in the whole elaborate chain. But nothing was going to be easy, was it? Not for fifty grand.

Paul continued. 'A friend of my mate Steve works in the offy, right? He's going to earn himself a couple of grand by keeping an eye out for you both. When you get opposite, leave Claire, and walk away. But judge it, mind. Make sure no one's watching.'

'OK.'

'He'll come out, wheel her in, phone the filth. Job done. Claire's back in the bosom of her loving family, safe and sound. The mother-in-law draws out the reward money, pays it to the kid in the offy, who takes his cut when it clears, passes the rest to my mate Steve, who then takes his three grand for acting as the middle man, before giving the other forty-five to me. Us, I mean. Obviously.'

'It's so complicated.'

'Has to be.'

'But can you trust all these people? Your friend Stephen, is it?'

'He's like a brother to me.'

'But all that money, surely—'

'Not Steve. Never. Trust me.'

Susan chewed her bottom lip. It wasn't her intention to criticise, she simply wanted to know. After all she was implicated, and therefore just as vulnerable to hidden flaws. 'And the man who works in the off-licence?'

'Steve says he's OK. Just a kid. Needs a few bob.'

'But all that money clearing through his bank account? What if he just runs away with it?'

Paul smiled. 'He'd never run anywhere again. Besides, he wouldn't try it. Steve and I will know the very day the money clears. Steve'll be on his doorstep at nine, down the bank with him at nine thirty. He won't try anything.'

'And then?'

'What?'

'What about us?' Susan insisted. 'When we've got the money? Where do we go, how long does it take?'

'As soon as the wife chucks me out, we're away. The strain's already telling. She hates me even more than usual. Blames me for the whole Claire thing. Going bloody nuts she is. My reckoning is that if I keep winding her up enough, she'll go for divorce within a couple of months.'

'But why wait that long?'

'Dust has got to settle, Suzy. It'd look pretty suspicious, wouldn't it, me moving in with you the moment her mum hands the life savings over? This way, she chucks me out, instigates the divorce, and we collect forty-five big ones. I tell you, we can't lose. Just trust me, Suzy, trust me.'

By the time he returned home, the place was in darkness. It was nearly eleven, and as far as he could gather, his mother-in-law had gone back to her own house for the night. He knew this because a bed hadn't been made up for him on the couch. Laughing to himself, he slowly walked upstairs.

Amy sat in bed reading a magazine by a small bedside light. 'The hero returns,' she said frostily.

He quickly stripped off and slid between the sheets and tried running an experimental hand up her warm thigh.

'Sod off,' she quickly replied. 'How is she?'

'Claire or the girl?'

'Claire, of course! I couldn't give a stuff about your stupid little girlfriend!'

'Claire's fine. Enjoying her little holiday. Spends most of her time playing with the toys I left in the flat before Suzy took her there. And by the way, she ain't my girlfriend.'

Amy put down the magazine, met him in the eye. 'So what's taken you all this time, then, eh? Nearly three hours, Paul?'

'She needed reassurance.'

'I know your kind of reassurance.'

He yawned, anxious for sleep. 'Look, I've got to play the part, haven't I?'

'Shut your eyes and think of England, do you?' Amy mocked.

'Nope. Just fifty thousand lovely pounds. That does it for me, no worries.'

Amy turned angry. 'I want Claire back, Paul. Really. I'm not doing the psycho act this time, I really want her back. I mean, is she safe? Is your bimbo qualified to look after her?'

Paul sighed. 'Christ, we've been over this a thousand times! Suzy's great with kids. She lost one of her own at birth. She's spoiling Claire rotten.'

'Day after day in a tiny flat? How?'

'Claire's fine. Trust me.'

Amy put down the magazine and turned out the light. An uneasy silence descended. 'God only knows how you managed to talk me into this.'

'Because,' Paul replied, bored with the constant explanations, 'it was the only way to stop your mother willing the lot to the bloody cats' home.'

'Animal sanctuary,' Amy corrected.

'Whatever. Either way, we'd not see a bloody penny of it. Besides, who needs it more, us in this dump, or a dozen broken-down donkeys in a muddy field?'

'And what if she finds out it's all another of your scams?'

'My master scam,' Paul corrected, his voice edged with pride. 'How? Are you going to tell her?'

Amy thought for a moment in the oppressive darkness. 'The girl might. Your lover. Once she finds out you've no intention of running away with her.'

'Nah. She can't. Already up to her neck in it, see? I'll let things run their course, then gently cool it off with her. Besides, she's just a kid, too scared to say boo to a goose. I spent a lot of time choosing her, remember?' He moved in for a secondary hugging attempt. 'This way, love, we get forty-five big ones, and believe you me, no one's going to be any the wiser.'

'Just trust you, right?'

'Took the words right out of my mouth.'

Ten days passed, during which time all went according to Paul's master plan. Claire was indeed spotted outside an off-licence on the Monday night, and returned by police to scenes of massive family jubilation some hours later. During careful interviewing by police specialists, she was unable to give any concrete clues as to her abductor's identity, save that it was most probably a woman.

Local press and TV crews swamped the small council house, as the tearful Rogers family told of their agonising days of despair and sleepless nights of worry. It was a happy-ending story, smiling child, deliriously happy parents, proud grandmother.

The eagle-eyed sales assistant, as instructed, insisted on anonymity, asking only to be introduced to the family in order to collect the advertised reward. If the police had any suspicions, they were soon dispelled when a computer search revealed the young lad had nothing more serious on his record than three parking offences.

For Paul, life couldn't have been rosier. Suzy returned to work and her own house after her 'holiday', ears ringing with his promises that it was only a matter of a few short weeks before their new life together would finally begin to happen.

He returned to the garage, busied himself tinkering with cars, repairing some faults, starting others for future business, and all the time dreaming about the money ...

The Monday after Claire's safe return was pay-day. Paul phoned in sick at work, then drove straight round to Steve's after lunch in order to collect the forty-five grand the young sales assistant had drawn out during the morning, then passed on to the trusted middle man after taking two thousand for his trouble.

His heart raced as he knocked on the door.

Steve answered, flustered. 'We've been stuffed.'

'You what?'

'He's not shown with the money.'

Paul began to tremble. An old nervous twitch suddenly resurfaced. 'Not shown?'

Steve ushered him into the living-room. 'I went round at half-nine to collect, the little sod wasn't there.'

'Oh Jesus!'

'Must've done a bunk or something.'

'Or something?' Paul's eyes narrowed as he scrutinised his most trusted friend. 'You straight about this?'

'What you gassing about? He's gone, I tell you!'

'Maybe he never,' Paul replied coldly. 'Maybe you got the dough and now aren't being straight with me.'

An ugly silence followed, before Steve protested, 'Listen, the kid's gone. I'm as sick as you, Paul, trust me. I had an easy three grand tied up in all this!'

'Yeah, or an even easier fifty. Put the frighteners on the kid and take the bloody lot!'

'It's the truth, I swear! Search me, search the house, do whatever! I ain't got your money!'

Something in the terrified eyes and desperate voice told Paul his old friend was telling the truth. They'd been conned. But how? 'What happened?'

'He never went to the bank. I was waiting there all morning. It's his branch, the only place they'd allow him to withdraw that amount of cash. And today's the first day it would have cleared. I knocked round his place, I tell you, he ain't there. Just disappeared off the face of the earth.'

Paul sat, thought for a minute, struggled to slow his heart. 'All right. OK. Listen, if he ain't been to the bank, chances are it's still all in there. Maybe he's sick in bed or something. Had an accident, in hospital, I don't know.'

'Yeah, maybe.'

'Tell you one thing though,' Paul said menacingly. 'If he's

tried to pull one over us, he'll bleeding end up in his own episode of *Casualty*, I promise you that.'

Amy jumped as the key turned in the lock. It was past ten, Paul had been due back for hours. His supper lay cold and congealed on the thin wooden table.

She watched him enter the room, then slump in the sofa. He stank of stale beer and cigarettes. 'Well?' she asked, tight-lipped.

He held up a hand to silence her.

But she persisted. 'The money, Paul? Not left it in the car, have you?'

'It's going to take a little longer than I thought,' he whispered.

'What are you saying?'

'I haven't got it. Spent all bloody day looking for the little bastard who can draw it out for us. God knows where he's got to. But I'll find him. And he'll get us the cash. It's safe where it is.'

'And where's that, Paul?'

He looked up, surprised at her quiet intent. 'The kid's bank. He ain't been there today, so it's still in there. All of it.'

'You stupid man.'

'You what?'

'You expect me to believe that? From a man who'd spend months seducing a tart in order to have his own daughter kidnapped so he can get his hands on his mother-in-law's money?'

Her tone worried him. Too calm, measured. 'Steady on, Amy.'

'You've already got it, haven't you? Sorted it away somewhere. And now you're giving me this cock and bull about not collecting it—'

'It's the truth! Tru—'

She stood, moved towards him, still contained, but struggling. 'Trust you? Ha! Why should I? My mother was right. You're a no-good common criminal. And a very poor liar.'

'It's not a lie!'

'You wanted all of it for yourself!'

'No, you're wrong, you're . . .' The last thing he saw was the flashing kitchen knife.

Susan Morgan turned slightly on the sun-lounger and cast a critical eye over the new man in her life. Young, reasonably honest, OK-looking. Certainly an improvement on Paul, although Keith Miller wasn't the brightest of men. He hadn't even heard about special clearance until she told him during one of her many visits to the off-licence where he worked.

She smiled, listening as the distant waves gently washed the golden sand some way below the hotel balcony. What else could Paul have expected? That she keep dear Claire a virtual prisoner in the poky room he'd rented? It made sense that she sneak the girl out for some fresh air every now and again. Besides, she had to check that she could trust the young sales assistant, had to be sure for Claire's sake.

Just three visits on consecutive nights it took, late night strolls, just as Keith left for home. On the second night, they held hands. On the third they kissed, and she told him about special clearance allowing withdrawal after just forty-eight hours.

It was nice here – warm, friendly. They even had copies of the English tabloids in the lobby, and she'd read with some interest the story of the poor mother who'd killed her husband in self-defence after a drunken row. Apparently, they'd just gone through a horrendous kidnapping ordeal, and the stress was showing. Police were reluctant to charge the woman after all she'd gone through.

Susan Morgan took a sip from the long cool cocktail and settled back down to bask in the sun once more. She'd have another child of her own soon, which would complete her happiness.

And maybe, she'd also finally found a man to trust.

Keith Miles

Keith Miles is a versatile and talented writer whose work always bears the hallmark of the true professional. He contributed a historical tale to last year's CWA anthology using the pen-name which he uses for his tales of past crime, Edward Marston. Here he offers under his own name a story which is very different, but equally pleasing.

BY THE TIME YOU READ THIS

by Keith Miles

By the time you read this, I will be dead. You have finally driven me to it.

After changing the wording of his suicide note a dozen times, Malcolm Hilliard came to a decision. He sat back to admire the result. It was perfect. Short, sharp and guaranteed to give his wife maximum shock. He imagined her reaction when she read it. There would be a surge of pain and guilt followed by an immediate sense of panic. Denise would flail around madly, wondering where he was, what had provoked him, why he had given no earlier warning, how he intended to take his own life and whether or not he could be found before he did so. She would *suffer*.

Fifteen years of marriage were being ended by a terse note which he did not even bother to sign. The fact that it was typed out on her own machine gave it additional impact. It was cold and impersonal. In the past, even the briefest of notes to her had contained ritual endearments. This one was comprehensively different. It was an unequivocal rejection of Denise. That would hurt her deeply. She had an obsession about being loved. She needed to float on a cloud of domestic adoration. It would never occur to her that her devoted husband actually hated her.

No husband – Malcolm reminded himself – could have been more devoted. He took an interest in her when she had only limited education and moderate prospects. Until she met him, her boyfriends consisted of a series of no-hopers, usually unemployed and always chasing some futile dream about being a pop star or a professional football player. The most she could have expected from any of them was a miserable existence in a grotty bedsitter or a disgusting squat. Malcolm rescued her from all that. He gave her security and respectability. He gave her something which made the other girls at the office gape with envy.

When they heard that Denise Wallace was going to marry the boss, they were devastated. Malcolm recalled the look on their faces when he told them. Three of them at least had aspirations of their own with regard to their employer and there were two others with whom he had fleeting moments at office parties. Yet they were all beaten by the shy young newcomer with the long red hair and the nervous smile. Denise lost that shyness with amazing speed. The nervous smile became a quiet grin of triumph. She was soon Denise Hilliard and the world was at her feet.

Malcolm gave her all that and she repaid him with lies and betrayal. It was time to get his revenge. The note would be the start of it. When she recovered from the initial blow, she would be tormented by the thought of what others would say about her. Denise's whole pretence as a loyal wife would be shattered beyond recall. She would be terrified to lose her father's love, her sister's indulgence and the uncritical affection of her friends. She would feel cast adrift. Her impulse to try to find her husband would take on new urgency. She would ring the police. That was the one thing of which Malcolm could be absolutely certain.

A policeman would be involved.

He was late. Denise became increasingly annoyed. Having organised everything so carefully at her end, she expected a similar efficiency from him. They had agreed that she would get there first and check into the room so that they were not actually seen together but he promised to arrive soon after her. Over two hours had now elapsed. Staring out at the car-park, her annoyance slowly deepened into fury. Denise was taking an enormous risk on his behalf and she made sure that he appreciated that. Then there was the emotional significance. It was the first and only time in her entire marriage that she had agreed to spend a whole night with another man. He ought to feel honoured. And very grateful.

When a police car swept into the drive, she was both relieved and alarmed, glad that he had finally come but disturbed that he should travel in such a conspicuous vehicle. It was a false alarm. The police car was merely using the motel as a convenient means of turning in a circle before rejoining the road and heading back in the direction from which it came. Secondary anxieties surfaced. Did one of his colleagues know about his tryst at the motel? Had he come in search of Royston's car? Or had Royston himself been driving the police vehicle and got cold feet at the last moment? Denise was torn between fear and anger.

Five minutes later, her ordeal was over. His blue Escort slid quietly into the car-park and came to a halt beside her Clio. The twitch of the curtains told him the number of the room. When she let him in, he took her in his arms and kissed away her doubts and recriminations. He was there. He was hers. Everything would be fine now.

'Sorry I'm late,' he said, still holding her. 'Problem at the nick.'

'Why didn't you ring?'

'Too tricky, love.'

'I thought you'd be here ages ago.'

'So did I. One of those things.'

'I was beside myself with worry,' said Denise, letting her anguish show in her face and her voice. 'I've been here for *hours*, Royston. I began to think that you'd changed your mind. If you couldn't ring me from the station, why didn't you get me on our mobile?'

'Don't have it with me.'

'Then you could have stopped at a call box.'

'I didn't want to waste another second before I got here. Drove at top speed all the way until I caught up with one of our squad cars. That slowed me right down. Nearly had a fit when I saw it turning in here.'

'It went straight out again.'

'Yes, I cut down a side road when it headed back towards me. Last thing we need is for me to be recognised by two of my pals. So I waited in a lay-by until I felt sure they'd be out of sight then I came straight here.' He kissed her again. 'Am I forgiven?'

'No,' she said, pouting playfully.

'Denise!'

'But I'll work on it.'

'You do that.'

Police Constable Royston Mansfield picked her up in his arms and carried her effortlessly to the bed. He set her down gently then beamed at her with that friendly grin which she had noticed the very first time they met. He had looked so tall, manly and reassuring in his uniform. Even in a sports jacket and trousers, he was still unmistakably a policeman. Denise trusted him. When he solved a small problem for her – her missing dog whom he found within a day – she had no idea that he might be able to help her solve the much bigger problem of an unhappy marriage.

'You're beautiful,' he said, slipping off his coat.

'Then why did it take you so long to get here?'

'Look, I told you. I'm sorry.'

'How sorry?'

'I'll show you.' He began to undress. 'Where's your husband?'

'At home.'

'What did you tell him?'

'That I was driving up to Birmingham to see Vicky.'

'What if he rings?'

'He won't.'

'But what if he does?'

'Vicky will cover for me. She's a good friend. It's one of the reasons Malcolm dislikes her so much. He thinks that Vicky is a bad influence on me. He loathes having to speak to her. No, Malcolm won't ring. He'll be too busy downing whiskies at the golf club.' She raised a foot so that he could remove her shoe. 'What about your wife?'

'Pat has gone to see her parents in Devon.'

'Has she taken the children with her?'

'Yes,' he said, slipping off her other shoe before rubbing his cheek against her toes. 'They won't be back until Sunday night.'

'Won't she ring you at some stage?'

'If she does, I won't be there. I'm a copper. Pat is used to it.'

'Used to you spending a night with another woman?' she teased.

He chuckled. 'Used to me working all hours.'

'Do you miss her?'

'What – now? Of course not.'

'What about the kids?'

'Denise!' he protested. 'I didn't come here to talk about them. Any more than you came here to discuss your husband. Or perhaps you did. Is that what this is all about? Are you missng Malcolm?'

'Oh, yes,' she said with a giggle. 'Blissfully!'

The dog was the giveaway. Denise hardly went anywhere without it. On previous trips to Birmingham, she had always taken Coco with her. This time, the animal had been left behind with a list of feeding instructions. Malcolm did not believe for one minute the lame excuse that Vicky now had a cat and that Coco could no longer be invited. He gave a hollow laugh. Vicky *was* a cat. He had never met such a feline creature. The one time he was foolish enough to get close to her, she left scratches all the way down his back. It was a fortnight before he dared to let Denise see him naked or she might have recognised her best friend's trademark. Vicky had no cat. It did not matter if she now had a whole menagerie because Denise had not gone to Birmingham at all. The whining terrier had been left behind because Coco would have been an encumbrance.

Malcolm coaxed him down into the cellar with a bowl of food. He considered it to be a masterstroke. When his wife read the suicide note, she would soon fear for Coco's safety, knowing how strongly Malcolm had resisted the idea of her owning a dog. Denise would search the house at once. Coco's yelps would probably guide her to the cellar where he was chained to the wall. Directly above his head was the reinforced box in which Malcolm kept his shotgun under lock and key. His wife was bound to see that it was empty. It would intensify her agony.

As he left the house and walked to his car, one of the neighbours drove past. Malcolm gave him a cheery wave. When the search for him began, he knew that the neighbour's evidence would pinpoint the time of his departure. That was good. It would give the police a starting point. They could follow the trail that led to him and his shotgun. He wondered how long it would take Denise to work out where he had gone and why. She was an intelligent woman. She might have little formal education, but she had gifts of deduction and manipulation which a graduate like Malcolm could never hope to match.

When she found the note, the dog and the missing shotgun, she would be too dazed to think properly at first. Once she reported to the police that her husband was missing, however, they would calm her down and make her search for the clues which only she could find. It would not take her all that long before she realised that Malcolm, with his passion for order and symmetry, would seek to end his marriage in the place where it first began. Before flying off on their honeymoon in Hawaii, the couple spent their wedding night at his cottage on the Sussex coast. It had been idyllic, the one secure memory to which he anchored himself. Whenever they had difficulties, a weekend at the cottage usually helped to resolve them. It was their puncture outfit. Denise refused to go any more. It was another warning sign. She felt their marriage was beyond repair.

He was driving down a country road when the thought struck him. What if Denise had taken her lover to the cottage? What if she had decided to get back at her husband by making use of a place which meant so much to him? The very notion brought Malcolm out into a cold sweat. What if he arrived there and caught them in bed? He pulled over involuntarily to the kerb and switched off the ignition. Getting out of the car, he opened the boot and took out the shotgun to load it. Every contingency had to be taken into account. When he drove on, his temples were pounding.

It was almost as if he *wanted* them to be polluting his cottage.

*

'We should have done this in that cottage of yours,' he said lazily.

'Why?'

'It would have saved us some money, for a start.'

'Royston!' She slapped his naked thigh.

'Obvious place to go to spend our first night together.'

'It would remind me too much of our honeymoon,' she said with a shudder. 'I can't bear the cottage. It's Malcom's, not mine. I never really enjoyed going back there. It's creepy.'

'Not when you have a copper to look after you.'

'Look after me here.'

'I just did.'

They shared a laugh then he kissed her before hauling himself off the bed and walking to the refrigerator. Denise marvelled at him. He was everything that her husband was not. Royston was five years younger than her instead of being ten years older. He had a firm, well-muscled body instead of a flabby paunch. Most important of all, her lover was so spontaneous. His clothes were scattered all over the floor where he had flung them before making love to her. Malcolm would have folded his trousers neatly before hanging them up. Royston was now uncorking the post-coital champagne which Malcolm would have seen as an essential preliminary. Royston simply made it up as they went along whereas her husband, a true accountant, did everything by numbers. Even the most intimate marital moments had a hideous mathematical logic to them.

Royston poured her champagne and laughed when it dripped on the carpet. Malcolm would never have done that. He was so careful to spill nothing which cost him money. Denise sat up and took her glass. Royston filled his own glass then clinked hers before taking a first approving sip. He sat on the bed and slipped an arm around her. Denise had never felt such a glow of contentment. It was tinged with a sense of danger which made her feel so alive. After a long, arid marriage, she was getting the kind of physical and emotional satisfaction which was impossible in the cottage on the Sussex coast. Real pleasure had been programmed out by Malcolm. He could never let himself go.

'This is the life!' said Royston, sipping his champagne.

'Yes,' she agreed. 'It's what we both deserve.'

'And now we can have it – thanks to your dog.'

'My dog?'

'If Coco hadn't got himself locked up in your neighbour's shed, we might never have met. I mean, I only came to your house out of kindness. A missing dog was well down my list of priorities. I had burglaries and a case of GBH to look into that day. You were lucky.'

'I know that now,' she purred.

'And so was I.'

'Don't you forget it, PC Mansfield.'

'No, Mrs Hilliard.'

He gave her a hug and they lapsed into reminiscences. They talked about each time they had met or exchanged letters or called each other on the telephone. They were drawn closer and closer together. Sensing that he was in the right mood, she chose her moment to broach the subject which was uppermost in her mind.

'Have you spoken to your wife yet?' she said.

'What about?'

'The future.'

'I've dropped hints.'

'Hints?'

'Yes, you know,' he said dismissively. 'Sort of preparing the way. I have to do that. Pat and I have been together a long time. I owe her something. I've got to let her down gently.'

'Malcolm and I go back much further,' she said bitterly, 'but I intend to give it to him straight between the eyes. That's all he deserves.'

'Hell hath no fury, eh?'

'He's been dreadful.'

'So you tell me.'

'He has, Royston,' she said, snuggling into his shoulder. 'Malcolm spent fifteen years stopping me from doing things I wanted to do. He stopped me working, stopped me getting qualifications, stopped me seeing certain friends, stopped me having the holidays I wanted and stopped me ...' Her voice broke off as she recalled the deepest wound. '... and stopped me having children. I cried myself to sleep for years over that. Every woman should have the right to bring children into the world. But Malcolm wouldn't let me. He said that children would come between us. It took ages before I could persuade him to let me have a dog.'

'Does he like Coco?'

'He resents him like mad.'

'I bet he's having fun looking after the dog.'

'I made him do it.'

'Real sod, is he?'

'Malcolm? You don't know half of it.'

'He's far too old for you, Denise.'

'Too old and too old-fashioned.'

'Bit of a control freak, by the sound of it.'

'Oh, yes. I've had no real freedom.'

'Why have you stayed with him so long?'

'Because I was waiting for you to come and rescue me.'

He gave a laugh and kissed her. Denise made her first mistake.

'I want us to get married, Royston,' she said.

Long before he reached the cottage, he came to see that she would not possibly be there. It held too many memories for her and they could not be obliterated by a night with an off-duty policeman. Those memories would embarrass and hamper Denise. Wherever she had gone, it was not to the cottage where they initiated their married life. Malcolm was safe from having to take impetuous action with a loaded shotgun. The object of the exercise was to make an erring wife suffer agonies of remorse not to get himself arrested for shooting her lover. The cottage was inviolate. He would be safe there and his plan could slowly unfold.

A light drizzle was falling as he parked his car on the little drive and let himself into the building. It was dark and musty. He could almost feel its accusation of neglect. Malcolm opened the shutters to let in light then lifted a few of the sash windows to allow fresh air to blow through the cottage. He felt invigorated simply by being there. He was surrounded by his things.

His books, records and CDs were all neatly arranged on their shelves. His video cassettes were stacked alphabetically along the wall behind the television. Even his collection of professional magazines was in chronological order. The cottage was designed to fit him like a suit. It was a refuge which never let him down.

His one regret about the place was that he had once invited Vicky to spend the night. She was an uninhibited lover and he had luxuriated in her wildness at first but the scratches down his back had dampened his ardour at once. It was not only the pain but the deliberation with which it was inflicted. Vicky was leaving her tattoo on him as if wishing that her best friend would see it but Denise had long since outgrown any curiosity about her husband's naked body. A fortnight had seen the marks made by Vicky's fingernails fade to invisibility but those scratches remained in Malcolm's mind. If he did not despise the woman so much, he might have been tempted to invite Vicky to spend that very night with him. What better way to scotch his wife's alibi than by bedding the very woman with whom she claimed she would be staying in Birmingham?

Malcolm unpacked the car then unloaded the shotgun and hid it in the roof space. There was never any intention of using it on himself. He wished to be a missing person and not a suicide victim. Much as he hated her for what she did to him, he wanted his wife back. She was his possession. Malcolm would share with nobody. Regaining Denise and his ascendancy over her would be the best punishment of all. It was only a question of biding his time. Then he could make her life a misery. Until then, of course, she was in the arms of another man and there was only one way to banish that thought from his mind.

He opened the first bottle of wine and poured himself a large glass. Reclining in his favourite chair, he switched on the television and went systematically through the channels. David Attenborough came on to the screen, talking about the insect life in Sumatra. That was just what Malcolm wanted. A complete escape from his situation. The time to return to it was when that situation had been markedly improved.

*

'What do you mean, you haven't really thought about it?' she demanded.

'Come back to bed, Denise.'

'Answer my question.'

'Not while you're in such a state.'

'I'm not in any kind of state.'

'Calm down, will you?'

'And stop telling me to calm down!' she yelled, stamping a foot. 'I'm not some madwoman in a council flat. You're not on duty now.'

'More's the pity!' he murmured.

'What was that?'

'Nothing.'

'I heard, Royston.'

'Come over here,' he said with an appeasing smile. 'Why argue like this? It's pointless. We can talk properly in bed. Come on, Denise.'

'No!'

'Why not?'

'Because you're not touching me until we've had this out.'

'It's two o'clock in the morning.'

'I don't care what bloody time it is.'

'Well, I do.' He rolled over. 'Goodnight, Denise.'

'Don't you dare go to sleep on me!'

'I'm tired.'

'We're both tired,' she said, marching around the bed to stand over him, 'but this has to be settled. It's the reason I agreed to come here in the first place. Are you listening? You promised that we'd be together one day,' she said, wagging a finger. 'You promised faithfully.'

'We *are* together – or hadn't you noticed?'

'You know what I mean, Royston.'

'I thought I did but, obviously, I got it wrong.'

'I spelled it out loud and clear.'

'You never mentioned children.'

'Yes, I did.'

'Not in the way you talked about them tonight.'

'For heaven's sake!' she wailed. 'You knew that I wanted

children of my own. That's why I want to leave Malcolm. To be with someone who can give me those children.'

'Oh, I see,' he said, sitting up angrily. 'You didn't want me because you loved me. All I am to you is a walking sperm bank!'

'I need to have children, Royston.'

'But I already have two.'

'Your wife will get custody of those.'

'I'm not ready to think that far ahead.'

'Well, I am. So were you a couple of hours ago when you were inside me. It's amazing how quickly you change your tune when you've had your money's worth out of me.'

'But I haven't had it yet!' he retorted. 'When a woman agrees to spend a night with me, I expect the full works. I don't want some silly cow ranting at me about how she loves children.'

'That's a vile thing to say!'

Striking out at him was her second mistake. Royston had drunk far too much to remember the rules of gentlemanly behaviour. He parried her blow then swung his forearm viciously against her face, catching her on the temple and sending her sprawling against the wall. Her head struck solid concrete and she went dizzy. Denise was only dimly aware of what was going on. She could neither stand up nor compose her thoughts. Vague sounds filled her ears but she had no idea what they were. It was only when the door slammed that her head cleared enough for her to sit up and take stock. Royston had gone. His car was heard starting up and driving off.

It was over.

Malcolm did not even wake up until well after noon. A heavy meal, two bottles of Merlot, some stiff whiskies, late-night films which kept him mesmerised by the television screen until the small hours and sheer nervous exhaustion combined to knock him senseless until Sunday lunchtime. His head ached and his mouth was dry but he was rallied by a delicious thought.

Denise would be home by now. She would already have read his note and felt the first searing pangs of guilt. His revenge had been set in motion.

A bath revived him enough to face a late breakfast of toast and coffee. Then he watched a football match on the television and the afternoon disappeared in a haze. By mid-evening, he was wondering why she had not rung to check if he was there. He had his speech ready, calculated to turn the screw even more. When there was no word from her by ten, he rang the house himself but all that he heard was his own voice on the answerphone. Denise had to be there – unless she was out searching for him. Yes, that was it. She was probably driving down to the cottage at that very moment, desperately hoping that she could find him still alive before he took an irrevocable step with the shotgun. Malcolm retrieved the weapon from its hiding place and reloaded it. If his wife burst in, he needed the scene to look convincing.

By midnight, he was on his second bottle of wine. When that was empty, he was fast asleep in his chair. He awoke at dawn, shivering with cold and aching all over. Where *was* she? The note had been left on the mantelpiece in their bedroom. She must have seen it when she unpacked her overnight bag. Coco would have known that she was back in the house and howled for attention. Malcolm had worked it all out. Yet still there was no visit and no telephone call. Mild panic eventually gripped him and he rang home once more but his own voice came back at him. Malcolm lost his nerve. Slamming down the receiver, he got dressed and gathered up his things. He was soon driving homewards at top speed.

Two police cars were waiting outside his house. Malcolm wished that he had been more patient but it was too late to turn back now. Neighbours had seen him. One even gave a smile of sympathy. Malcolm stopped his car and ran into the house. Policemen seemed to be everywhere but there was no sign of Denise. He asserted his authority.

'Who's in charge here?' he shouted.

A thickset man in an ill-fitting suit turned to him.

'I am, sir,' he said quietly, producing a warrant card to show to Malcolm. 'Detective Inspector Ellis, Metropolitan CID. Mr Hilliard?'

'That's me.'

'Mr Malcolm Hilliard?'

'Yes, yes. Call off the search. I'm back now.'

'But we haven't been searching for you, sir.'

'Oh?'

'No, this is about your wife.' The inspector heaved a sigh. 'I have some bad news, I'm afraid. Our colleagues in Sussex actually found her. Mrs Hilliard drove her car over the edge of a cliff.'

Malcolm was distraught. 'Denise is dead?'

'I'm afraid so, Mr Hilliard. You have my deepest sympathy.'

'A cliff in Sussex, you say?'

'Yes, sir. The car burst into flames and we had difficulty identifying both the vehicle and its occupant. That's why there was a delay. Once we knew that the vehicle was registered to a Mrs Denise Hilliard at this address, we came straight here. Since you were not at home, we broke in to see if we could find some indication of your whereabouts. It was then that we learned the truth.'

'Truth?' whispered Malcolm.

'I understand from your neighbours that you have a cottage on the Sussex coast. We wondered if your wife might have been making for that late on Saturday night and simply come off the road in the dark. When we searched your house, however, we realised that it was no accident. Mrs Hilliard committed suicide.'

'Suicide!'

'No doubt about it, sir.'

'Denise would never do that!' cried Malcolm. 'Never!'

'She did, I'm afraid. Mrs Hilliard left a note for you.'

'A note?'

'Here it is.'

He handed over the note and Malcolm read the words which he himself had typed out two days earlier with such gloating pleasure.

By the time you read this, I will be dead. You have finally driven me to it.

There was a long and painful pause.
'I think you have some explaining to do, sir,' said the inspector.

Ruth Rendell

Ruth Rendell needs no introduction to anyone who likes the best in crime fiction. This account of the misadventures of a detective story fan is a typically stylish offering from an outstanding writer. Unlike the other contributions to this volume, it has been published before, but it is so satisfying that I was keen to include it in *Missing Persons*, and most grateful when Ruth was happy to allow me to do so.

PEOPLE DON'T DO SUCH THINGS

by Ruth Rendell

People don't do such things.

That's the last line of *Hedda Gabler*, and Ibsen makes this chap say it out of a sort of bewilderment at finding truth stranger than fiction. I know just how he felt. I say it myself every time I come up against the hard reality that Reeve Baker is serving fifteen years in prison for murdering my wife, and that I played my part in it, and that it happened to us three. People don't do such things. But they do.

Real life had never been stranger than fiction for me. It had always been beautifully pedestrian and calm and pleasant, and all the people I knew jogged along in the same sort of way. Except Reeve, that is. I suppose I made a friend of Reeve and enjoyed his company so much because of the contrast between his manner of living and my own, and so that when he had gone home I could say comfortably to Gwendolen:

'How dull our lives must seem to Reeve!'

An acquaintance of mine had given him my name when he had got into a mess with his finances and was having trouble with the Inland Revenue. As an accountant with a good many writers among my clients, I was used to their irresponsible attitude to money – the way they fall back on the excuse of artistic temperament for what is, in fact, calculated tax evasion – and I was able to sort things out for Reeve and show him how to keep more or less solvent. As a way, I suppose, of showing his gratitude, Reeve took Gwendolen and me out to dinner, then we had him over at our place, and after that we became close friends.

Writers and the way they work hold a fascination for ordinary chaps like me. It's a mystery to me where they get their ideas from, apart from constructing the thing and creating characters and making their characters talk and so on. But Reeve could do it all right, and set the whole lot at the court of Louis Quinze or in medieval Italy or what not. I've read all nine of his historical novels and admired what you might call his virtuosity. But I only read them to please him really. Detective stories were what I preferred and I seldom bothered with any other form of fiction.

Gwendolen once said to me it was amazing Reeve could fill his books with so much drama when he was living drama all the time. You'd imagine he'd have got rid of it all on paper. I think the truth was that every one of his heroes was himself, only transformed into Cesare Borgia or Casanova. You could see Reeve in them all, tall, handsome and dashing as they were, and each a devil with the women. Reeve had got divorced from his wife a year or so before I'd met him, and since then he'd had a string of girlfriends, models, actresses, girls in the fashion trade, secretaries, journalists, schoolteachers, high-powered lady executives and even a dentist. Once when we were over at his place he played us a record of an aria from *Don Giovanni* – another character Reeve identified with and wrote about. It was called the 'Catalogue Song' and it listed all the types of girls the Don had made love to, blonde, brunette, redhead, young, old, rich, poor, ending up with something about as long as she wears a petticoat you know what he does. Funny, I even remember the Italian for that bit, though it's the only Italian I know. *Purche porti la gonnella voi sapete quel che fa*. Then the singer laughed in an unpleasant way, laughed to music with a seducer's sneer, and Reeve laughed too, saying it gave him a fellow-feeling.

I'm old-fashioned, I know that. I'm conventional. Sex is for marriage, as far as I'm concerned, and what sex you have before marriage – I never had much – I can't help thinking of as a shameful secret thing. I never even believed that people did have much of it outside marriage. All talk and boasting, I thought. I really did think that. And I kidded myself that when Reeve talked of going out with a new girl he meant going out with. Taking out for a meal, I thought, and dancing with and taking home in a taxi and then maybe a goodnight kiss on the doorstep. Until one Sunday morning, when Reeve was coming over for lunch, I phoned him to ask if he'd meet us in the pub for a pre-lunch drink. He sounded half-asleep and I could hear a girl giggling in the background. Then I heard him say:

'Get some clothes on, lovey, and make us a cup of tea, will you? My head's splitting.'

I told Gwendolen.

'What did you expect?' she said.

'I don't know,' I said. 'I thought you'd be shocked.'

'He's very good-looking and he's only thirty-seven. It's natural.' But she had blushed a little. 'I am rather shocked,' she said. 'We don't belong in his sort of life, do we?'

And yet we remained in it, on the edge of it. As we got to know Reeve better, he put aside those small prevarications he had employed to save our feelings. And he would tell us, without shyness, anecdotes of his amorous past and present. The one about the girl who was so possessive that even though he had broken with her, she had got into his flat in his absence and been lying naked in his bed when he brought his new girl home that night; the one about the married woman who had hidden him for two hours in her wardrobe until her husband had gone out; the girl who had come to borrow a pound of sugar and had stayed all night; fair girls, dark girls, plump, thin, rich, poor ... *Purche porti la gonnella voi sapete quel che fa.*

'It's another world,' said Gwendolen.

And I said, 'How the other half lives.'

We were given to clichés of this sort. Our life was a cliché, the commonest sort of life led by middle-class people in the Western world. We had a nice detached house in one of the right suburbs, solid furniture and lifetime-lasting carpets. I had my car and she hers. I left for the office at half-past eight and returned at six. Gwendolen cleaned the house and went shopping and gave coffee mornings. In the evenings we liked to sit at home and watch television, generally going to bed at eleven. I think I was a good husband. I never forgot my wife's birthday or failed to send her roses on our anniversary or omitted to do my share of the dishwashing. And she was an excellent wife, romantically-inclined, not sensual. At any rate, she was never sensual with me.

She kept every birthday card I ever sent her, and the Valentines I sent her while we were engaged. Gwendolen was one of those women who hoard and cherish small mementoes. In a drawer of her dressing table she kept the menu card from the restaurant where we celebrated our engagement, a picture postcard of the hotel where we spent our honeymoon, every photograph of us that had ever been taken, our wedding pictures in a leather-bound album. Yes, she was an arch-romantic, and in her diffident way, with an air of daring, she would sometimes reproach Reeve for his callousness.

'But you can't do that to someone who loves you,' she said when he had announced his brutal intention of going off on holiday without telling his latest girlfriend where he was going or even that he was going at all. 'You'll break her heart.'

'Gwendolen, my love, she hasn't got a heart. Women don't have them. She has another sort of machine, a combination of telescope, lie detector, scalpel and castrating device.'

'You're too cynical,' said my wife. 'You may fall in love yourself one day and then you'll know how it feels.'

'Not necessarily. As Shaw said—' Reeve was always quoting what other writers had said ' – "Don't do unto others as you would have others do unto you, as we don't all have the same tastes."'

'We all have the same taste about not wanting to be ill-treated.'

'She should have thought of that before she tried to control my life. No, I shall quietly disappear for a while. I mightn't go away, in fact. I might just say I'm going away and lie low at home for a fortnight. Fill up the deep freeze, you know, and lay in a stock of liquor. I've done it before in this sort of situation. It's rather pleasant and I get a hell of a lot of work done.'

Gwendolen was silenced by this and, I must say, so was I. You may wonder, after these examples of his morality, just what it was I saw in Reeve. It's hard now for me to remember. Charm, perhaps, and a never-failing hospitality; a rueful way of talking about his own life as if it was all he could hope for, while mine was the ideal all men would aspire to; a helplessness about his financial affairs combined with an admiration for my grasp of them; a manner of talking to me as if we were equally men of the world, only I had chosen the better part. When invited to one of our dull modest gatherings, he would always be the exciting friend with the witty small talk, the reviver of a failing party, the industrious barman; above all, the one among our friends who wasn't an accountant, a bank manager, a solicitor, a general practitioner or a company executive. We had his books on our shelves. Our friends borrowed them and told their friends they'd met Reeve Baker at our house. He gave us a *cachet* that raised us enough centimetres above the level of the bourgeoisie to make us interesting.

Perhaps, in those days, I should have asked myself what it was he saw in us.

It was about a year ago that I first noticed a coolness between Gwendolen and Reeve. The banter they had gone in for, which had consisted in wry confessions or flirtatious compliments from him, and shy, somewhat maternal reproofs from her, stopped almost entirely. When we all three were together they talked to each other through me, as if I were their interpreter. I asked Gwendolen if he'd done something to upset her.

She looked extremely taken aback. 'What makes you ask?'

'You always seem a bit peeved with him.'

'I'm sorry,' she said. 'I'll try to be nicer. I didn't know I'd changed.'

She had changed to me too. She flinched sometimes when I touched her, and although she never refused me, there was an apathy about her love-making.

'What's the matter?' I asked her after a failure which disturbed me because it was so unprecedented.

She said it was nothing, and then, 'We're getting older. You can't expect things to be the same as when we were first married.'

'For God's sake,' I said. 'You're thirty-five and I'm thirty-nine. We're not in our dotage.'

She sighed and looked unhappy. She had become moody and difficult. Although she hardly opened her mouth in Reeve's presence, she talked about him a lot when he wasn't there, seizing upon almost any excuse to discuss him and speculate about his character. And she seemed inexplicably annoyed when, on our tenth wedding anniversary, a greetings card arrived addressed to us both from him. I, of course, had sent her roses. At the end of the week I missed a receipt for a bill I'd paid – as an accountant I'm naturally circumspect about these things – and I searched through our wastepaper basket, thinking I might have thrown it away. I found it, and I also found the anniversary card I'd sent Gwendolen to accompany the roses.

All these things I noticed. That was the trouble with me – I noticed things but I lacked the experience of life to add them up and make a significant total. I didn't have the worldly wisdom to guess why my wife was always out when I phoned her in the afternoons, or why she was forever buying new clothes. I noticed, I wondered, that was all.

I noticed things about Reeve too. For one thing, that he'd stopped talking about his girlfriends.

'He's growing up at last,' I said to Gwendolen.

She reacted with warmth, with enthusiasm. 'I really think he is.'

But she was wrong. He had only three months of what I thought of as celibacy. And then when he talked of a new girlfriend, it was to me alone. Confidentially, over a Friday night drink in the pub, he told me of this 'marvellous chick', twenty years old, he had met at a party the week before.

'It won't last, Reeve,' I said.

'I sincerely hope not. Who wants it to *last*?'

Not Gwendolen, certainly. When I told her she was incredulous, then aghast. And when I said I was sorry I'd told her since Reeve's backsliding upset her so much, she snapped at me that she didn't want to discuss him. She became even more snappy and nervous and depressed too. Whenever the phone rang she jumped. Once or twice I came home to find no wife, no dinner prepared; then she'd come in, looking haggard, to say she'd been out for a walk. I got her to see our doctor and he put her on tranquillisers which just made her more depressed.

I hadn't seen Reeve for ages. Then, out of the blue he phoned me at work to say he was off to the South of France for three weeks.

'In your state of financial health?' I said. I'd had a struggle getting him to pay the January instalment of his twice-yearly income tax, and I knew he was practically broke till he got the advance on his new book in May. 'The South of France is a bit pricey, isn't it?'

'I'll manage,' he said. 'My bank manager's one of my fans and he's let me have an overdraft.'

Gwendolen didn't seem very surprised to hear about Reeve's holiday. He'd told me he was going on his own – the 'marvellous chick' had long disappeared – and she said she thought he needed the rest, especially as there wouldn't be any of those girls to bother him, as she put it.

When I first met Reeve he'd been renting a flat but I persuaded him to buy one, for security and as an investment. The place was known euphemistically as a garden flat but it was in fact a basement, the lower ground floor of a big Victorian house in Bayswater. My usual route to work didn't take me along his street, but sometimes when the traffic was heavy I'd go through the back doubles and past his house. After he'd been away for about two weeks I happened to do this one morning and, of course, I glanced at Reeve's window. One always does glance at a friend's house, I think, when one is passing even if one knows that friend isn't at home. His bedroom was at the front, the top half of the window visible, the lower half concealed by the rise of lawn. I noticed that the curtains were drawn. Not particularly wise, I thought, an invitation to burglars, and then I forgot about it. But two mornings later I passed that way again, passed very slowly this time as there was a traffic hold-up, and again I glanced at Reeve's window. The curtains were no longer quite drawn. There was a gap about six inches wide between them. Now whatever a burglar may do, it's very unlikely he'll pull back drawn curtains. I didn't consider burglars this time. I thought Reeve must have come back early.

Telling myself I should be late for work anyway if I struggled along in this traffic jam, I parked the car as soon as I could at a meter. I'll knock on old Reeve's door, I thought, and get him to make me a cup of coffee. There was no answer. But as I looked once more at that window I was almost certain those curtains had been moved again, and in the past ten minutes. I rang the doorbell of the woman in the flat upstairs. She came down in her dressing-gown.

'Sorry to disturb you,' I said. 'But do you happen to know if Mr Baker's come back?'

'He's not coming back till Saturday,' she said.

'Sure of that?'

'Of course I'm sure,' she said rather huffily. 'I put a note through his door Monday, and if he was back he'd have come straight up for this parcel I took in for him.'

'Did he take his car, d'you know?' I said, feeling like a detective in one of my favourite crime novels.

'Of course he did. What is this? What's he done?'

I said he'd done nothing, as far as I knew, and she banged the door in my face. So I went down the road to the row of lock-up garages. I couldn't see much through the little panes of frosted glass in the door of Reeve's garage, just enough to be certain the interior wasn't empty but that the greenish blur was the body of Reeve's Fiat. And then I knew for sure. He hadn't gone away at all. I chuckled to myself as I imagined him lying low for these three weeks in his flat, living off food from the deep freeze and spending most of his time in the back regions where, enclosed as those rooms were by a courtyard with high walls, he could show lights day and night with impunity. Just wait till Saturday, I thought, and I pictured myself asking him for details of his holiday, laying little traps for him, until even he with his writer's powers of invention would have to admit he'd never been away at all.

Gwendolen was laying the table for our evening meal when I got in. She, I'd decided, was the only person with whom I'd share this joke. I got all her attention the minute I mentioned Reeve's name, but when I reached the bit about his car being in the garage she stared at me and all the colour went out of her face. She sat down, letting the bunch of knives and forks she was holding fall into her lap.

'What on earth's the matter?' I said.

'How could he be so cruel? How could he do that to anyone?'

'Oh, my dear, Reeve's quite ruthless where women are concerned. You remember, he told us he'd done it before.'

'I'm going to phone him,' she said, and I saw that she was shivering. She dialled his number and I heard the ringing tone start.

'He won't answer,' I said. 'I wouldn't have told you if I'd thought it was going to upset you.'

She didn't say any more. There were things cooking on the stove and the table was half-laid, but she left all that and went into the hall. Almost immediately afterwards I heard the front door close.

I know I'm slow on the uptake in some ways but I'm not stupid. Even a husband who trusts his wife like I trusted mine – or, rather, never considered there was any need for trust – would know, after that, that something had been going on. Nothing much, though, I told myself. A crush perhaps on her part, hero-worship which his flattery and his confidences had fanned. Naturally, she'd feel let down, betrayed, when she discovered he'd deceived her as to his whereabouts when he'd led her to believe she was a special friend and privy to all his secrets. But I went upstairs just the same to reassure myself by looking in that dressing table drawer where she kept her souvenirs. Dishonourable? I don't think so. She had never locked it or tried to keep its contents private from me.

And all those little mementoes of our first meeting, our courtship, our marriage, were still there. Between a birthday card and a Valentine I saw a pressed rose. But there too, alone in a nest made out of a lace handkerchief I had given her, were a locket and a button. The locket was one her mother had left to her, but the photograph in it, that of some long-dead unidentifiable relative, had been replaced by a cut-out of Reeve from a snapshot. On the reverse side was a lock of hair. The button I recognised as coming from Reeve's blazer, though it hadn't, I noticed, been cut off. He must have lost it in our house and she'd picked it up. The hair was Reeve's, black, wavy, here and there with a thread of grey, but again it hadn't been cut off. On one of our visits to his flat she must have combed it out of his hairbrush and twisted it into a lock.

Poor little Gwendolen... Briefly, I'd suspected Reeve. For one dreadful moment, sitting down there after she'd gone out, I'd asked myself, could he have ...? Could my best friend have ...? But no. He hadn't even sent her a letter or a flower. It had been all on her side, and for that reason – I knew where she was bound for – I must stop her reaching him and humiliating herself.

I slipped the things into my pocket with some vague idea of using them to show her how childish she was being. She hadn't taken her car. Gwendolen always disliked driving in central London. I took mine and drove to the tube station I knew she'd go to.

She came out a quarter of an hour after I got there, walking fast and glancing nervously to the right and left of her. When she saw me she gave a little gasp and stood stock-still.

'Get in, darling,' I said gently. 'I want to talk to you.'

She got in but she didn't speak. I drove down to the Bayswater Road and into the Park. There, on the Ring, I parked under the plane trees, and because she still didn't utter a word, I said:

'You mustn't think I don't understand. We've been married ten years and I daresay I'm a dull sort of chap. Reeve's exciting and different and – Well, maybe it's only natural for you to think you've fallen for him.'

She stared at me stonily. 'I love him and he loves me.'

'That's nonsense,' I said, but it wasn't the chill of the spring evening that made me shiver. 'Just because he's used that charm of his on you—'

She interrupted me. 'I want a divorce.'

'For heaven's sake,' I said. 'You hardly know Reeve. You've never been alone with him, have you?'

'Never been alone with him?' She gave a brittle, desperate laugh. 'He's been my lover for six months. And now I'm going to him. I'm going to tell him he doesn't have to hide from women any more because I'll be with him all the time.'

In the half-dark I gaped at her. 'I don't believe you,' I said, but I did. I did. 'You mean you along with all the rest ...? My wife?'

'I'm going to be Reeve's wife. I'm the only one that understands him, the only one he can talk to. He told me that just before – before he went away.'

'Only he didn't go away.' There was a great redness in front of my eyes like a lake of blood. 'You fool,' I shouted at her. 'Don't you see it's you he's hiding from, *you*? He's done this to get away from you like he's got away from all the others. Love you? He never even gave you a present, not even a photograph. If you go there, he won't let you in. You're the last person he'd let in.'

'I'm going to him,' she cried, and she began to struggle with the car door. 'I'm going to him, to live with him, and I never want to see you again!'

In the end I drove home alone. Her wish came true and she never did see me again.

When she wasn't back by eleven I called the police. They asked me to go down to the police station and fill out a Missing Persons form, but they didn't take my fear very seriously. Apparently, when a woman of Gwendolen's age disappears they take it for granted she's gone off with a man. They took it seriously all right when a park keeper found her strangled body among some bushes in the morning.

That was on the Thursday. The police wanted to know where Gwendolen could have been going so far from her home. They wanted the names and addresses of all our friends. Was there anyone we knew in Kensington or Paddington or Bayswater, anywhere in the vicinity of the Park? I said there was no one. The next day they asked me again and I said, as if I'd just remembered:

'Only Reeve Baker. The novelist, you know.' I gave them his address. 'But he's away on holiday, has been for three weeks. He's not coming home till tomorrow.'

What happened after that I know from the evidence given at Reeve's trial, his trial for the murder of my wife. The police called on him on Saturday morning. I don't think they suspected him at all at first. My reading of crime fiction has taught me they would have asked him for any information he could give about our private life.

Unfortunately for him, they had already talked to some of his neighbours. Reeve had led all these people to think he had really gone away. The milkman and the paper boy were both certain he had been away. So when the police questioned him about that, and he knew just why they were questioning him, he got into a panic. He didn't dare say he'd been in France. They could have shown that to be false without the least trouble. Instead, he told the truth and said he'd been lying low to escape the attentions of a woman. Which woman? He wouldn't say, but the woman in the flat upstairs would. Time and time again she had seen Gwendolen visit him in the afternoons, had heard them quarrelling, Gwendolen protesting her love for him and he shouting that he wouldn't be controlled, that he'd do anything to escape her possessiveness.

He had, of course, no alibi for the Wednesday night. But the judge and the jury could see he'd done his best to arrange one. Novelists are apt to let their imaginations run away with them; they don't realise how astute and thorough the police are. And there was firmer evidence of his guilt even than that. Three main exhibits were produced in the court: Reeve's blazer with a button missing from the sleeve; that very button; a cluster of his hairs. The button had been found by Gwendolen's body and the hairs on her coat ...

My reading of detective stories hadn't been in vain, though I haven't read one since then. People don't, I suppose, after a thing like that.

June Thomson

June Thomson has long been recognised as one of our leading crime writers. She first achieved fame through her series of novels about Inspector Finch and in recent years she has produced splendid collections of Sherlockian pastiches together with a biographical study of Holmes and Watson. June's fans will be delighted to learn that, after quite a hiatus, a new Finch book is currently in the works. In the meantime, I hope her latest short story will keep them entertained.

COMING HOME

by June Thomson

I hadn't thought about Ashdene for years. There was, after all, no reason why I should. I'd left the village in 1946 when I was ten, not long after the end of the war when my father was demobbed from the army. He was offered a job in Ilford and so we moved from our brick and stone cottage to a suburban semi with a proper bathroom.

For a time I missed the fields and the wide, open skies of rural Essex. But I'm not by nature nostalgic and my new life soon blotted out those old memories. I grew up, went to university, married, moved to London, had children and eventually was widowed. Ashdene never entered my head until a few weeks ago.

I had gone to stay for the weekend with my son and his family in Cambridge and was driving back to London on the M11. Not far from Bishop's Stortford, the traffic, which had been moving quite normally until then, began to slow up and within a mile had practically come to a halt.

It was a hot, late afternoon in July and, after an exasperating quarter of an hour spent crawling forward a few yards before grinding again to a complete standstill, I decided to leave the motorway at the next exit and take to the minor roads. I was certain that, by making a detour to the left, I could eventually rejoin the M11 at the Harlow junction at which point I hoped the bottleneck would have cleared.

I set off along the A120, the road to Great Dunmow, which I realised after a few miles was taking me too far to the east, so I turned off again into a network of minor byways which led, I discovered later, through a part of Essex known as the Rodings, named after the cluster of such villages as Margaret Roding, Abbess Roding and so on.

I drove slowly, enjoying the peace of the countryside after the hubbub of the motorway, and admiring the blond fields of corn and the grass verges rich with wild flowers, the names of some of which I remembered from my own country childhood – cow parsley, ragged robin, ladies' bedstraw. Through the open windows of the car, I caught, too, scents which were also familiar but which were buried deeper in my subconsciousness and which brought with them a yearning similar to homesickness though not so clearly defined.

Even then I didn't think of Ashdene. I only recalled in a half-realised fashion other cornfields like those I was passing and for a moment caught again the rich, dusty scent of ripe wheat and the rasp of dry stalks against my bare legs.

I should have been prepared for what happened soon afterwards. The names of the Roding Villages should have given me at least a clue but I had not made the connection. After all, I was only ten when I had left and, in those days, not having a car, we had always taken the bus in the other direction to Chelmsford on those rare occasions we travelled out of the village.

I had drawn up at a crossroads to read the names on a signpost which stood on a small triangle of grass in the middle, it seemed, of nowhere. I was hoping to find the direction to Harlow. I had now come nearly ten miles out of my way and had begun to think that I ought soon to turn right and rejoin the M11.

Harlow was not signposted. The arm to the left led to Beauchamp Roding, to the right Little Laver. Straight ahead, down a road even narrower than the one along which I had come, lay a place the name of which I read but did not at first properly register.

Ashdene.

It was like coming face to face with someone I thought was a stranger and then, a moment later, realising with a shock of recognition that it was a friend from the past whom I had not seen for years and thought I had forgotten.

I could, of course, have turned to the right and continued on my way to Harlow which must lie in that direction. Instead, almost instinctively, like a bird making for its nest, I drove straight on.

If I had hoped for instant recollection, a sense of homecoming, I was disappointed. The fields, the woods, the occasional cottage or farmhouse were unfamiliar. In fact, I had still recognised nothing when I came to the name of Ashdene in black letters on a white-painted sign planted low down on the grass verge to my left. It was at this point that I decided to park the car and walk the rest of the way. Perhaps on foot I'd more easily recollect certain landmarks which in the car, with my attention largely fixed on the road ahead, I might miss. So, a little further on, I drew the car on to the verge, locked it and set off towards the village.

Almost at once, I had a sense of familiarity. In much the same way as I had recalled the scrape of corn-stalks against my legs, I remembered the drag of this particular hill as I had toiled up it as a child, longing for the moment when I would turn the corner and see the houses and the village school in front of me and the oblong tower of the church, like a beacon, rising above its surrounding trees.

Recollection now came quickly. There on the left was the big chestnut tree which as children we had stoned in order to bring down the conkers. And a little further on, round the corner and to the right, there would be a narrow lane which led nowhere except to a single clapboarded cottage, painted over with some dull black substance, pitch perhaps or creosote, to keep out the damp. It had seemed sinister to me as a child, like the house of a wicked witch or the big bad wolf. But in fact it was occupied by no one more frightening than Fancy Nancy and her father.

Although I could not recall their surname, her name came back to me instantly as if it had been lying quietly at the back of my mind all those years waiting to be resurrected.

Fancy Nancy. That's what we children used to call her because of her bright ginger hair and her scarlet lipstick and the way she used to look sideways at the men, even the married ones, her upper lip lifting eagerly to show her teeth and gums.

She was no better than she ought to be, according to the grown-ups, who predicted a bad end for her, just like her mother who had run off with the baker's roundsman, leaving three-year-old Nancy with her father.

As usual, the adults were right. During the war, Fancy Nancy had also run away, in her case with a soldier they said she'd been meeting in Chelmsford on her Saturday afternoons off.

It was the talk of the village at the time, how she used to come home on the last bus with love bites on her neck.

'Good riddance to bad rubbish,' the women said darkly. 'Although, you mark my words, she'll come slinking back here one of these days with a baby, expecting her father to take her in.'

But she never did come back and, after a while, the police stopped calling to ask questions and Fancy Nancy was no longer a topic of conversation.

As for her father, he stayed on in the cottage and was rarely seen about the village except cycling slowly to and from Chitty's farm where he worked as a cowman. He never spoke. He never even raised his head to acknowledge anyone else's presence. It was as if none of us existed.

I assumed he was dead by now. At the time Fancy Nancy ran away, he must have been in his forties which would mean he was in his nineties if he were still alive; not impossible, of course, but not very likely.

Yet for some odd reason, I imagined the cottage would still be there. Houses seemed more permanent than people. I was therefore taken aback when, having turned the corner near the top of the hill, I saw that not only had the cottage disappeared but the lane as well. In their places were now a hard-surfaced cul-de-sac, named Church View, and a double row of bungalows, three a side, each with its own integral garage and satellite dish.

It was an unsettling moment and I was relieved when, a little further on, I came to the entrance drive to Ashdene Hall on the crest of the hill and within sight of the village. That at least was still standing and appeared relatively unchanged. The garden, however, looked neglected and the house itself seemed empty. An estate agent's 'Sold' sign which stood by the gate suggested it had recently changed hands, although the new owners had not yet moved in.

Seeing the place with adult eyes, I realised it was a charming example of a Regency house, elegant and beautifully proportioned. As a child, I had thought of it only as 'the big house' where the two ladies lived. At that moment, as if my memory was now working quite freely, I suddenly recalled not only their appearances but also their names. The short, dark one with the cropped hair and the sharp, fox-terrier features was Miss Kay, the plump, fair one who smiled a great deal was Mrs Collinson.

The Ashdene Hall ladies, as they were often referred to, were something of a mystery in the village, largely because they were hardly ever seen except on occasions being driven past in their big, black car, by the chauffeur, Maurice, whose name I only heard of later. Apart from him, there was a married couple who acted as cook and gardener; obviously foreign because of their olive skin and black hair but whose names and exact nationality were unknown.

All of this tended to make the household a centre of curiosity. What was the exact connection between the two ladies who looked too dissimilar to be related? And, more suspiciously, what was their relationship with the chauffeur?

The adults always dropped their voices at this point but from the occasional word or phrase I could piece together what they were saying. Mrs Collinson was presumably a widow; at least, there was no Mr Collinson about. The other one was apparently not married. And then there was *him*, so young and good-looking, just like Douglas Fairbanks with that little, dark moustache of his. Well, it made you wonder, didn't it?

After she left school at fourteen, Fancy Nancy went to work for them to help with the cooking and cleaning and, if the village women hadn't considered it demeaning to question her directly, they might have learned a lot about the Ashdene Hall ladies. As for Fancy Nancy, she paid the women back for their contempt by saying nothing about her employers and if anyone had the temerity to refer to them, she merely shrugged and lifted her upper lip in a sly, provocative smile.

Eventually, quite by chance, I was to learn more about the Ashdene Hall ladies than anyone else in the village, with the exception of Fancy Nancy. I was about seven when it happened. I had gone to pick blackberries in the field behind our house where the hedges were full of ripe, black fruit.

I was about half-way down the field when I heard whimpering and, searching about, I found a little liver and white spaniel caught up in the brambles. I knew it came from Ashdene Hall because I had seen Maurice taking it for walks whenever he went to the village shop to buy cigarettes. I assumed it was Mrs Collinson's. Miss Kay looked too sharp and impatient to own a pet dog; certainly not a spaniel.

After I had freed it from the hedge, I slipped the belt of my dress through its collar and, abandoning the pudding basin half-full of blackberries, I set off to walk to Ashdene Hall through the fields. My decision not to go back to the house to tell my mother where I was going was quite deliberate. I knew what would happen if I did. She would give me all kinds of instructions about remembering my manners and not staying too long but this would be nothing to the cross-examination I'd be put through when I got home. Who did I see? One of the ladies or that chauffeur of theirs? Did I go into the house? What was it like?

I cut back on to the road through the gateway leading from the paddock which lay directly behind Ashdene Hall. It was part of the grounds of the house and was probably meant for grazing the family horses when the house was first built. But nobody used it except for some of the local children, usually boys, who sneaked in there occasionally to collect frogspawn from the pond. My mother had forbidden me to go anywhere near it. It was too dangerous, she said. The banks were steep and the water too deep. Later on, the ladies had some workmen in to fence it off with barbed wire and to put up a 'Trespassers Will Be Prosecuted' notice, so I suppose they were aware of the boys' incursions and the danger the pond was to children.

I remember standing for a few seconds at the gate, as I was now doing, looking up the gravelled drive towards the house. On that occasion, I'd had to gather up my courage to approach it and, if the little dog, realising it was safely home, had not tugged eagerly at its improvised lead, I might have turned away. But now there was nothing to stop me. The house was empty and there was no one about.

I took the same route I had taken all those years before, not up to the front door but round to the back of the house. In the village, no one except strangers or the vicar ever came to people's front doors, which were usually kept locked and bolted.

As on that earlier occasion, I found myself in the cobbled yard with outbuildings and stables grouped round it and, at the far end, a high brick wall with a wooden door set into it.

The chauffeur was there, I remember, hosing down the black car. Or, at least, that was what he was supposed to be doing. In fact, his attention was not on the car but on Fancy Nancy who was standing beside him, a laundry basket balanced on one hip. She was wearing a blue, button-through dress with white piping, a maid's uniform, I suppose, and the colour accentuated the redness of her hair which burnt like flames in the autumn sunlight.

I stood there overcome with a form of stage-fright so extreme that I was incapable of either speech or movement. Partly it was timidity at finding myself in this unfamiliar situation. What should I do? What should I say?

But mostly it was caused by an awareness of some alien and dangerous energy which fizzed and crackled between the two of them like an unseen current and which brought with it a whiff of forbidden delights.

I might have stood there indefinitely because they were too absorbed in one another to notice me. The sound of running water which was carelessly pouring over the car and sluicing away across the cobblestones covered up the little whining noises the dog made in its pleasure at being home although it seemed subdued as if, like me, it was unsure how to behave.

Whether the dog's whimpering finally caught Maruice's attention I do not know, but he looked across at me and instantaneously that current was switched off. With the same abruptness, he dismissed Fancy Nancy with a curt gesture of his head. She left immediately, disappearing through the wooden door in the yard wall which led, I assumed, to some part of the garden where washing could be hung.

Turning off the tap, Maurice came to stand over me. There was a jaunty, swashbuckling air about him which I found intimidating. Even the dog seemed affected by it for it crouched low on the ground in a submissive manner, squirming forward on its belly as if uncertain of its welcome.

'So you've found 'er,' Maurice said. 'I've been out twice lookin' for 'er, the stupid little bitch. Mrs Collinson's nearly gone off 'er 'ead.'

I had never been so close to him before and the proximity of his physical presence was overpowering. There was, too, a strange glitter about him. His eyes and each separate hair on his head shone while his lips below the neat dark moustache had a red brilliance as if the blood was pulsing just below the skin.

As I stood there, still tongue-tied, he assumed control, picking up the dog and shoving it roughly under one arm before, releasing the belt of my dress from its collar, he handed it back to me with a wink.

'Come on,' he said. 'I'd better take you both to see the missus. As for you,' he added, rapping the spaniel hard on the top of its head with his knuckles, 'you ought to be in the dog-house, the trouble you've bleedin' well caused.'

Grinning at his own joke, he led the way into the house through the back door.

I have no memory now of the route we took. All I can recall is entering a large room full of sunlight sparkling on shiny surfaces and the two ladies sitting having tea in front of a log fire.

Miss Kay remained seated, watching with an expression of amusement on her sharp little face as Mrs Collinson jumped to her feet in a flurry of skirts and bangles.

'Oh, Maurice!' she cried. It was the first time I'd heard his name. 'You've found my darling Flora!'

Taking the dog, she cradled it like a baby, letting it lick her face in an ecstasy of joy and love.

'Not me, ma'am,' Maurice said. 'It was this young lady 'ere as brought 'er back.'

Young as I was, I realised how his manner had changed in front of the two ladies. That swaggering look had been replaced by a much more deferential air.

'How perfectly sweet of you!' Mrs Collinson exclaimed,

addressing me in a tone of voice I had never heard before except on the wireless. 'You must have some reward, my dear. Dorothy, take a five-pound note from my bag, there's a darling.'

It was more money than I had ever been given before, even on my birthdays or at Christmas, but in the end it turned out to be something of an albatross. I didn't want to tell my mother about the afternoon's events, not on account of the two ladies but because of Maurice and Fancy Nancy. Without knowing why, I realised that what I had seen should be kept a secret. So the five-pound note remained hidden in the bottom of a drawer until, not long before we moved from Ashdene, I found the courage to change it in a shop in Chelmsford and to spend it guiltily little by little over the next few weeks.

I'm not sure exactly when Fancy Nancy ran away. I have the feeling that it was not long after the incident with the dog but I can't be sure. The past has a tendency to telescope in upon itself so that one event seems to follow closely on another. I only know that, after she had gone, I associated her disappearance with the occasion I had seen her going out of the stable-yard through the wooden door at the far end with the laundry basket on one hip and the sunlight glistening on her red hair.

On a more rational level, I knew this couldn't be the case. According to the gossip, she had last been seen on a Saturday afternoon, her half-day off, waiting for the twenty past one bus into Chelmsford. She failed to return home that night and the following morning her father reported her missing.

The police made enquiries. I remember one coming to our house and my mother sending me out into the garden so that I wouldn't overhear what was said. But it was common knowledge that she hadn't been on the last bus home from Chelmsford that evening.

The search was finally called off and it was assumed that the gossip was true and that she'd run off with a soldier she'd been meeting on the sly. There was an army camp at Swanham and a couple of American airbases only a few miles away.

Again, I can't be sure of the exact timing but I think it was in the same year that Maurice was called up into the army and the Ashdene Hall ladies, together with the married couple, moved out of the village, some said to Wales, others to Devon. It was assumed they couldn't manage without a chauffeur and, besides, petrol was rationed. Nothing was heard of any of them again and, for the remainder of the war, the house was taken over by some military organisation which no one knew anything about.

The memory of that last occasion when I had stood in the yard and, in particular, the image of Fancy Nancy disappearing through the wooden door into, it seemed, oblivion, prompted me to walk towards it to see what lay on the other side.

It was a kitchen garden with overgrown vegetable beds and fruit trees at the far end. A washing-line, perhaps the same one Fancy Nancy had used, sagged disconsolately between two wooden posts. Beyond the trees was a high hedge with a gap in it which must lead, I assumed, into the paddock behind the house.

The sound of men's voices coming from the other side of the hedge caught my attention and I went towards the gap, curious to find out what they were doing on these otherwise deserted premises.

They were cleaning out the pond, no doubt on the orders of the new owner, using grappling hooks attached to ropes which they threw out into the water before dragging them to the edge. Already the bank was littered with dead branches, an old car seat and a tangle of barbed wire.

A yellow van parked nearby with 'Thornton's Landscape Gardening' and a telephone number painted on its side suggested that, once the pond was cleaned out, the site would become a feature of the grounds, stocked perhaps with fish and planted with water lilies.

I had no intention of going over to talk to them. It was none of my business and I had begun to turn away when one of the men gave a shout. There was a horrified urgency in his voice and, like a fool, I turned back to look.

His colleague had dropped his own rope and was helping the other man to drag something to the bank. At first, I could not understand the horror. It appeared to be nothing more than a crudely wrapped bundle, like an old carpet, tied round with wire to which were attached several pieces of heavy, rusty metal. And then I saw the feet sticking out at one end; or at least, the bones of feet, partly dismembered. At the other end, a skull emerged, discoloured by the black slime of mud and decayed leaves. Water poured from its nose and eye sockets.

I backed away, leaving the men to their gruesome task of lifting the dreadful bundle on to the bank.

There was no doubt in my mind whose body it was and who had murdered her. She hadn't come home from Chelmsford on the last bus so someone must have brought her back in a car and the only likely person who had the use of a vehicle was Maurice. The motive, too, seemed perfectly straightforward. She had become a liability, perhaps even a danger: the old story of the pregnant girlfriend who demanded marriage or threatened to ruin him by telling her father or the police. She was, after all, under-age.

My only uncertainty concerned the two ladies. Had they known of the plan? Or had they acted as accessories after the murder, helping him to cover up the crime because their own relationship with him was, as the local women had hinted, not the sort they'd want made public? Although I couldn't remember the date, the construction of the barbed wire fence round the pond seemed now to take on a new significance.

I walked quickly back to the car and drove away in the direction from which I had come without going into the village. It was pointless to get involved. There would be people still living in Ashdene who could give a better account than I of Fancy Nancy, Maurice and the two ladies. And besides, it was all so long ago that it seemed futile to try uncovering the truth when most of the participants were, like Fancy Nancy, probably dead.

I have never again attempted to return to Ashdene and I know now I never will. To me, it is simply a place I once knew long ago. Fancy Nancy may have come home but I no longer feel the least desire to follow her example.

Alison White

Like several other contributors to this book, Alison White is a member of the new generation of crime fiction authors. Her first story, a historical mystery, appeared in last year's CWA anthology, *Past Crimes*, and she recently wrote a contemporary tale for a book put together by members of the CWA's Northern Chapter, *Northern Blood 3*. 'A Busy Afternoon' is perhaps the most chilling story so far to come from the pen of a writer of whom much more, I am sure, will be heard in the future.

A BUSY AFTERNOON

by Alison White

'Will you come then? On Saturday?'
 'I've told you. There's lots of things I'm supposed to do on Saturday. People expect me.'
 'I'm a person too. Don't I count as one of the people?'
 She laughed. He could be very persuasive.
 'Please? You know how much it means to me.'
 'I'm not supposed to. And I don't want to let anyone down.'
 'You won't. Just for an hour then. Besides,' he said, smiling, 'Who's going to know?'

At half-past two, Ernest went into the kitchen and got the tray ready. The best china cups, saucers and plates. Then he got Helen's favourite biscuits out of the cupboard. He always had his grandchildren's favourites in. Not that Kim and David came much. He had to watch the sell-by dates on the packets he bought for them. Helen was different though. She was reliable. Good thing too. Her favourites were coconut marshmallows. They didn't keep as long as the others. Not once they were opened anyway.

Of course she'd roll her eyes in exasperation when she saw the tray all laid out and tut-tut about it. The way fifteen-year-olds could. But she'd enjoy them, that was for sure. She usually ate them the same way too. Nibbling half-way down each side and then saving the jam in the middle for the end. Sucking stray bits of coconut off her fingers. Ernest loved to watch children eat their favourite foods. There was a concentration and a delight that couldn't be matched. She'd be here soon.

*

A BUSY AFTERNOON

'I always go to Grandad's on my way back from shopping.'

'Lucky Grandad.'

'And Mum will have my tea ready for me. I usually rush in, eat and then dash out again. I'm going to the pictures. Just with my friends.'

He sighed. 'Lucky friends.'

She laughed. He was funny. And persistent. 'Actually . . .'

'What?'

'Grandad doesn't live that far from you . . .'

'Was it expensive?' Rosemary reluctantly held the front door open so her ex-husband could come inside the home they'd once shared.

'Not so bad. Don't worry, I'll take care of it.' He handed her the car keys. 'It needed a new clutch. It's probably my bad driving that did it anyway.'

'You've not driven it for a long time,' she said quietly. 'Could I pay you in instalments?' She didn't want to feel indebted any more than necessary.

'I've told you, forget it.' He didn't look at her. A year apart hadn't made things any easier between them. She was still bitter and had every right to be, he supposed. But from what he could gather, she kept her feelings to herself. Certainly Helen never gave any hint that she'd been badmouthing him when he saw her.

'Where's Helen?'

'It's Saturday afternoon. Where do you think she is?' She glared at him. Obviously he was as interested in their family routines as ever.

'Just asking. How is your dad anyway?'

'The same.'

He perched on the edge of the settee, trying to think of something else to say and failing. 'I'll be off, then. I'm not seeing Helen till next Sunday. She's doing some sort of skating thing tomorrow?' He frowned, trying to remember the details.

'Rollerblading,' Rosemary said. 'It's the latest thing. To be honest,' she smiled faintly, 'I think she's got her eye on someone. That's why she's so keen all of a sudden.'

He nodded. 'Well, I suppose it had to happen. She is fifteen. I used to wonder how I'd feel when she brought boyfriends home. Thinking I'd sit there with my arms folded and give them the third degree.'

'Well, that's one embarrassment she'll be spared, then. You don't live at home any more, do you?'

She glanced at her watch. Plenty of time. She'd finished shopping early and it didn't really matter that she shouldn't be there. Like he'd said, who would know? She was smiling as she rang the doorbell, and he was too when he answered.

'You came.'
'You knew I would.'
'Yes, I did.'
She laughed and followed him inside.

Rosemary waved half-heartedly as John left. She shouldn't have made that cheap jibe about him not living there any more. Didn't even know why she had. It wasn't as though it made her feel any better. She watched from the front door as he walked down the road, hands deep in his pockets, head bent. So familiar. And so not a part of her life any more. Except to do the residue of his duties for now, like fixing the car. Or taking their daughter out, when rollerblading didn't get in the way.

Helen. She'd promised to iron her blue top for her. She wanted to wear it to the pictures tonight. Sighing, Rosemary hung the car keys up on the hook in the kitchen and set up the ironing board.

'Isn't this lovely?' *She smiled and turned back to face him.*
'I'm glad you like it. I wanted to make it special for you.'
She blushed and put down her bag. 'Shall I sit down then?'
'Please do. Sit by me.' *He patted the seat beside him.* 'You've had a busy afternoon, haven't you?'
'It's not over yet.' *There was something a bit different about him today. She wasn't sure what it was.*

'I'm glad you managed to fit me in.' He was smiling at her. 'I wanted to make today nice for you.'

'You have. You are.'

'Good. So nice . . .' He smiled again. '. . . that you never wanted to leave.'

Rosemary had to treat Helen's top with a stain remover, but it seemed to have worked at last. Then she'd rinsed it where the mark was and ironed it again. It was on the hanger now, waiting for her to come home. Of course it would have been helpful if Helen had thought to mention the stain, but that was teenagers for you. And she was a good girl really.

Time was marching on. Normally Helen was home by now. She must be coming on the later bus. So she put the kettle on, convinced that by the time the tea had brewed, her daughter would be with her, kicking off her shoes, rubbing her feet and telling her all about her day. Before the mad rush for her evening out.

'It's been lovely,' Helen said with a sigh. 'But I really have to go.'

'No. Not yet.'

'I've got to. I told you, I'm going out and—'

'Not just yet. Soon. There's something I want to show you first. Please?'

There was a plea in his eyes as well as his voice. 'All right,' she said. 'What is it?'

He smiled and took hold of her hand, 'Close your eyes. I want it to be a surprise.'

Rosemary's second cup of tea was cold. Helen hadn't been on the next bus. Or the one after that. And it was growing dark outside. She didn't want to draw the curtains over. She wanted to keep them open so that she'd see her daughter when she came walking down the road. Well, running now probably, because she was late. It couldn't be that the buses hadn't turned up, because she'd seen them herself at the top of the road. It must be something else that was delaying her. But what?

If John was here still, he'd tell her to stop flapping. That she was being silly, that Helen was fifteen and was probably just chatting with her friends somewhere. But he wasn't here to say that. Besides, she was meeting up with her friends later. Not this afternoon.

The phone rang and she snatched at it. It was Stacey, Helen's best friend from school. Something about the arrangements for tonight.

'She's not back yet, Stacey. I'll take a message, shall I?'

Rosemary forced herself to sound cheerful. She knew it was ridiculous to worry like this. It was Saturday afternoon, for heaven's sake. Helen went out every Saturday and did the same things. So what if she was a bit late? She was hardly the type of girl who'd get into a stranger's car or anything. Was she?

'Oh.' Stacey's disappointment was obvious. 'I just wondered if I could borrow something, that's all. Can you get her to ring me when she gets in then?'

'No problem,' Rosemary said. Then couldn't stop herself. 'Stacey?'

'Mmm?'

'Helen didn't mention doing anything different this afternoon, did she? Only she's usually back by now. I wondered if she'd arranged to see a boy in town or anything.'

There was a long pause.

'If she did, then she didn't tell me,' Stacey said at last. 'Maybe she's just chatting at her grandad's. Or doing a job for him. You will get her to ring me, won't you?'

'I will,' Rosemary promised, 'as soon as she comes home.'

'Well, I've seen it now.' Helen shivered. It was cold down there. Damp too. 'You've done wonders, you really have.'

'Do you like it?'

'Mmm. But I've got to go now. I did tell you—'

'I know you did. Oh.' He turned his head. 'Someone's at the door. Won't be a minute.'

'I'll come with—'

But he'd gone. Quickly. Closing the door behind him. Honestly. She'd told him she had to go. She shouldn't even be here anyway and felt bad about deceiving people, but had known it was important to him. She'd managed to get here, hadn't she? Didn't that prove she cared?

She went up the steps that took her to the cellar door and reached for the handle. But before she could reach it, she heard him turn the key in the lock.

'Could I speak to John, please?' Rosemary smarted with humiliation as the woman who had stolen her husband went to bring him to the phone.

'Rosie? What is it? The car?'

'No.' Hearing his voice, she couldn't keep the strain out of her own. Not now.

'What then?'

'It's Helen. It's half-past six and she's normally back by five. She's meeting her friends in half an hour, supposedly. I mean, she's not left herself enough time to eat or anything . . .'

She heard him take in a breath, as though willing himself to be patient with her. 'It's all right,' she heard him say in the background to the woman he'd left her for.

'Sorry, Rosie, but don't you think you're getting worked up about nothing?'

'No – '

'Maybe she's running an errand for your dad. You know what she's like for trying to help people.'

'John . . .'

'What?'

'I've just spoken to Dad. Helen hasn't been there all afternoon. Now will you listen to me? She's never missed going there, has she? Not once. There's something wrong, I just know it. The buses are running fine, so it's not that. She's just . . . disappeared.'

*

Helen wasn't sure how long she'd been asleep. Or why she'd slept. Not down here where it was freezing cold, and still, unmistakably, a cellar, however nice he'd tried to make it.

She sat up and rubbed her eyes. There was a blanket over her. A big checked one, slightly scratchy. Like a car rug. She hadn't noticed it before. He must have been back down here then, maybe put it over her. What was going on?

She tried to stand up but her legs felt a bit funny. She stretched out her arms, she'd been squashed on the sofa bed and felt achy. There was a crick in her neck too. Focusing more clearly now, she saw a fancy screen was around her makeshift bed. She remembered the screens. He'd told her they were Japanese.

There was a chest in the corner. On top of it was a tray with a glass of water and she was about to drink it, when she stopped short. Perhaps he'd drugged her and that's why she felt like this. She couldn't drink it, then. She'd just have to wait. She'd have to stay alert and as soon as he came back in, then she'd have to get past him.

Maybe it was just a game. But she didn't want to play. She wanted to go home.

'Why don't you ring round her friends to begin with,' the police officer said. 'See if they've got any ideas.'

'She's supposed to be meeting them now,' Rosemary said. 'But she always comes home first.'

'Maybe she's gone straight there.' The officer was kind, but not unduly worried at this stage. He had a teenage daughter himself who was in a world of her own.

'My husband's gone to the cinema, to see if she has,' Rosemary said. She'd had to talk him into it, but he'd agreed in the end.

'And he'll give her a piece of his mind if he finds her, eh? Well, why don't you give me a ring back if she's not there, and we'll see what's what. I'm sure she'll turn up. They usually do.'

There was one last year that hadn't, Rosemary remembered. And not far from here. Katy something. But then maybe the policeman was right. It was just that, as a parent, the missing ones were what stuck in your mind. You didn't think about the hundreds of times teenagers worried their parents by being late, or wandering off to do their own thing for a while. But Helen was a sensible girl. Wasn't she?

'This is emotional blackmail.' Liz stood with her arms folded as John tied his shoelaces. 'You've already been over there once today with the car. How long's she going to lay this guilt trip on you?'

'It's Helen, Liz. It's nothing to do with Rosie. Not really. She's right. Helen is very reliable. Every Saturday, it's shopping, Grandad's, then home and out with her friends.'

'And she's growing up.'

'And she's my daughter. Who's not where she's supposed to be. I'll just check she's not gone straight to the cinema.'

'Why can't Rosemary do that?'

'She wants to stay by the phone in case Helen rings.'

Liz groaned. 'If she was in trouble and couldn't get her mother, she'd phone here, wouldn't she? Are you going to do this every time she's a bit late?'

John hesitated. 'I have to check it out, Liz. It's just not like her.'

'Helen? Are you awake? Helen?'

He was knocking on the door. She went over as quietly as she could but he heard.

'You are! Oh good. Are you feeling better now? I'm sorry you were so sleepy before.'

'What did you give me?'

'Don't be annoyed.' He sounded sad. And she heard him dragging something, a chair, across the floor, breathing heavily.

'Why not?'

'Helen,' he gasped, short of breath as he sat down. 'I had to make you sleep. You would have just gone otherwise. I didn't want you to go.'

'I came, didn't I?' She couldn't keep the sob out of her voice. 'I promised I would and I did.'

'But you might not have come back, you see. I need you with me.

Helen, you must believe that I don't want to hurt you. But I don't want you to go.'

'You can't keep me here for ever.'

He sighed. 'There's some food for you. I left it before. In a cardboard box on the chair. See it? It's all stuff you like.'

She banged on the door with her fist. 'I don't want it. I want to go home.'

'You can't go home, Helen. You can't ever go home. But you must eat.'

'I won't.'

He sighed heavily. 'You've got to, Helen. She didn't eat so I lost her.'

'Who?'

'That wasn't what I wanted. It really wasn't. All I want is for someone to talk to me. I enjoy your company, Helen. You know that. That's why you came today. I've got lots of food in that you'll like. And I'll take care of you. I know it's not what you planned, but you'll get used to it. You'll like it, I promise. You enjoy helping people, don't you? And you know you're helping me. We'll be fine.'

She heard him get up slowly, then push the chair back against the wall. She couldn't see through the keyhole, he'd put some tape over it. It was still locked.

'Maybe you could give us a recent photograph? Just so's we've got it ready.' The police officer smiled kindly at Rosemary and John, sitting side by side on the sofa. 'And we can run through some details. Probably we'll do all that and she'll walk through the door.'

'I hope so,' said Rosemary.

'You checked out the boyfriend, you say?' The officer looked at John.

'Her friend told me there was a boy she liked. Someone she saw at rollerblading. She knew where he lived, so I went round there. He's been at home all day with a stomach bug. I don't think I made myself popular with his parents. I guess I'll have to apologise. But Stacey – her friend – said there was no one else she'd go off with. I don't understand it. It's just not Helen to do something like this.'

'Even her friends are worried now,' Rosemary said. 'They didn't bother going to the pictures.'

'Well, we can speak to them,' the officer soothed. 'And the boy.'

The phone rang and Rosemary snatched at it. Then shook her head at the two men looking at her expectantly.

'I know,' she said quietly into the mouthpiece. 'And I'm sorry, Dad. No, she's not home yet. Well, I'm sure she'll be back soon. Look, can I maybe ring you later?'

'Rosie's dad,' John explained to the police. 'Crotchety old bastard. Hates everybody. And not many are keen on him either. Helen still goes there every Saturday. Says she thinks he's just lonely and he'd miss her if she didn't. He does nothing but moan though. Doesn't so much as make her a cup of tea. Usually he has a list of jobs for her to do when she gets there. But she does them. That's the kind of girl she is.' He looked away then, feeling choked up. Where the hell was she?

'But she didn't go there today?'

'No. And he's been moaning about it. Doesn't occur to him that we're worried about her. All he's bothered about is she promised to sew on some buttons for him. That's the third time he's phoned.'

Helen was shivering. She was only wearing her thin blouse and skirt. Her coat was in the house somewhere. She didn't want to eat his stupid food. What if he'd put something in it again? She wanted him to open the door, so she could get out. He'd only managed to trap her here because he'd drugged her somehow. But what had he meant before? He'd said 'she' hadn't eaten and so he'd lost her. Who was 'she'?

Helen fought the tears that threatened to come and tried to think rationally. It didn't make sense that he could have kept someone else down here. People died if they didn't eat. And what would he do with them then? No, he was just trying to frighten her.

He'd made it like a little home down here. A couple of screens partitioning it off. Cushions, comfy chairs and a sofa bed. A table with a lamp on. He'd tried to make it cosy.

For the first time, she became aware of a humming noise. An electrical hum, and she stepped behind a screen and saw a freezer. One of those big chest freezers like they had in supermarkets. How much food did he have stashed away? How long was he planning to keep her there?

She opened the lid, then screamed at what she saw. There was no frozen food inside. Just the very dead body of another young girl.

Ernest sat in his living-room, the tray wth china cups and saucers still on the table in front of him. She'd left a couple of biscuits earlier on. He'd finish them off now. She certainly wouldn't be eating them today anyway, he'd just heard her scream. Which must mean she'd found Katy. That was a shame. But at his age, he could hardly move a body, could he? That's where the freezer had been useful.

Sadly, he licked the coconut from his fingers as he finished the last biscuit. He could see why she liked them so much.

Of course, Katy was very different to Helen. And he'd try and explain that to her when she'd calmed down. Katy had been after his money. She had a paper round and he'd asked her to do a little job for him for a pound or two. She was quite happy to do that. But she didn't want to be there just for the pleasure of his company.

'I thought you had something for me to do,' she'd moaned another time when he'd asked her in after her round. 'You can get kids to come and just sit round with the elderly, you know, if you want. Adopt a grandad or something. I've got work to do.'

He'd been hurt. Shocked even. All this time, she'd done odd things round the house for him with a smile that he thought was for him. Not for his cash.

So he'd asked her to look in the cellar and bring up a box of photos for him. Then he'd locked her in.

He sat for hours outside the door trying to explain that he just wanted to be friends, and she should think more about helping people, rather than just making money. But she hadn't listened.

When he was sure Katy slept, he'd left her food. He couldn't risk going in there when she was awake. At his age, and with her temperament, she might rush at him and overpower him. He'd popped some sleeping pills in the water he left for her too.

But she didn't eat. Not for ages. Days. Longer. And after a while she stopped whimpering. She stopped making any noise at all. And so Ernest stopped talking to her. There was no point.

He'd been sad, the way it had turned out. It wasn't the way he'd planned things. All he wanted was for someone to talk to. And it had taken him for ever to get her body into the freezer. Once, he could have lifted a little thing like her easily. But at his age, it was a different matter. Still, he'd done it in the end.

Helen was a different matter though. Katy had been right about schoolkids visiting the elderly. He'd found out the local school did it and got himself on the list. Then he'd got Helen. He loved her visits. She was always on time. Enjoying tea and biscuits with him and they'd chat for ages. She genuinely loved his company. Like a real grandchild. She was a good girl. Not a money grabber like Katy.

And she'd proved it by coming today. Their visits were arranged by the school and she wasn't supposed to call unless it had all been pre-arranged. But he told her how weekends were the worst and that he just wished he could see her then. She'd said that actually he lived by her grandad, and so she'd come. Not because she had to, but because she wanted to.

She was upset now, of course. But she'd settle down. Realise that he just wanted to talk to her and things would be back to normal for them. Except that she'd be staying. It was like a little palace down there for her. He'd make sure she had everything she needed. Including her favourite biscuits.

Better leave her for a while though. Let her settle in. He yawned widely and moved to his favourite chair beside the fire. Maybe he'd have a little sleep now. It had been a very busy afternoon.

Biographical Notes of Contributors

Mat Coward was born in 1960 and became a full-time freelance writer and broadcaster in 1986. Having written all manner of material for all manner of markets, he currently specialises in book reviews, magazine humour columns and short stories – crime, SF, humour, horror and children's. His first crime story was shortlisted for a CWA Dagger. Since then his stories have appeared in numerous magazines, anthologies and e-zines in the UK, US and Europe as well as being broadcast on BBC radio.

Judith Cutler is at present Secretary of the CWA. After immediate success with short stories – she won the *Critical Quarterly* prize at the age of eighteen – she was blocked for many years, not returning to writing until she was in her late thirties. Since then she has produced two detective series, one featuring college lecturer Sophie Rivers, the other Detective Sergeant Kate Power. She still enjoys writing short stories. Judith lives in Birmingham, teaching for Birmingham University after many years at an inner-city college.

Carol Anne Davis has been described as 'an ucompromising new literary talent'. Her second crime novel, *Safe as Houses* has just been published. Four reviewers chose her mortuary-based novel *Shrouded* as their début of the year in 1997. Both books are published by The Do-Not Press. Carol's short stories have appeared in anthologies and magazines and have been placed in national competitions. Her dark crime collection is available for publication and she says that no reasonable offer will be refused.

Eileen Dewhurst was born in Liverpool, read English at Oxford, and has earned her living in a variety of ways, including journalism. When she is not writing, she enjoys solving cryptic crossword puzzles and drawing and painting cats. Her nineteenth and latest novel is *Roundabout*. Her other works include *A Private Prosecution, The House That Jack Built,* and *Death in Candie Gardens*. She wrote five novels featuring the policeman Neil Carter; currently, her principal series detectives are actress Phyllida Moon and the Guernsey policeman Tim Le Page.

Marjorie Eccles was born in Yorkshire and spent her childhood there and on the Northumbrian coast. Later, she lived for many years in the Midlands, where her crime novels are set. Her series featuring Detective Chief Inspector Gil Mayo has achieved an enthusiastic following; the most recent title is *The Superintendent's Daughter*.

Martin Edwards has written six novels about the lawyer and amateur detective Harry Devlin; the first, *All the Lonely People*, was shortlisted for the CWA John Creasey Memorial Award for the best first crime novel of 1991. The series has been optioned for television. He has published about twenty short mysteries, including several with a historical setting, and is also the author of six non-fiction books on legal topics. His latest novel is *First Cut Is the Deepest*.

John Hall worked as an analytical chemist and systems analyst before becoming a full-time writer. He contributes regularly to *Sherlock Holmes: The Detective Magazine* and to the *Sherlock Holmes Journal*. His books include two commentaries on the Sherlock Holmes cases, *Sidelights on Holmes* and *The Abominable Wife*. He has written several new Holmes novels, but is now concentrating on a series featuring his medieval investigator Martyn Byrd.

Edward D. Hoch has dominated the market for short crime fiction of quality over the past forty years. Although he has written occasional novels, it is his gift for (and ability to make a living from) the short form that has earned him a unique reputation. In the course of writing many hundreds of stories,

Hoch has employed a wide range of pen-names and created series characters such as Captain Leopold, Dr Sam Hawthorne, the cipher expert Rand, Ben Snow and Simon Ark, who claims to be two thousand years old. Recent collections of selected cases of Hawthorne and Snow are, respectively, *Diagnosis: Impossible* and *The Ripper of Storyville*.

Bill Kirton lives in Aberdeen. He has been a university lecturer, written, dictated and acted in revues and plays for stage and radio, presented TV programmes and still does voice-overs for radio and television commercials and video programmes. He is married with two daughters, one son, a stepson and a granddaughter.

Janet Laurence writes two series of crime novels. Nine featuring Darina Lisle, cook, have been published, each set in a different area of the food world. The second in her historical series set in mid-eighteenth-century London and featuring Italian painter Canaletto is her latest book. She lives in Somerset with her husband, Keith. Her stepson, Tim, is married to actress Serena Gordon and they have two small sons. All the family loves to travel.

Peter Lewis has lived in the North-East for more than thirty years. He is an academic and teaches courses in crime at one of the institutions for which Durham is famous. Among his books are 'bio-critiques' of Eric Ambler and John le Carré; the latter received an Edgar Allan Poe award from the Mystery Writers of America. He and his wife run Flambard Press, which has published *Northern Blood 2*, an anthology of regional crime stories, and collections of the work of Chaz Brenchley and H. R. F. Keating.

Phil Lovesey is the son of award-winning crime writer Peter Lovesey. Born in 1963, he took a degree in film and television studies and had a career as London's laziest copywriter at a succession of the capital's most desperate advertising agencies. He turned to 'proper' writing in 1994 with a series of short stories, and was runner-up in the prestigious MWA fiftieth anniversary short-story competition in 1995. His first novel, *Death Duties*, was published last year.

Keith Miles has written over forty plays for radio, television and the theatre and thirty crime novels, one of which, *The Roaring Boy*, was nominated for an Edgar Award by the Mystery Writers of America. His 1999 publications are *Saint's Rest*, set in 1930s Chicago, and, as Edward Marston, *The Foxes of Warwick*, the latest Domesday Chronicle, *The Wanton Angel* set in Elizabethan London and *The King's Evil*, first in a series of Restoration mysteries. He is a former chairman of the Crime Writers Association.

Ruth Rendell under her own name, and as Barbara Vine, has achieved both critical and popular acclaim for her achievement in showing the rich potential of the crime novel. Her first book about the Kingsmarkham policeman, Reg Wexford, *From Doon With Death*, appeared in 1964. Her non-series novels under her own name include *A Demon In My View* which won the CWA Gold Dagger in 1976 and the even more remarkable *A Judgement In Stone*. *Lake of Darkness* won the Arts Council National Book Award for Genre Fiction in 1981. The much-praised Vine novels include *A Fatal Inversion* (another CWA Gold Dagger winner) and *The Brimstone Wedding*; the most recent is *The Chimney Sweeper's Boy*.

June Thomson has published eighteen crime novels featuring her series detective Jack Finch and his sergeant Tom Boyce. In addition, she has written collections of Holmes pastiches and a 'biography' of the famous pair, *Sherlock Holmes and Dr Watson*. A collection of her own short stories, *Flowers for the Dead*, was published in 1992. Her books have been published in hardback and paperback in this country and abroad, including the USA, France, Germany, Portugal, Japan and Russia.

Alison White was born and bred in Liverpool, but returned to the North-West after some time living and working in London and is now based in Southport. She has published many stories in magazines and her work has also been broadcast on BBC Network Northwest, Radio 4 and the World Service. In recent years, she has concentrated increasingly on crime fiction, writing for magazines such as *Ellery Queen's Mystery Magazine*. She is now at work on her first mystery novel.